A mistress, a werewolf, a screenwriter and a shapeshifter walk into your heart in these two sexy paranormal stories of love and redemption.

Shifting Flames

Shunned screenwriter Eve Perez has something to prove. Shut out of the industry after a scandal, she's ready to do whatever it takes to climb back to the top, even if it means working with notoriously difficult author Celeste Quon.

Reclusive best-selling author Celeste Quon is adored by a generation of fans, but would they love her if they knew her truth? Under pressure from her fans, Celeste agrees to bring her best-selling novel to the screen but on her terms.

After a freak spring snowstorm strands Eve at Celeste's home she discovers Celeste's incredible secret. Amid their fiery attraction should she let their relationship burn out, or surrender to the flames of their desire?

The Fire Inside

For Clara, crafting pain into pleasure is her job. For Selena, it's her salvation. When submissive Selena hires Clara as her Domina, it seems like the best of business arrangements. But when their emotions infiltrate what was meant to be only professional, both women are rocked by the possibilities that their relationship might be changing into something... more.

Selena has given her submission to Clara for months, but faced with the idea of giving her heart, she runs. Loving

Clara means revealing her secret, the one that sent her seeking pain in the first place, and it's a risk Selena can't take.

Clara, confused and terrified by the glimpse she had of Selena's true self, can't keep herself from wanting more. And, as Selena's Miss, she's not afraid to demand she be given the chance to take it. Snowed in at Clara's mountain cabin, the women must face the truth about themselves and about each other.

Can true love grow from a business relationship, and can it conquer even the darkest of fears?

Soul Burn

Brenda Murphy
Megan Hart

A NineStar Press Publication

Published by NineStar Press
P.O. Box 91792,
Albuquerque, New Mexico, 87199 USA.
www.ninestarpress.com

Soul Burn

Printed in the USA
First Edition
January, 2020

Print ISBN: 978-1-951880-33-0

Also available in eBook, ISBN: 978-1-951880-29-3

Warnings: This book contains sexually explicit material, which is only suitable for mature readers, pain play, deceased family members, graphic violence, and references to physical abuse.

Table of Contents

SHIFTING FLAMES

Brenda Murphy

To C, Always

This book is the result of a long ass ride to Chicago and brilliant suggestion by my co-author, Megan Hart. Here's to horror movies, Regency libations, and another road trip.

Chapter One

A chill breeze lifted the edge of Eve's cocktail napkin, and she slapped her hand over it to keep it from blowing off the table. She took a sip of her bourbon and ginger ale before she checked the time on her phone. *Why did I say yes? And why the hell can't Michelle show up on time? For once. Just once.*

"Sorry, Eve." A warm hand on her shoulder and an air kiss in the vague vicinity of her cheek announced her manager's arrival.

"It's fine." *It's not. But what the hell am I going to say about it? I need her. Need this job.* Eve placed her phone on the table face down.

The waiter arrived, and Michelle perused the wine menu and ordered. She waited until he had left before she raised her gaze to Eve's. "Well?"

"Well what? I told you on the phone it was yes to whatever you had for me. What's the problem? A dog of a book? I can make chicken salad out of chickenshit if that's your concern." Eve took another sip of her bourbon, the smoky sweet taste of the alcohol smoothing off the rough edge of her anxiety.

"I'm not concerned about your ability to write a decent screenplay."

"What then?" Eve leaned back in her chair.

"I'm going to be honest." Michelle pressed close to the table and placed both hands flat.

Eve snorted. "I've been around too long to know that phrase means anything. What is it?"

"I'm not sure it's right for you. After…"

Eve spoke over Michelle. "I know I screwed up. I can't go back in time to change anything. Are you really dropping me as a client?"

Michelle looked up at the ceiling before she brought her gaze back to Eve's face. "How can you ask that? I've stuck by you. If I was going to drop you, I would have done it…" Michelle tapped the table, drawing Eve's attention. "Look, Shelia did you dirty and stole your work. I can't change the past. But I have a job for you. Though your name wouldn't be the only one on the screenplay."

Eve took a sip of her bourbon. "Come on, spill."

The waiter arrived and placed Michelle's wine on the table. "Ready to order? Another drink?"

Eve lifted her glass. "Another of these. And an order of fries, please, with the trio of dips."

Michelle waited until the waiter had left them to speak. She glanced at the other tables and then leaned closer to Eve. "You ever read Celeste Quon's *Stone Gate*?"

"Yes. Along with millions of other people. It was on the *Times*'s Best Seller list for what, four years? Back when you actually had to go into a bookstore to buy a book." Eve curled the edge of her napkin and then smoothed it out.

"Want a shot at adapting it?"

Eve inhaled sharply. "Who wouldn't?" She met Michelle's gaze. "For real?"

"Yes."

"Why now? It was optioned years ago."

"Her contract has her with the final and full approval of the screenplay."

Eve groaned. "Oh no. No wonder."

Michelle covered Eve's hand with her own and squeezed gently. "Right? But good for us."

"Because I'm desperate?" *'Cause I am.* "Do I get paid no matter what? For my time? Or is it tied to the script being approved? I'm not doing this on spec."

"You get paid when it's finished, approved or not." Michelle traced the flower design on the tabletop with her nail.

"What are you not telling me?" Eve rested her hand on top of Michelle's, stilling her motion.

"You'll have to go to Denver to work with her."

"What?"

The waiter placed Eve's drink in front of her before he centered the platter of French fries between them, along with two small plates. "Anything else, ladies?"

"Yes, please, another glass of wine." Michelle lifted her half-full wineglass and drained it. She waited until the waiter was out of eavesdropping range. She picked up a fry and dipped it into the small cup of sriracha mayonnaise. "She doesn't travel. Or leave her home. Hasn't been off the place in years. And wants to work 'closely' with the screenwriter, according to her people."

Eve failed to stifle her grimace. "Ugh. She has 'people' and what the hell, she writes the scariest stories ever, and she's agoraphobic? Why can't we skype or something?"

Michelle's expression softened. "We all have our demons. And she insists on meeting the screenwriter in person."

"What's the time frame?" Eve fidgeted with her fork. "When do I leave?"

Michelle popped another fry in her mouth and chewed slowly. "When can you leave? The option runs out in eight weeks."

Eve raised both brows. "What the hell? I'm supposed to drop everything to run off to Denver and work with someone notorious for being difficult and come out with a screenplay she'll sign off on in eight weeks, for one of the most beloved books of all time? No pressure, Michelle."

"You can say no." Michelle tapped her phone's screen with a turquoise-painted nail.

"Tell me the payout."

Michelle turned her phone screen toward Eve. "You get half on completion of the screenplay, approved by Ms. Quon or not. The full amount if she signs off on it."

Eve took the phone from Michelle's hand and stared at the screen. *Damn. Enough to keep Mom in care. Enough to keep the lights on. Enough to say yes.* "Besides Denver, what's the catch?"

"Her compound backs up to Estes Park. It's too far from Denver to commute. She expects you to live on the estate."

The waiter deposited Michelle's glass of wine on the table and nipped away.

"Thank you," Michelle called at his retreating back before she took a large sip of her wine. "You know Barbara Davis?"

"Yeah. She's good people. I worked with her on the *Night is the Hunter* project." Eve picked up a fry and bit into it. "Why?"

Michelle grimaced. "She left within twenty-four hours of meeting Quon. Quon's burned through six screenwriters in the last two years. The longest stayed three days."

"Maybe they didn't have the right motivation to stay." *They weren't worried about their mom getting tossed out of a mental health institution. No one here for me. Mom doesn't know who I am anymore. Not that she wanted me when she did. Why not? Maybe I can get back to where I was. Only as good as your last success. Or flop. Fuck, I loved that book. I have to do it. How scary can she be?* Eve passed Michelle's phone back to her. "When do I leave?"

Michelle leaned back in her chair and lifted her glass of wine in salute. "I knew you were the perfect person for the job."

Eve failed to stifle her eye roll and raised her own glass.

*

The snow was deep, and Celeste's muscles burned as she ran, stretching out and surrendering to her beast. The scents of smaller creatures, pica and marmots cozy in their burrows under the snow, failed to tempt her from her run. She bounded up the rocks and stopped when she reached the peak overlooking her property and range. The valley below was quiet; a thick layer of spring snow muffled the usual sounds of birds and small prey.

Celeste settled on her haunches. She lifted her head and inhaled, breathing in the wet scents of the valley. Along with the faint smell of fir and pine came the sharp smell of gun grease, and the stench of a man. She inhaled again, tasting the air, and the scent of death assaulted her senses. The whine of a snowmobile approaching from the east filled her ears and she turned toward the sound. *Hunter. In my territory. Trespasser.* She crouched and flattened her body behind a large outcrop.

The snowcat plowed its way through the fresh powder snow of the valley. The rider, dressed in a camouflage snowsuit, stopped shy of the base of the mountain that flanked Celeste's home, the edge of her territory and border of the park. An entrenching tool and a rifle were strapped to the back of his snowcat. The disembodied head of a bear peered lifelessly from the back of the snowmobile alongside the bodies of two cubs. *Trophy hunter. Murderer.*

The man stopped the snowmobile and dismounted. He slipped the strap of his rifle across his chest before he lifted binoculars to his eyes and scanned the valley. Celeste focused on the scene below her. The lifeless eyes of the bear stared back at her and her rage built. *Killed them in their den. Fucking trophy hunter. Scum. Let's see how he likes being prey.*

Celeste lifted her head and growled, roaring her fury to the sky. The man dropped the binoculars to his chest and scrabbled for his rifle. She charged down the mountain toward him. He lifted his rifle to his shoulder. Celeste barreled into him and knocked him down. He swung the rifle and the barrel clipped her nose. Snarling, she rose up on her paws and batted at the gun. She caught it in her claws and shredded the strap. The man cursed and drew a sidearm, his arm trembling as he aimed at her face.

She wheeled, swatted at the gun, and raked his leg, digging her claws deep. He screamed as blood spouted from his thigh, pulsing in an arterial fountain. A thud against her ribs made her spin, and she turned toward the pain, baring her teeth. He clubbed at her with his fists. She placed a paw on his chest, curling her claws into his flesh, and held him still as she closed her jaws over his throat. A satisfying gush of blood filled her mouth and spilled over the snow. She shook him like a rag doll, unleashing her fury. He struggled once and then relaxed as he bled out.

Celeste wiped her paw over her face, scrubbing at the blood that coated her fur. *What to do? He'll be missed. The cave.* She closed her eyes and shifted into her human form. The cold of the snow bit into her naked flesh as she shifted. *Can't tolerate this cold for long.* Celeste roughly stripped the snowsuit off the dead man and shuddered as she drew it on. After collecting his guns, she wiped them clean of fingerprints and stowed them on the snowcat. She stroked the soft fur of the cubs, her anger swelling anew as she imagined him killing them while they slept. She used the entrenching tool and hollowed out a place in the snow under a fir tree. Celeste gathered the small bodies of the cubs and placed them next to their mother's head in their makeshift den and covered them.

The tattered wet fabric stuck to her skin and she stifled the urge to vomit as the human stink that clung to the suit filled her senses. She dug into the blood-soaked pocket of the man's snowsuit and retrieved the snowmobile keys. After she closed his eyes, she lifted him and tossed his body over the back of the cart.

Celeste piloted the snowmobile away from the blood-soaked snow. At the base of a steep mountain, she shut the engine down before she unloaded the body of the hunter and settled him over her shoulder. She climbed up the winding narrow path to the cave opening. Sweat stung her eyes, and she was breathing hard by the time she arrived at the mouth of the cave. She dumped the man's body on the ground and wiped sweat from her forehead with the point of her wrist.

Celeste tugged aside the brush she had piled up to hide her lair from hikers. The comforting dank smell of old dry earth greeted her. She ran her hand over the cool stones lining the walls and drew her weatherproof box from its hiding place. The spring-loaded lock clicked open with a snap. She opened the box and lifted her headlamp clear, flicked it on, and then settled the strap over her head.

Celeste hooked her hand under the man's shoulders. With a steady stream of curses, she dragged his body into the cave. Fifty feet into the cave, the roof sloped down, and she had to crawl while dragging his body behind her. At the rear of the cave, she stopped and clawed away the cairn of stones that blocked her way. She rolled him into the alcove and shoved his body over the bones and half-rotted corpses of others who had died before him. Vile trespassers with no respect, killing for "sport" and to satisfy their blood lust rather than to eat. She wiped the blood from her hand on his snowsuit, stripped it off, and crammed it next to him, desperate to be rid of it.

Celeste restacked the rocks with precision to disguise the underground tomb and seal his body inside. After replacing her headlamp in its hidden storage box, she exited the cave and camouflaged the entrance to her den. At the base of the mountain, she put the keys in the ignition of the snowcat and left it there with the motor running. *When they search for him, they'll assume he ran out of gas and tried to hike out. Lost to the wild. Like many before him.* She knelt in the snow and focused, relaxing into the twisting of her joints and the sharp ripple of pain and pleasure as she morphed into her tiger form. Celeste rolled in the clean snow, letting it wash away the events of the morning, before she shook her fur out and bounded away toward her home.

*

The line at the rental desk stretched to oblivion and beyond, surpassed only by the line at the ridiculously overpriced coffee shop. Skipping both, Eve picked up a bottle of water and snacks for the road trip ahead of her before she joined the queue at the rental car counter. As she waited in line, she studied the fat gray clouds clinging to the tops of mountains surrounding the airport.

"Eve Garcia. You have a car for me." Eve thumbed her phone to her itinerary. "I have the reservation number."

A smarmy smile spread over the face of the nattily dressed desk clerk. "Of course. I just need you to sign the contract."

Eve filled out the paperwork and passed her license and credit card to the desk clerk.

He entered her information and swiped her card. "Do you want to purchase insurance?"

"No. My car insurance covers me."

"Are you sure?" His expression morphed into one of practiced concern. "It's not that much more a day." He inclined his shiny bald head toward the flat-screen television. "Late spring storms can be pretty bad."

"No. I'm good. Just the car."

"Suit yourself." He tipped his head toward the glass doors to the left of the desk. "Second lane to the left. Orange van will pick you up and take you to the lot."

*

A flash of brown and white and then the sickening crunch of metal as a mountain sheep glanced off the bumper of the car. Eve swore and lifted her foot off the gas pedal. White-knuckled, she clung to the steering wheel. Her stomach cramped as the car whipped around twice, the wheels gliding over the fresh snow, before it made one final turn and slammed against the guardrail.

The impact wrenched the wheel from Eve's hands, and she banged her knee on the console. A gust of wind rocked the car. *Fuck. Out. I need to get out.* She unlocked her door and shoved. Her sweaty hands slipped off the door handle. She shoved hard with her shoulder against the frame. Bitter bile rose in her throat when the door refused to open. Giving up, she levered her body into the back of the car and climbed out of the rear door.

A bighorn sheep lay still on the far side of the road with a deep gash in its hip. A river of bright-red blood stained the stark white snow under its body. She walked to the rear of the car and peered over the guardrail. *Close. Too fucking close to going over.* A wave of nausea hit her, and she deposited her breakfast of chips on the side of the road.

She spit and wiped her mouth with the back of her hand and rested her head on the cold metal of the trunk. A blast of snowflakes stung her face, and she hunched her shoulders to shield her face as she straightened. She shoved her hands into her coat pockets and walked to the front of the car. It had lodged firmly against the guardrail. The front tires were flat, and the hood boasted a ripple of accordion folds. Clouds of steam seeped from the buckled edges of the hood.

Just fucking great. Eve entered the car and clambered back into the front seat to search for her phone. After locating it under the dash opposite the driver's side, she pressed the button to turn it on. *No service. Because of course.* She leaned back on the seat. *Don't panic. You're close to her house.* She closed her eyes. *Should have downloaded a map. Printed one out. Fuck, I'm an idiot.* A blast of wind rocked the car, and she flailed her arms as the vehicle creaked and shifted.

Scrambling to the back seat, she banged her elbow on the doorframe, setting off another round of nausea. *Can't stay here. Walk to her house. Can't be more than a mile.* She shoved her phone into her back pocket before she pulled on her thin black leather gloves. *Why'd I pack a fashion statement? Stupid.*

Eve wrestled her large suitcase from the back of the car and shouldered her messenger bag. Snow had already covered the tracks from the car. She took a long swallow from her water bottle. A movement on the rocky cliff above the road caught her attention, and she glanced up. She choked and spewed water as her gaze fixed on gleaming amber-colored eyes staring back at her from a furry white-and-orange striped face. She wiped the spilled water from her mouth with her sleeve and focused on what she could see of the beast. *What the fuck? A tiger? Did I hit my head?*

Eve pinched the bridge of her nose and closed her eyes. *Breathe. Calm down.* She lowered her hand and opened her eyes slowly before she scanned the embankment. *Nothing. Stressed, that's all.* After another drink of water, she stuffed her water bottle in the mesh pocket on the side of her messenger bag. A stronger gust of wind rocked her body, and she hunched her shoulders as snow and small rocks pelted her. The scree and scrape of metal made her turn in time to see the rental car tip over the rail. The distant sound of the crash sobered Eve.

Me. I could have been in there.

*

Celeste focused on the fat flanks of the male bighorn sheep as he charged over the ragged rocks, scrabbling over the loose stones and scree. She swiped at his flank, a glancing blow, and cursed herself for striking too soon. Too frightened to hear the sound of approaching tires, the wounded sheep charged ahead, and made a final desperate leap. Rocks gave and slid under Celeste as she skidded to a stop on the embankment above the highway. Panting, she stopped and crouched behind the rocks. The sheep's hooves slipped on the fresh snow, and a small blue car skidded before it struck the animal.

The car spun out, tracing large circles across both lanes of the highway before it crashed against the guardrail. Curious, she risked a glance over the boulder. A tall woman leaned against the back of the car and vomited. The sharp smell of bile stung her nose, and Celeste snarled. *Who the hell would be crazy enough to be driving in this? Must be a fool. Or desperate. Or a desperate fool.* Celeste brushed a paw over her face and rested her head on her folded paws to study the woman.

Her belly rumbled, a loud reminder that her would-have-been dinner lay dead in a large pool of blood on the far side of the road. The woman disappeared into the car and emerged with a huge suitcase and a messenger bag. Celeste let her gaze roam over the woman's thin frame. Even at a distance she could sense her determination and anger from the set of her shoulders. The woman glanced up and into Celeste's eyes. Her gaze locked onto Celeste's face.

Celeste fell into her dark brown eyes. *Beautiful eyes. Commanding. Haunted. Wistful. Hungry. I've seen her. Where?* Celeste remained still with a predator's practiced ease. *Writer. She's the screenwriter.* A blast of wind drove snow and loose stones against her fur. A violent screech assaulted her ears, and Celeste turned in time to see the wrecked car tumble over the guardrail into the deep ravine below. Celeste turned her attention back to the woman and the road.

The woman turned and walked away from the car, dragging a wheeled suitcase through the snow. The messenger bag on her shoulder banged against her hip with each determined step. *Too cold. Fool. She'll die in this. I need to get back.*

*

Celeste entered the dark shed. The stale smell of old gasoline and motor oil stung her nose. Her gaze skittered around the shed. She shrugged off her fears of being discovered. Secure on her estate, safe from those who would harm her in her most vulnerable state, she lifted her head and focused her energy on transforming into her human form. Her body sunk into itself as she morphed and shifted.

Celeste's thick brown-and-white tiger fur vanished as her skin regenerated. Her fangs sank back into her jaw and the bones of her face resumed their human shape. Celeste stifled a groan as her joints reconfigured themselves. The pain and pleasure of shifting shot through her body like heat lightning. She stretched her arms overhead and relaxed into her human form.

The floor was cold under her bare knees and she shivered, already missing her warm thick fur. Her clit ached, thick and needy, and she brushed her fingers over herself. A quick soothing stroke to defuse her sexual energy. *No time. Damn it. Later. When I can take my time. Play with my new toy. Why did I say yes? She's obviously an idiot, trying to walk to my house in a spring blizzard. Why did I ever agree to an option? Vanity. My vanity. And money. Damn it.*

Celeste trembled as she pulled her underlayer on. Her hair was still wet from the snow. Unwilling to risk the woman's life to vanity, she pulled it back and secured it with a rubber band. She tugged her snowsuit on and then took the keys for the Arctic Cat from their hook. *Fool. Another desperate idiot. I should let her die. But that would bring investigations. And trouble.* She turned the key, and the snowmobile rumbled under her. *Time to play cavalry.*

Chapter Two

Eve trudged forward. The desolate stretch of road mirrored her thoughts. The snow stung her cheeks and clung to her eyelashes. Skin wet with sweat and out of breath from the change in altitude and the effort of dragging her suitcase, she stopped and rested. Panting, she leaned over and placed her hands on her knees. *Damn altitude. Fuck.*

Wind buffeted her body, and her shoulder bag shifted and slammed against her knee, knocking her to the rough pavement. Her hands skidded on the snow. Pain ripped through her as the skin of her palm tore, and she fell flat and lay in the snow. Eve gasped and struggled to breathe in the frigid air. *Fuck, I'm gonna die out here. Stupid. Why did I say yes to this ridiculous job? Need to get up. Not going to quit.* Slowly, she raised herself to her knees and pushed up from the snow. Her bloody hand trembled as she drank the last of her water.

The snow fell in a steady seamless sheet of white, and the fat flakes coated the highway. She looked behind her, trying to gauge how far she had traveled from the car. Vague outlines of her footprints dotted the road, and the twin yellow lines marking the centerline were barely visible. Eve pulled her phone from her pocket. A red "low battery" warning flashed across the screen. *No service. And the car isn't due back for eight weeks. If I don't show, Celeste Quon will let Michelle know. And then what?*

Hours. Days until someone knows I'm out here. Fuck. Mom. She'll never know if I die. Doesn't even know who I am. What will happen to her? I have to survive this. Get it together. I've run twenty-six miles. I can make it to her house. It can't be far. Not going to die today.

The high-pitched whine of an engine cut through the air and her despair. *Snowmobile? Mountain patrol? Help.* Eve pushed the handle down on her suitcase and sat on it, facing the direction of the sound. She shivered and pulled her scarf up over her face, leaving a small gap for her eyes. A bright-green snowcat roared down the road. *Probably some insane mountain man, and instead of dying in the cold, I'll end up some kinda kidnapped wife. Fuck.* Eve pulled her messenger bag across her stomach and held it like a shield. *Damn, what was I thinking?* The snowmobile slid to a stop a few feet from Eve. The driver dismounted and strode toward her.

He's small. I could take him if I have to. Maybe a kid? Be cool. You already look like an idiot trying to walk in this with your suitcase. Brass it out. Eve stood and pulled her scarf away from her face, plastering on the biggest smile she could manage with her teeth chattering.

She waved. "Hey there."

The driver took two steps closer and unfastened her chin strap. Long white hair pulled into a low ponytail spilled free of the helmet as she removed it and tucked it under her arm. "Out for a stroll?" Her wide cheekbones were flushed, and her amber-colored gaze burned with annoyance.

Celeste Quon. Herself. Rescuing me. Great way to make an entrance. "Oh fuck." Eve covered her mouth and cleared her throat. "Sorry. I'm your screenwriter. Eve Garcia."

Celeste arched an eyebrow. "Indeed. I hope your screenplays are better than your survival instincts."

"Excuse me?" Eve lifted her chin.

"Any idiot knows not to leave their car in the middle of a snowstorm."

"Well, this idiot has an aversion to toppling over the sides of cliffs."

Celeste's nose wrinkled, and she tilted her head to the side as if listening for something. "We need to go." She turned and walked back to the snowmobile.

The set of Celeste's shoulders was all the indication Eve needed to know she was expected to obey without question. *Oh, fuck that. She needs to understand I'm not going to let her act like she's the fucking queen of the world.* Eve blew out a breath and followed Celeste to the snowmobile. She opened her mouth to complain and then shut it quickly. She clenched her teeth and gripped the handle of her suitcase tighter. *Deal with it. You need the money. Don't blow it.*

Celeste rested a hand on the windscreen of the snowcat. She eyed the suitcase Eve pulled behind her. "We don't have room for your bag."

Eve pressed her lips together in a thin line and counted to ten before she replied. "What the hell am I supposed to do? Work naked?"

Celeste raked her gaze over Eve. A soft smile played about her mouth. She met Eve's hard glare with a smirk. "Intriguing concept. However, I prefer to work without distractions, no matter how minor."

Me naked would be a "minor distraction". Fuck her. Eve flushed at Celeste's blatant appraisal and planted her feet. "I'm not leaving my bag."

Celeste's eyes narrowed. "You will. There's not room for us and your bag. Take whatever essentials you need. Leave the rest here. You can be foolish on your own time. I prefer to be safe."

Eve chewed her lip as she studied the toes of her wet snow-covered boots and shivered. *I'm a fool. An idiot for saying yes to this job. She's already made her mind up about me. She'll never listen to my suggestions. She thinks I'm an idiot.* The adrenaline rush of the accident faded. Too tired to fight, only too aware of her utter dependence on Celeste to survive, she unzipped the suitcase and flipped back the lid.

Eve extracted her toiletries bag, her extra pair of glasses, and favorite T-shirt and jeans and stuffed them into her messenger bag. Rummaging through her suitcase, Eve cursed herself for not being a more organized traveler. She wadded up three pairs of briefs and three bras before she stuffed them into her coat pockets. *Shoes.* She plucked out her favorite trainers and jammed two pairs of athletic socks into them before she tied the laces together and slung them over her shoulder. She glared at Celeste before she dug into the outside pocket of her suitcase and pulled out her running shorts and crammed them inside the front of her coat.

Celeste stood off to the side, her arms folded, her intense gaze fixed on Eve. The short hairs on the back of Eve's neck rose as she sensed Celeste's scrutiny. She zipped her bag shut and straightened. With both hands wrapped around the strap of her messenger bag, she glanced around at the rough terrain on either side of the road. "I can't just leave it here."

"Allow me." Celeste picked up the case with one hand and tossed it over the guardrail as if it weighed no more than a paper cup. "There. Shall we?"

Damn. Stronger than she looks. Freakishly strong. Eve eyed the snowmobile. "Uh. Sure."

"Give me your shoulder bag."

Eve hesitated.

Celeste quirked her mouth. "Promise I won't toss it."

Eve passed her bag to Celeste.

Celeste took Eve's satchel and secured it to the rear frame of the snowcat with bungee cords. The ski suit pulled tight over her ass. Eve stared at Celeste's shapely curves on display. *Definitely works out. Don't act like a creeper. Stop staring.* Eve averted her eyes.

Celeste straightened. "Now the shoes."

Eve frowned.

"Unless you'd prefer to be pummeled by them on the ride?" Celeste's smirk was back. "If you're into that kind of thing."

Eve snatched the trainers from around her neck and passed them to Celeste.

After tying her shoes in place, Celeste slung a leg over the seat of the snowmobile and twisted at the waist, turning her body toward Eve. She raised an elegantly shaped eyebrow. "Have you ridden on a snowmobile before?"

Eve mounted the seat behind her. The cold of the wet seat seeped into her pants. "No. But I've ridden a motorcycle."

"Well, I doubt you've ridden a motorcycle in the middle of a snowstorm." She squinted at Eve's coat and quirked her mouth. "Do you have a hat?"

"Scarf."

Celeste's expression softened and she passed her helmet to Eve. "Tuck your scarf into your coat and put this on."

Eve frowned. "What about you?"

Celeste retrieved a pair of goggles from a pocket under the dash of the snowmobile. "I'll be fine. The helmet will keep your head warm. Sit close to me. It will keep most of the wind off of you. It's a twenty-minute ride to my home."

She's concerned. Not as much of a hard-ass as she makes out. The way she handled my suitcase. Fuck, she must work out. Hard to tell with the snowsuit. The engine roared to life, and Eve pulled the helmet on and adjusted the chinstrap.

The padding of the helmet muffled the noise of the engine. She slid forward on the seat, maintaining a polite distance between them, unwilling to press her intimate flesh against Celeste's shapely ass. The faint scent of sandalwood clung to the helmet. *Must be her perfume. Hella sexy. Like her eyes. Where did that come from? Get a grip.*

Celeste reached back and grabbed Eve's wrists, tugged her forward, and settled her hands around her waist. Eve scooted forward, obeying Celeste's silent command. She was taller by a head. Celeste turned the handlebars of the snowmobile and rolled the throttle. The snowcat lurched forward and Eve's body made full contact against Celeste's back and thighs.

Even with the bulk of the snowsuit, Eve was aware of Celeste's muscles as they bunched and flexed as she steered the snowcat through the fresh powdery snow. The wind cut through Eve's clothes, pricking her skin with needle sharpness. She crouched behind Celeste's sturdy frame and clung to her warmth. Eve's body blazed everywhere she touched Celeste. *Be cool. She's your boss. And freakishly strong. And hot as fuck. Damn it.*

*

The ride back to her house with Eve's arms firmly settled around her waist did nothing to cool Celeste's cravings. Her foiled hunt had left her beast restless and hungry. Not hungry. Famished. Starving. The press of Eve's body against her fanned the embers of a long-banked fire. It had been ten years since she had even entertained the idea of indulging her needs with another. A wet ache settled between her legs. Eve's surprising pushback was refreshing after the succession of spineless screenwriters sent to work with her, each one convinced working with Celeste to bring her perennial best-selling novel to the big screen would make their careers. *Not this one. She knows her worth. Owns her power.*

The anger and rage that flashed in her chestnut-brown eyes when Celeste challenged her had stirred her blood and ignited a red-hot flare of desire in Celeste. Thoughts of Eve's wild mane of dark hair framing her high cheekbones and the way her full mouth had pulled into a snarl after Celeste had teased her about working naked made her smile and her nipples hard as she thought about kissing Eve. *Kissing Eve. And then what?* Celeste gave over to delicious fantasies of seducing Eve as she navigated the track back to the house. *What would she do if I pushed harder? Would she push back? Own her power? Or become another obsequious disappointment? Or would she recognize me for what I am and give me what I crave? No. Too dangerous. And inappropriate. She's here to work.*

The things Eve had chosen to take with her intrigued Celeste. *Her running shoes. An athlete's choice. She's built like a long-distance runner.* Eve's long legs rested against Celeste's thighs, and Celeste imagined what it would be like to kneel between them and see Eve's cruel beauty above her, one of her elegant hands wrapped in Celeste's hair as she ordered her to do all kinds of deliciously dirty things. She stifled her groan and promised herself another hunt as soon as she had Eve settled.

*

The welcome warmth of the mudroom melted the last bits of snow clinging to Eve's hair. Icy rivulets ran down her neck. Eve tugged off her sodden leather gloves and flexed her hands. The skin was a mottled red, and her joints were stiff. She laid the gloves over the bench before she toed off her boots and slipped off her wet socks. The white tile of the floor was cold on her bare feet. Her hands ached and she struggled to unbutton her coat.

"Allow me." Celeste brushed Eve's hands away.

"I can do it." Eve lifted her chin.

"I'm sure, but I don't have all day." Celeste unbuttoned Eve's coat. "Hang it there, over the tray."

Eve shrugged out of her coat and hung it on the hook Celeste had indicated. She tightened her shoulders against the shivers that racked her body.

"You need to get out of those wet clothes."

"They'll dry."

"Yes. But you becoming ill is not on my agenda."

Eve raked her hand through her hair. "I don't have anything dry to wear. Or did you forget?"

"I have a very good memory." Celeste eyed her and tilted her head to the side.

Eve shivered and crossed her arms over her chest, only too aware of her nipples, hard from the cold, pressing against the wet fabric of her shirt.

Celeste lifted her hand and pointed to a door. "Bathroom's through there. Strip and shower. I'll bring you some clothes."

Eve opened her mouth to protest and shut it. She tucked her hands under her armpits, desperate to warm them. *A hot shower. Dry clothes. Be sensible. She's right. If you get sick, it won't help anything. Don't act like an idiot any more than you have. She saved your dumb ass.*

"Thank you." Eve met Celeste's gaze. "I'm not usually this much of a mess. The accident rattled me."

"You're welcome. There are towels in the closet next to the shower." Celeste turned away and left her to marvel how her day had gone so sideways so fast.

*

Eve removed her phone from her pocket and placed it on the vanity top before she stripped out of her clothes. While the water heated, she located a towel and placed it on a hook next to the shower door. The shower was large with bronze taps and natural stone walls and a glass door. The stall had six different showerheads, and Eve indulged herself by standing in the hot water until her fingertips were wrinkled and the cold that had embedded itself in her body was vanquished.

As she scrubbed her hair with shampoo, she heard the click of the latch as the bathroom door opened. The faint scent of Celeste's sandalwood perfume seeped into her consciousness. Her body responded as she remembered the way Celeste's powerful body had pressed against her on the snowmobile. Desire, unwelcome and undeniable, surged through her. *What would it be like to control someone so powerful? To have her kneel and serve me as I wish? To see nothing in those amber eyes but a willingness to please?*

Eve kept her eyes tightly closed, unwilling to acknowledge Celeste's presence, desperate to avoid any more awkwardness, hating her vulnerable position as Celeste's house guest. The sensation of being watched hardened her nipples. *She's looking at me. Wants me. Does she like what she sees? What would she do if I opened the glass and dragged her in here? Kissed her until she begged to serve me? She wishes.* Eve allowed her arrogance and body confidence to drive her. She arched back to display her breasts as she rinsed her hair.

Aware of her audience, Eve cupped her breasts and thumbed her nipples before she smoothed her hands over her hips to sluice the rest of the suds off her body. With two fingers she pushed through her wet curls and gave her clit a languid stroke before she raised her arms over her head and worked the rest of the soap from her hair. She held the pose long after her hair was clean of shampoo. Eve waited until the snap of the door latch signaled Celeste's departure before she opened her eyes and shut off the taps.

Steam wafted into the bathroom when she opened the shower door and clouded the mirror over the sink. A tidy stack of clothes was arranged on the counter. Eve donned a black tank top, a bit too large, a matching cotton long-sleeved T-shirt too short in the sleeves, and a pair of soft black yoga pants too roomy in the hip. The hem of the pants stopped a full two inches above the top of the thick wool socks that completed the outfit. A glance in the mirror confirmed Eve's suspicion that she looked as ridiculous as she imagined. She picked up her phone from the counter and pressed the on button. *Dead. At least the socks fit. Clean and dry. What the hell did she do with my dirty clothes?*

Eve studied her reflection and stifled a shudder. *I would have died. What was I thinking? Maybe I hit my head? No tender spots when I washed my hair. No bruises on my face. What would've happened if she hadn't rescued me? Damn lucky. How did she know about the accident? Duh. She knew I didn't walk from the airport. But still. Those eyes. She sees right through me. Or into me. Fuck. Get it together. I'm here to work.*

*

Celeste opened the bathroom door. Eve's back was toward her with both hands buried in her long dark locks as she washed her hair. Thick suds cascaded down her back and slid over the smooth curve of her flank. Celeste looked down at the floor as a flush stole over her. Her hands trembled as she placed the stack of clothing on the counter. She gathered Eve's discarded clothes from the floor before she risked another glance at Eve's naked form.

She stared as Eve rinsed her hair. Drawn to the naked flame of Eve's beauty, Celeste crept closer and settled her hand over the glass, imagining the sensation of Eve's lean muscles and soft curves under her palm. Eve arched her head back under the spray as she rinsed her hair. She brought her hands up and cupped her breasts, thumbs sweeping over her nipples before her hands dipped and flowed over her hips, carrying the lather with them.

Celeste's nose tingled with the unmistakable scent of Eve's excitement, rising on the steam from the shower and laced through with the crisp apple scent of the shampoo and the honey essence of the bath soap. Celeste lifted her head and inhaled deeply, bathing her senses in Eve. Desire roiled through her. *She wants it too. Is she teasing me? Does she know I'm here? How she's affecting me? Will she try to seduce me into agreeing to her script?*

Celeste bit her lip. *She's gorgeous. And strong. I want. I want her. No. Not like this. She's here to work.* Her vision blurred. A rush of desire overwhelmed her, and she yanked her hand back from the glass. *Out. I need to get out of here. Run. A long run. A hunt. Meat. Fresh meat. Now.* She clutched Eve's clothes to her chest as she backed out of the door, gaze locked on Eve's stunning form until the moment she closed the door.

*

After her shower, Eve followed the smell of brewing coffee to the kitchen to the left of the mudroom. A blue sticky note was pressed to the side of a huge coffee cup. Adjacent to the mug was a plate covered with plastic wrap. A sandwich cut into four neat triangles with a stack of potato chips artfully arranged around the edge filled the plate. Eve lifted the note and read the tidy printing.

> *Make yourself comfortable. Juice and water in the refrigerator.*
>
> *C.*

Eve peeled off the plastic wrap and inspected the sandwich. *Peanut butter and strawberry jelly. How odd. A kid's meal. Whatever. Comfort food. Did she make this? Does she think I need to be comforted? Fuck me, I'm overthinking this.* She searched through the cabinets and found a glass and filled it with water from the refrigerator. Eve sat on one of the tall stools and ate at the kitchen island. Her gaze flitted around the room as she tucked into the sandwich and chips. The kitchen was large. A six-burner stainless-steel stove occupied one wall, flanked by banks of cabinets.

The top of the stove had a well-used patina, the dark stains around the burners evidence it was not a showpiece but used for cooking. A round teak table with four chairs sat in front of three floor-to-ceiling windows that offered a view of the mountains sheltering the valley the house occupied. Gusts of wind blew the snow sideways. The tops of the mountains disappeared into the heavy gray clouds that scuttled across the sky.

Eve strained her ears, listening for sounds of activity. Her skin prickled. *Damn quiet. It's a big house. Where is she?* Eve glanced out the window. *She's sure as fuck not outside. She must have assistants. A housekeeper? Probably a groundskeeper too.* She loitered in the kitchen, grateful for the pot of coffee. She sipped the dark brew, closing her eyes as she savored the flavor. A bold blend, perfectly balanced. She already wanted a second cup even as she drank her first.

Make myself comfortable. Dressed like a clown. Fuck, I need to check my laptop. The neoprene should have kept it dry. Eve rinsed her plate and placed it in the dishwasher. She walked back to the mudroom. Her messenger bag was on the bench on top of a hand towel. The fabric was mottled with wetness. She carried the bag to the kitchen and placed it on the center island.

She poured herself another cup of coffee and then opened her bag. The flap and zipper had done a fair job of keeping the contents dry. Her notes were curled and damp at the edges. The neoprene laptop sleeve was dry. Eve opened the sleeve and removed her laptop and started it to reassure herself. Satisfied the machine was in working order, she shut it down, preferring to enjoy her second cup of coffee without the stress of email. She emptied the contents of her bag onto the wide surface of the kitchen island. Her notes were stuck together. Gingerly, she separated the pages before she spread them out to dry on the scarred and stained butcher block top. She traced her fingers over deep gouges marring the wood surface. *What the hell made those marks? Cleaver? No. Not cuts. Gouges. Like a scratching post. Awful big kitty. What did I see after the accident? Maybe a bobcat? Or mountain lion? Do they have mountain lions here?*

She draped her jeans and T-shirts over the dining chairs and hung her underwear alongside her running shorts. *My underwear all over Celeste Quon's kitchen. Bizarre. What a way to meet your rich and famous co-author.*

*

Belly full, sated after her hunt, Celeste sauntered into the kitchen. The overhead light splayed out over Eve, casting her in a warm glow as she hunched over her computer typing. She tapped her lip with a pen, seemingly oblivious to Celeste's presence. Celeste grimaced at the assorted clothing draped about the kitchen to dry.

"Are you hungry?" Celeste rested her hands on the countertop and noticed the rust-colored stains under her nails, a faint reminder of her successful hunt. She curled her fingers into her palm.

Eve startled. "Sorry, what? Have you been there long?" She twisted in the chair, turning her gaze to Celeste.

"Are you hungry?"

"I'm almost always hungry. Thank you for the sandwich." Eve rested her hand on the top of her computer as if to close it.

"Don't stop working on my account." Celeste turned away and gathered ingredients from the pantry. After setting a pot of broth on the stove to boil, she watched Eve from under her lashes as she chopped garlic and peeled ginger to add to the broth. Eve's brow was furrowed as she bent over her laptop, her elegant fingers flying over the keys.

After heating the oil, Celeste browned the garlic and ginger. The spicy scent of Sichuan pepper filled the air as she added crushed peppercorns to the sauté. Celeste tipped the broth into the pan and a cloud of fragrant steam filled the kitchen. She dropped winter melon and mushrooms into the pot.

Eve looked up at her, a broad smile on her face. "Smells delicious."

"If you don't mind moving your undergarments, we could eat at the table." Celeste inclined her head toward the small dining table.

Eve blushed. A dull-rose color painted her cheeks and Celeste lost focus as she imagined what else would make color rise in Eve's face.

"Sorry. Of course." Eve closed her laptop and gathered her clothes into a loose pile on one of the chairs.

Celeste placed a large bowl of noodles and broth in front of Eve. She refilled her teacup before she returned to the table and sat across from her.

Celeste leaned back in her chair and indulged herself in watching Eve's mouth as she ate.

"You're not eating?" Eve dabbed her mouth with her napkin.

"I ate earlier." Celeste met Eve's gaze.

Eve rolled the edge of her napkin between her fingers. "Thank you. For everything. I'm usually the one who rescues people. I'm grateful. You saved my life."

"I'm sorry about your car. And my intemperance before." Celeste sipped her tea.

"No problem. I'm going to consider it your contribution to remind me not to over-pack." Eve shifted in her seat. "Do you live alone?"

Celeste filled her teacup. "In the winter, yes. My housekeeper hates the winter. She and her partner winter in Florida."

Eve spooned the soup into her mouth. Celeste forced her gaze from Eve's face and turned her teacup in her hands.

"What year was this house built?" Eve gestured with her spoon. "The woodwork is amazing."

"Nineteen twenty-three. It was a hunting lodge to begin with. During Prohibition they expanded it, turned it into a speakeasy and brothel."

"How long have you owned it?"

"On paper, it's been in my family for many years. My great-grandfather was a banker in Singapore. He accepted the house as collateral for a loan. The man defaulted on the loan, but we couldn't take possession due to the Chinese Exclusion Act. It was the first thing I purchased as soon as I could afford it."

"Wow. That's quite a story." Eve sipped her tea. "This soup is fantastic."

Celeste soaked up Eve's praise like a dry sponge. "Thank you. It's a family recipe."

Eve's gaze settled over Celeste. "I appreciate everything you've done for me. I don't know what I was expecting but not this."

Celeste sighed. "Rumors of my being difficult are not unfounded."

Eve laughed. "If tossing my suitcase down the side of a mountain is typical, I understand the rumors."

Celeste shifted in her seat. "I'm terribly sorry. I'll pay to replace your things."

Eve reached out and touched the back of Celeste's hand. "I'm not attached to my clothes, but thank you for the offer." She waved her spoon over the soup. "How about we call it even and you promise to cook this for me again?"

Celeste's skin burned under Eve's touch, and she turned her hand up and entwined their fingers. "It would be my pleasure." She met Eve's hungry gaze with one of her own.

*

Eve yanked her hand away from Celeste's touch, rattled by the intimacy of Celeste's gaze, and spooned another bite of the fragrant soup into her mouth. Celeste's expression shuttered, and she drew her hand away slowly before she leaned back in her chair and sipped her tea. The small hairs on Eve's neck stood up as she sensed Celeste's scrutiny.

Eve dabbed her mouth with her napkin. "What do you do here all winter by yourself?"

Celeste tipped her head back and her lustrous hair slid over her shoulders. "Enjoy my solitude."

Eve blinked at Celeste's cool tone and looked out of the window. Chastised, she returned her attention to her meal. She lifted the bowl with both hands to drink the last swallow of rich broth. The silence between them was thick and uncomfortable. Eve shifted in her seat, unsure how to proceed.

"If you're still hungry there is more in the pot." Celeste waved in the direction of the stove. Her icy tone and detached manner added to Eve's concern she had somehow offended Celeste.

"Thank you." Eve refilled her bowl. She studied Celeste's face from under her lashes as she ate. Celeste's hands encircled her teacup, her thumb rubbing the rim of the cup in idle patterns. Her expression was closed, her eyes distant, and her posture as rigid as the straight-backed chair she occupied. The wind shifted and snow pelted the glass before melting in intersecting rivulets.

Eve finished her soup in silence. *Eggshells. Fucking walking on eggshells. What did I say? Because I asked a personal question? Fuck. Okay, business only. Stick to business.* Eve folded her napkin and placed it beside her bowl. "When do you want to start working?"

Celeste started and stared briefly at Eve. "Sorry. What did you say?"

"When would you like to start working on the adaptation?"

Celeste huffed out a breath. "Tomorrow." She stood abruptly before she snatched Eve's empty bowl and silverware off the table.

Eve's chair scraped over the tiles as she rose. "You cooked. Let me wash up."

"No need." Celeste called over her shoulder.

Eve frowned. "What can I do to help?"

"Nothing." The dishes clattered as Celeste rinsed them and placed them into a dishwasher.

Eve leaned against the kitchen island and admired Celeste's practiced and efficient movements as she cleaned the kitchen. Her back was to Eve as she washed the soup pot. Eve studied Celeste as she worked. A good five inches shorter than Eve, Celeste's body was tightly muscled. Her broad shoulders, trim waist, and well-rounded ass were strong evidence Celeste attended to her physical health meticulously.

Eve traced her fingers over the wood grain of the kitchen island and tried to remember the scant details of the various internet biographies of Celeste she had read on her flight. While she had found reams of information about her work and accomplishments, she had found little personal information other than her age, listed as fifty years old. Her relationship status stated she was single; a brief mention of a partner in an early bio from fifteen years prior hinted Celeste was lesbian. No mention was made of any family or partner. *Is she closeted by choice, or did her publisher force her?*

Eve's gaydar had pinged solidly the moment Celeste had pulled off her helmet and made eye contact. Observing the elegant and sexy woman before her, Eve wondered about Celeste's fierce insistence on privacy and how she was ever going to work with her. The tantalizing prospect of breaking down Celeste's walls while keeping her own boundaries in place titillated Eve.

"Would you like some wine?" Celeste used the sprayer to rinse the sink.

"I would."

Celeste turned to her and dried her hands on a dishtowel. "Red?"

Eve smiled. "Do I look like a red wine drinker, or are you guessing?"

She inclined her head toward a walnut-paneled cabinet. "That's the wine chiller. See if anything there suits you. If not, we'll make a trip to the cellar." She hung the towel to dry and opened the cabinet behind her. She extracted two red wine glasses and a corkscrew and placed them on the kitchen island.

Eve worried her lip with her teeth, wondering at the shift in Celeste's demeanor as she examined the labels on the wine bottles. *Charming hostess or stoic loner? Which one is the real Celeste?*

*

Celeste let the ritual of cleaning clear her mind. *What is it about her? Why now? Ten years of avoiding entanglements and here I am practically throwing myself at her. Breathe. Stay in control. Shut the pain away. Breathe. She's here to do a job not become my plaything. Work. She's here to work.*

"Is this claret?"

Eve's giddy tone dissolved every firm intention Celeste had set to keep this arrangement business only. *But it's already beyond that, isn't it? It was from the moment I saw her dragging that damn suitcase through the snow. And the shower. Oh goddess, the shower.* The soft pop of the cork along with the clink of glassware and the splash of wine being poured and the memory of Eve's delectable body in the shower further softened Celeste's resolve. *One drink. What harm could one drink cause?*

"Love it. I take it you like it?" Celeste wiped the counter one last time, before she hung the dishcloth on its hook and turned to face Eve.

"Yes. Although I have to confess feeling a little like an old lady drinking it." Eve's gaze skittered away from Celeste.

Celeste raised an eyebrow. "Old age is a privilege denied many, as they say. Are you tired?"

"Wired." Eve met Celeste's gaze over the rim of her glass.

Celeste picked up her wineglass and swirled the blood-red wine once before she sipped it. "You've had a traumatic day. What would help you relax?" She took another sip of her wine.

Eve fiddled with the edge of her shirt, Celeste's shirt, much too big in the shoulders and short in the sleeves. "This wine will help."

Celeste picked up the bottle. "I have a lounge. We don't have to stand in the kitchen. Come with me." She led Eve out of the room.

*

The lounge was a cozy viewing room filled with a large copper-colored leather sectional, and a tall basket with assorted crocheted throws. A coffee table was centered across from a large flat-screen television. The walls on either side of the screen were filled floor to ceiling with DVD and Blu-ray discs.

Eve nodded toward the shelves. "You don't stream movies?"

Celeste laughed. "No. No, satellite internet is fine for some things but streaming here can be spotty because of the weather. And my tastes in film are often hard to find."

Eve walked over to the shelves and studied the titles. The films were arranged by language. Korean, French, English, Italian, German, Spanish, and Mandarin titles filled every inch of the shelves. Eve trailed her finger over the shelf and tilted her head to read the movie titles. "Pedro Almodóvar's *Tie Me Up! Tie Me Down!*" She pulled the DVD from the shelf and read the back cover. "It's seriously ridiculous. It always makes me laugh."

"We could watch it, if you like. It's been years since I've watched it."

Eve replaced the DVD on the shelf, careful to return it to its place and not disturb Celeste's meticulous filing system. "No." She reached up and pulled another disc from the shelf. "*The Handmaiden.* Park Chan-Wook is amazing and his adaptation of *Fingersmith* is delightful." She held it out to Celeste. "Could we watch it?"

"Delightful? You are deliciously dark, my friend." Celeste raised an eyebrow and her glass.

Eve flushed with Celeste's praise.

"*The Handmaiden* it is." Celeste placed her glass on the table, smiled, and took the disc from Eve's hand.

Eve bit her lip and tried to ignore the heat that raced up her arm when their fingers brushed. She stepped back and drained her wineglass.

Celeste tipped her head toward the bottle. "Help yourself."

Eve eyed Celeste's ass as she bent over and inserted the disc before she glanced up at the ceiling and reminded herself once again that she was here on business before she refilled her glass.

They sat quietly. Eve tucked herself into the corner of the couch, careful to avoid touching Celeste. Touching Celeste. She wanted to do more than touch. Much more. She had seen, in Celeste's eyes, the longing, the submissive craving direction and a Dominant's care. Celeste's need was palpable in the small room, a constant hum in Eve's body, unquenched by the wine.

She knotted her hands together in her lap and returned her attention to the movie as it unfolded before her. She focused on the lush cinematography, crisp dialogue, and twisty plotlines, becoming engrossed in the film. *This.* This was why she stayed in the business. She relished the chance to be part of something incredibly engaging and entertaining, designed to make people forget their problems. It was a Dominant's wet dream, the idea of controlling countless people's emotions in the dark with her words and storytelling. Eve sipped her wine and savored the twisted tale playing out on the screen.

The moment of seeming betrayal arrived in the film and a faintly audible pitiable moan sounded in the intimate room. Eve peered at Celeste in the dim light. White-knuckled, she gripped the crocheted blanket she had tucked over her legs, and her mouth pulled into a grimace. Her eyes were bright, as the woman on the screen screamed and called out as she was led away to the asylum.

"You okay?" Eve whispered, unable to stop herself from caring.

Celeste nodded, teeth set on her lip.

Eve tilted her head. "You sure?"

Celeste paused the movie, and a grim smile played over her lips. "Yes. I'm being silly. I've seen this. I know how it ends."

Eve stretched her arm along the back of the couch and turned to face Celeste more fully. "Doesn't mean it doesn't still give you the feels. A good movie is like a good book—no matter how many times you've read it, the words and plot still affect you."

Celeste met her gaze. "True."

Eve studied Celeste's amber eyes. *Pain. Longing. Desire. She feels it too. Nope. I can't go there. But I sure want to.* She looked away from Celeste's face and gestured to the screen. "Come on, let's keep watching so we can get to the sexy parts."

Celeste's laugh filled the small room and the empty parts of Eve's heart.

*

Eve shivered. The third-floor guest room was chilly after the cozy warmth of the viewing room and Celeste's company. She crossed the room and undid the braided silk cord holding the heavy red drapes in place. Eve's nipples pebbled as she tugged the left curtain closed. The ground was blanketed in sparkling blue-white snow under a full moon. She clasped the edge of the right curtain and a flash of orange and black drew Eve's gaze.

A tiger stood in profile, head lifted to the sky, fur glowing, haloed by the moonlight. Eve stared as the animal lifted its head and locked its gaze on Eve, pinning her in place. A shiver shook Eve and she had the sensation of her soul being stripped bare. She gasped, took a half step back, and yanked the curtain over the window.

Eve rubbed her eyes. *Too much wine after dinner. I'm drunk.* She raised her hand to her forehead. *Maybe I did hit my head? Is this how it started with Mom? The hallucinations, the voices? No. I'm okay. I'm tired. I'm going to open my eyes and it'll be gone.* She opened her eyes slowly before she pulled the curtain back with two fingers and scanned the snow. A broken line marred the satin surface. No tiger. The tracks led away from the house toward the mountains.

Eve yanked the curtain in place and turned her back. *My imagination. But the tracks. Must have been some random animal. The house borders the park. I'm tired. Exhausted. Bed. It will all be better in the morning.*

In the bathroom, Eve unwrapped a new toothbrush Celeste had left beside the sink and brushed her teeth. The black silk pajamas Celeste had laid out for her fit no better than the other clothes she had lent her. The sensation of the pajama pants climbing up her shin every time Eve turned over in bed was maddening. She tore off the pants and flung them to the floor.

Celeste had tended to Eve, prepared her a magnificent dinner, offered to pay for her clothes, and been the perfect hostess in every way. Eve's thoughts circled back to Celeste's methodical approach as she prepared dinner. The form-fitting plum-colored T-shirt Celeste wore had displayed her thickly muscled shoulders and trim waist to perfection. Eve had typed the same sentence of an email she was composing three times, unable to look away from Celeste's forearms as she chopped the vegetables for their dinner. *No indication of the unholy wildcat pain in the ass she was reported to be. Well, other than the suitcase. What's the difference between me and the others? Because they were straight? She's sure as hell not; not with that fuck-me vibe loud and clear even if she's not out. Not Domme enough? Or vanilla? No matter. Can't go there.*

Eve closed her eyes. *Her eyes. Intense. Hungry. Willing.* Images of Celeste's tightly muscled body, her silver hair twisted around her hands as she held Celeste in place, filled her mind. She imagined Celeste's gorgeous amber eyes looking up at Eve as she kneeled at her feet, her delicate mouth wrapped around her clit. She lowered her hand and brushed her fingers over her clit. Eve stroked herself. Gathering the slick heat between her legs, she jacked her clit. She rocked her hips, pressed into her hand, and thrust two fingers inside, while she rubbed her thumb over her clit in languorous circles.

Eve slid her other hand over her breast and rolled her nipple. She scraped her fingernail over the tip and the keen edge of pain detonated her orgasm. She arched into her palm and cupped herself and squeezed, setting off another orgasm. Gasping, she curled on her side and sank into delicious aftershocks. She stretched out under the perfectly weighted duvet, relaxed into the softness of the bed and postorgasmic lassitude, and slept.

Chapter Three

They met in the kitchen, and Eve nursed her coffee as Celeste sipped her tea. "You make damn good coffee for a tea drinker."

Celeste snorted. "I'm committed to caffeine in all its forms. I drink tea in the morning but usually indulge in coffee midafternoon."

Eve gathered her notes into a pile. "Where do you want to do this?"

A ghost of a smile played over Celeste's mouth. "This?"

Eve cocked her eyebrow. "Work?"

Celeste refilled her tea. "My study."

Eve picked up her coffee cup and tucked her laptop and notes under her arm. "Lead on."

In the wood-paneled study, Celeste brushed by Eve and opened the heavy blue drapes that covered a bay window. The brief contact ignited every sensuous thought Eve had tamped down during the night. The bay window offered a view of the valley floor and the mountains surrounding Celeste's home. The snow had stopped briefly overnight, only to start again as the sun rose. Now, it fell steadily. *Not going anywhere anytime soon. Stuck here. With a woman who is sexy and confusing as hell. Focus. Get it together.* The heady scent of Celeste's sandalwood perfume crowded Eve's senses. *Does she have to smell so good? Fuck me. Focus. Don't fuck this up acting like a thirsty teenager. Can't afford to blow this.* Eve stifled a surge of anxiety and stepped away from Celeste.

Celeste frowned at her. "Are you all right?"

"Fine." Eve placed her laptop on the library table that dominated the center of the room.

Floor-to-ceiling shelves lined the walls with a rolling ladder that rode along a brass rail and provided access to the uppermost shelves. Celeste sat at the head of the table, her posture regal. "I looked over your notes while you were sleeping."

Eve paced the room, anxious to keep distance between them. "And?"

"You're the first screenwriter to understand the core of *Stone Gate.* I don't know why they didn't send you to me two years ago."

"I was out of the business for a while." Eve rolled her pen in her hands.

Celeste tilted her head. "Why?" Her amber eyes were bright and locked on to Eve's gaze. "You're talented. I've seen *Miles to Go,* and *For All the Right Reasons.* Why did you drop out?"

Eve looked up at the ceiling before she brought her gaze back to Celeste's face. "I had a lover who claimed I plagiarized her work. She had a large fan base who believed her over me. No one would hire me. Until she tried it with someone more famous. The truth came out. Not that it did me any good." Eve sipped her coffee to chase the bitterness from her mouth.

Celeste tapped the top of the table, drawing her attention. "Have you already done a treatment? Or do we do this together?"

"Together. If both of our names are going on the screenplay."

Celeste crossed her arms. "I've never written with anyone before."

"First time for everything." Casting aside caution, Eve sat in the chair closest to Celeste. "Do you want to type? Or should I?"

Celeste frowned. "I've dictated my last ten books. I'd prefer you type."

"We need to scale your epic into one hundred and ten pages. Each page of a script is about a minute of film."

A thunderous expression crossed Celeste's face and Eve held up her hand, palm out. "If the studio accepts the script, depending on the producer and the director we may be able to convince them to expand it, but we need to start within the framework the studio has optioned."

Celeste scowled and sat back in her chair. "How? How can we do that without butchering it?"

Eve picked up her notes. "We strip your manuscript down, do a reverse outline, and then we choose the ten most important scenes. And then the next ten, and another ten until we have one hundred and ten pages."

Celeste drummed her fingers on the table. "Who chooses?"

Eve met her gaze. "We do. We do this together."

Celeste's nostrils flared. "What if we don't agree?"

"Then we keep talking until we do." Eve held out her hand. "If you want this, we can do it." She held Celeste's gaze. "*Stone Gate* saved my life. I saw people like me have a happy ending. Don't you want to bring it to the screen? Reach more people?"

Celeste's eyes glinted. "People like you? You mean non-white queer people? You mean us. You understand. I don't want *Stone Gate* to be some ridiculous version of queerness or stereotypes. I want it to be real, not some tarted-up version of what sells." She clasped Eve's hand, her grip strong, and tugged Eve close. "If nothing else comes of this, knowing *Stone Gate* helped you means more to me than any amount of money."

Eve's breath caught as Celeste leaned in and brushed a brusque kiss over her cheek. Her lips were soft and warm on her skin. She released Celeste's hand and ignored every warning thought going off in her head, cupped Celeste's face, and kissed her.

Celeste relaxed into her touch and Eve pressed her advantage, tightening her grip when Celeste growled into her mouth and opened to her. Eve teased her tongue over her teeth, and nipped Celeste's lower lip, before she soothed it with her tongue. *Take her. Now. Take what she's offering.*

*

Eve's lips were tender even as her hands on Celeste's face were firm. Celeste let herself linger. She relaxed with Eve's kiss, surrendered to her, let Eve take what she wanted and opened herself to Eve's control. Strong fingertips pressed into her skin as Eve held her in place. The pressure and promise rocketed through Celeste, and her clit ached. She clutched at Eve's shoulders, arching into her embrace, aching to appease the raging hunger no amount of hunting and blood-warm meat would ever satisfy. Her tiger-self rose up, restless, wanting, fierce, and desperate. *Her kiss. Her hands on me. Now. Let her. Give over. No. Too risky. Stop. Stop now.*

Celeste raised her hand and placed it in the middle of Eve's chest and pressed her back into her chair. Panting, she gazed into Eve's dark-brown eyes and melted under the desire she saw reflected in them. She closed her eyes.

Breathe. Celeste lowered her gaze and ignored the wet heat between her thighs. "We can't. I can't." She turned her face and nuzzled Eve's palm. "I'm sorry."

Eve jerked her hands away from Celeste's face. "Damn. Sorry. I didn't mean..." She stood and the chair teetered, and she caught it before it fell. "I don't. I'm not usually..." She raised her hands, palms out. "Please forgive me." She looked away from Celeste.

"Look at me, please?" Celeste tilted her head and met Eve's gaze. "It's not because I don't find you attractive. But it would complicate things."

Eve flushed, the dull red color blooming across her cheeks. "Thank you. And um, I agree. I'll sit over here." She pulled out the chair and sat opposite from Celeste.

Celeste spun her pen on the table. "You said *Stone Gate* saved your life. Tell me more?"

Eve pushed her thick black hair back with both hands. "Not much to tell. I was miserable as an adolescent. Every girl around me was ecstatic because they were looking forward to their *quinceañera* and dressing up and crazy about boys. I was flummoxed. All I wanted was to do was wear jeans and boots and ride motorcycles. I left home as soon as I could.

"I read *Stone Gate* so many times my copy fell apart. It made me feel like there were other people like me, that my tribe was somewhere. I ran away to San Francisco, hooked up with older, wiser women. Went to school at UCSF and started writing. Did what I could to pay my bills. Got lucky, made a connection at a party, landed in West Hollywood, and here I am."

Celeste raised an eyebrow. "You skipped a few years."

Eve smiled, the rakish smile Celeste was falling in love with. "I'm sure your agent filled you in on the pertinent details."

"I'm more interested in what you did to pay the rent. In *Stone Gate,* my main character works as a sexual Dominant. When you said people like me, were you referring to that also?"

Eve's eyebrows drew down. "Will it make a difference if I am?"

"No judgment from me. I'm curious. Based on your notes"—Celeste pinned Eve in place with her gaze—"and your kiss, you seem to have a deep understanding of my main character. More than a passing understanding. You get her. Get what it means to be a Domme."

Eve raised her chin and met Celeste's questioning gaze with a penetrating expression.

That look. She understands me. Knows what I am. Desire, bone-deep and devastating, rocketed through Celeste and she gripped the edge of the table, fighting her urge to slide to her knees and relax into Eve's control. Her mouth watered as she remembered Eve's kiss, the small nip, the way she tasted. Celeste lowered her gaze. "I see."

Celeste tapped the top of the table. "I can be professional. I didn't come here to seduce you. I came to do a job."

Celeste raised her head. "I didn't say you did. I'm not as easy, or desperate as you seem to think I am." She shoved her chair back and stood. "I need a break. Help yourself to whatever you want in the kitchen."

*

After lunch, Eve returned to the study. Celeste was standing at the window, her hand against the pane of glass, staring out at the valley.

"Are you okay?" Eve placed the cup of coffee she had

brought with her on the desk.

Celeste turned from the window and shrugged her shoulders. "I'm sorry for before. I'm ready to work now."

Eve sat and opened her laptop. "Why don't we set some guidelines, map out what is most important to you as a storyteller, then we'll work through the scenes and dialogue to make that happen."

"Are you a magician? You think we can really tell the story in one hundred ten scenes? I must have been mad to agree to this." Celeste turned back to the window with her hands clenched into fists.

"Look at me."

Celeste spun on her heel and faced Eve.

"We can do this. It may not be exactly what you want but if you're serious we can make this happen. Trust me. Please." Eve held Celeste's gaze. "Don't give up on this."

Celeste rested her hands on her hips and inclined her head toward the window and the snowstorm outside. "It's not like I could send you away."

Eve laughed. "You're stuck with me. Let's just try it. We can do this. I know we can."

Celeste paced as they worked. Eve had the sensation of stripping Celeste naked, as they discussed which scenes were most precious to her and other nonnegotiable aspects of her novel. Trusting her Domme's intuition, she was ruthless, demanding Celeste reveal her desires and vision for the film. Celeste prowled the library as Eve typed, adding her own thoughts as they worked on the outline.

Eve took her computer glasses off and rubbed her eyes. "Sit down before you wear a hole in the floor. You're like a long-tailed cat in a room full of rocking chairs."

Celeste frowned. "What?"

Eve quirked her mouth. "It's something my grandma used to say."

Celeste smiled and laughed. Eve stared at her over the top of her computer. *Her laugh. Rich. Sweet. Makes me want to kiss her. Again. Would it be wrong? She said no. Honor that. Honor her.*

Celeste stopped walking and rested her hand on her hip. "I haven't heard that expression in years. My mother's family lived in Greenville, Mississippi for a while. Did you grow up in the south? I don't hear an accent."

Eve lifted her thick hair with both hands and let it fall before she shook it back into place. "I grew up in Atlanta. I worked long and hard to eradicate my accent."

Celeste tilted her head. "I get that." She glanced at the time on Eve's computer screen. "It's late. Are you hungry?"

Don't say it. Stay classy. Still can't believe that kiss. What the hell was I thinking? "Yes. Should we stop for the day?"

"Yes. I need to start supper."

"You don't have to cook for me." Eve flushed. *Smooth. She said she was hungry. Stop talking.*

Celeste turned to face Eve. "I like to cook. It's a pleasure for me." She looked down and away. "I haven't had anyone to..." She twisted her fingers together in a tight knot in front of her waist. "It's not a hardship."

Eve eyed the dejected set of Celeste's shoulders. "I don't cook for myself either when I'm alone."

Celeste pursed her lips. "Don't feel like you have to stop working. You don't have to keep me company."

Eve studied her face and the sadness reflected in Celeste's eyes. "Let me back this up, and I'm at your service."

Celeste's lips pulled into a half smile. "Be careful what you say. I might take you up on it."

*

The claret was divine, and Celeste indulged herself by pouring another glass for both of them. Eve sat across from her, reclined on the couch, her long legs splayed out, one arm along the back of the couch and the other cradling her wineglass. Celeste sipped her wine, enjoying the tart sweetness of the vintage as it filled her mouth and senses. She toyed with the edge of the fleece blanket covering her legs.

Eve closed her eyes and stretched her legs out in front of her. "Long day."

Her eyes remained closed, and Celeste took advantage of it, letting her gaze travel over Eve's full mouth, the smooth line of her jaw and then lower as she admired her half-hard nipples obvious through her shirt and imagined the way they would feel on her tongue. *What would be the harm? She's only here for a few weeks. And then she'll be gone. What would it be like to have her hands on me?* Celeste bit her lip hard enough to draw blood, the coppery taste soothing. *That kiss. More. I want more. Of that. Of her. I want her. No strings.*

Eve opened her eyes and stared at Celeste. Her expression was sharp in contrast to her relaxed pose. "What?" She smoothed her hand over her shirt and brushed over her nipples. "Do I have something on my shirt?"

Celeste flushed and looked away. "No. Sorry. I didn't mean to stare."

"Didn't you?" Eve sipped her wine. "Like what you

see?"

"Are you always this forward?" Celeste brought her gaze back to Eve's face.

Eve lifted her chin and firmed her mouth. "I'm sorry about the kiss."

Celeste raised an eyebrow. "Sorry you kissed me? Or didn't you enjoy it?"

Eve quirked her mouth. "Because I did. I'm not going to deny I'm attracted to you. As unprofessional as it is." She looked away from Celeste. "I don't want to make you uncomfortable. Or fuck this job up."

Celeste placed her wineglass on the side table. "I'm not uncomfortable." She crossed to Eve and stood in front of her. "Out of practice."

She took Eve's glass from her hand and then settled it next to her glass on the side table. She straddled Eve's legs.

Eve smirked and raised her eyebrow. "Are you now?"

Celeste dropped a kiss on her mouth, kissing the smirk off Eve's face as she lowered herself to her lap. "Yes. And ready to change that." She wrapped her hands in Eve's hair and kissed her again. "Are you ready?" Celeste leaned in to Eve's body and indulged herself in the kiss she had been craving since their first. Eve's mouth was sweet and hot, the sharp taste of the wine flavoring their kiss. Celeste held Eve in place, taking her time with a slow deep kiss. She pulled back to look into Eve's face.

Eve gasped and clutched Celeste's shoulders, her eyes glazed with desire. "You sure?"

Celeste kissed her again, tasting the delicate vintage on her lips as she trailed her hand down and cupped Eve's breasts. She smiled as her nipples hardened under her palms. "Yes. You?"

Eve groaned and nuzzled Celeste's neck, her lips soft and teasing as she shifted her grip and dug her fingers into Celeste's ass. She pulled Celeste against her and rocked hard. "Does this feel unsure?"

"No." Celeste raised her chin as Eve kissed the hollow of her throat before she nipped the delicate skin there. Sharp sweet pain shot through Celeste.

Eve's tongue traced a line over the shell of Celeste's ear.

She lost herself in the sensation of Eve's strong hands on her hips, holding her in place, and the rocking of her hips as she ground against her, sending ripples of pleasure through her body. "Please."

Eve nuzzled her neck. "Please, what?" Her hands were firm as she gripped the curves of Celeste's ass.

"Please. I want you..." Celeste kissed the skin under Eve's ear. "I need you to..." She raised her head and held Eve's gaze as she lifted her body clear of Eve's lap. She lowered her eyes, kneeled, and then touched her forehead to Eve's feet. "Please."

Eve plucked out the hair sticks holding up Celeste's long moonlight-colored hair and it tumbled over her shoulders. She carded her fingers through Celeste's hair before she wound it around her hand and tugged her head back. She kissed the corner of Celeste's mouth and rubbed the backs of her knuckles over Celeste's taut throat. Celeste closed her eyes and hummed her delight, relaxing into Eve's touch.

"Look at me." Eve's dark gaze settled on Celeste's face. "What do you need? Do you want to serve me?" She rubbed her thumb over Celeste's lower lip.

Celeste shuddered at the raw need in Eve's voice.

"Yes."

She twisted in Eve's grip and bit her hand, stopping short of breaking the skin, and deliberately raised her gaze in challenge. *Let her show me if she's Domme enough.*

"You like it rough, naughty kitten?" Eve's gaze glittered.

"You have no idea." Celeste nipped Eve's palm again.

Eve's expression hardened. "Oh, I have an idea. And you are desperately in need of a lesson."

Celeste smiled. "Am I?"

Eve trailed a finger over Celeste's breast and then flicked her nipple as she tightened her grip on her hair. She yanked hard and arched Celeste's head back, forcing her to scrabble for balance. "You tell me."

Celeste hissed and moaned, reveling in the stinging pain that rocketed through her body from Eve's rough handling. She pressed her thighs together to stem the flow of need soaking her pants. "Yes."

"Safe word?"

"Am I going to need it?"

"I won't play without it."

"Smoke."

"Smoke." Eve kissed Celeste's forehead, cupped her breast, and squeezed hard enough to bruise before she released her. Celeste lost her balance and tumbled to the floor.

"Strip. Now." Eve leaned back on the couch.

Celeste took a shuddering breath and rose. Lust roiled through her and she swayed. Eve reached out with both hands and steadied her.

"You okay, kitten?"

Cruel but caring. A Domme. A Mistress. My

Mistress. For tonight. The gesture undid Celeste, and she bit her lip to stem the dark emotions swirling in her soul. *Take it. Give her everything. Let go.* "Yes."

*

"Good." Eve released Celeste and shifted on the couch, setting her feet wide. "Slowly. I want to see you."

Celeste raised her hands to the hem of her shirt and tugged it over her head. Her small firm breasts were topped by thick brown nipples, her broad shoulders were capped with rounded muscle. Sculpted biceps and thick forearms roped with muscle made Eve's fingers tingle with the desire to touch Celeste's toned body. "Oh my. Even better than I imagined."

Celeste lifted her chin. A dull red flush spread over her body and a hint of a smile played around her mouth.

Eve inclined her head at Celeste. "Continue."

Celeste turned away from Eve. A random pattern of scars covered her back, shiny and raised, hard evidence of her experience with rough play. She bent at the waist as she slipped out of her tights and tossed them to the floor. Her rounded ass and thick thighs made Eve's mouth water. *Damn she's built. Those scars. Not kidding about rough play. Her thighs. Can't wait to paddle that ass.*

Celeste turned to face her. A sheen of wetness glittered on the smooth, closely trimmed straight hair between her thighs.

"Commando? Hopeful? Did you plan this? Show me. Show me how much you want this."

Celeste spread her legs wide and used both hands to display her thick clit. She dipped her fingers between her legs and cupped herself. She held Eve's gaze as she lifted her fingers to her mouth and licked them. Eve tilted her head and smiled at Celeste as she licked and sucked her desire from her fingers. Celeste closed her eyes, her face blissful.

"Come here." Eve scooted to the edge of the couch cushion. "Kneel."

Celeste kept her eyes averted and kneeled between Eve's legs. Eve unbuttoned her shirt and shrugged out of it before she reached behind her and unhooked her black lace bra. She tossed her clothes aside. "You've been staring at my breasts all evening." She cupped her breasts and pinched her nipples into hard peaks. "You fantasized about having your mouth on me, imagined how my nipples would feel in your mouth, didn't you?"

"Yes." Celeste's voice was a soft drawl. "Are you one of those fortunate women who can come from having their nipples sucked?"

"Mmm." Eve lifted Celeste's fingers to her mouth and licked them. She inhaled, filling her senses with the sweet scent of Celeste as want surged through her. "I have come that way once or twice. You want to try? Show me how much you want to give me pleasure?"

"Yes. Please." She tipped her head to the side and glanced at Eve from beneath her lashes. "What should I call you?"

"Miss." Eve reached out and cupped the back of Celeste's neck. The silky tendrils of her silver-colored hair floated over Eve's knuckles. She reached between Celeste's legs and drew her wetness over her thick clit, the slickness and heat ratcheting up her desire. She fingered her, rubbing Celeste's clit in slow circles and watching her face as she sank into her attentions, her jaw slack. Eve slid two fingers inside Celeste's wet heat and rocked her thumb over the base of her clit before she eased the hood back to tease the hard tip.

Her breathing quickened. "It's been a long time, Miss. I'm not...I don't think I can stop."

Eve leaned down and nipped her ear hard. Celeste cried out and came over Eve's fingers. "Naughty kitten." She rotated her fingers inside and swept her fingers over her sweet spot. Celeste gripped her arms, digging her nails into Eve's flesh, and yowled as she came again. A gush of fluid spilled down her thighs and wet Eve's wrist. "Oh Miss. Sorry. I couldn't stop. Please forgive me."

Eve pressed a kiss to Celeste's mouth, drinking in her pleasure, kissing her hard enough to bruise. Celeste dug her fingers into Eve's arms as she kissed her.

"Don't apologize for squirting; it's sexy as hell. But we'll have to work on your control, kitten. Until then..." Eve straightened. "Show me what you can do." She pulled Celeste's head to her breast. "Suck me."

Celeste's hot mouth closed over Eve's nipple and she sucked hard once. Eve groaned and gripped Celeste's shoulders, and wrapped her legs around her waist. Her hot tongue flickered over the skin under the curve of Eve's breast. Celeste nipped her in between the tender licks. She circled her tongue around Eve's nipple, skirting it, as she nuzzled and kissed her breasts. Eve's fingers tightened on Celeste's shoulders when she finally took her nipple into her mouth. She sucked hard and rolled Eve's nipple with her lips and tongue. Eve panted as sharp sensation pulsed through her body. Her clit swelled, and she rubbed against Celeste's upper body, the pressure and drag increasing her pleasure.

Celeste hummed around her nipple, giving it a final lick before she cupped it with her hand and rolled the nipple. She covered Eve's other nipple with her mouth, and Eve groaned as the twin sensations roiled through her. She panted as the pressure in her clit built, and she rocked in place, rubbing against Celeste's firm stomach as she suckled her. The rough texture of Celeste's tongue on her nipple spiked her pleasure. Celeste hummed, the vibrations from her mouth like a rip current to Eve's clit. *What would that feel like on my clit? So fucking good.* Eve arched against Celeste, wanting more of her mouth.

Celeste strummed her nipple with her tongue before she bit down, sending Eve tumbling into a climax. She clung to Celeste as the waves of pleasure rippled through her. Celeste groaned, a deep rumble, and her body vibrated against Eve's thighs as she laved her nipple and sent a ripping aftershock through Eve.

"Enough." Panting, Eve tugged Celeste's mouth away from her sensitive nipple. "Look at me."

Celeste opened her eyes and locked on to Eve's gaze.

Eve stared into Celeste's eyes. *Her eyes. Like the ones on the cliff. Like the tiger outside my window. What the fuck? I'm drunk. Did she slip something in the wine? No. It's the light.* She closed her eyes, opened them again slowly. She peered into Celeste's face. A soft halo of light framed her body, her skin shimmering, and her cheeks were rounder, her nose flatter. Her amber eyes were bright, and her pupils were huge. Eve gasped and covered her eyes with her hand. *They're the same. No. What is wrong with me?*

"Eve?" Celeste's breath tickled Eve's cheek. "Eve?" Her hand massaged Eve's thigh. "Are you all right?" She rubbed her face against the curve of Eve's neck.

Eve inhaled sharply. "Fine. I'm fine. The wine. I must have had more than I realized."

"Lay down. I'll get you some water." Celeste's arm

settled around her shoulders and she lifted Eve's legs to the sofa. Eve sagged in Celeste's embrace and let her position her on the couch. Celeste smoothed her hand over her skin and then covered her with a blanket. She leaned down and pressed a kiss to Eve's cheek. "I won't be a minute."

Eve sagged against the couch and kept her eyes closed. She listened for the sound of Celeste's footsteps as she left the room before she opened them. She rolled to her back, pillowed her head in her hands, and stared at the coffered ceiling. *It's starting. Mom was my age. Seeing things. Just like her. Fuck.*

Chapter Four

She saw. I can't believe I lost control. Celeste chewed her lip. *Will she believe what she saw? Or question it? She thinks she was drunk. It can't happen again.* A flush crept over her cheeks as she remembered the sensation of Eve's fingers on her clit, inside her, and an ache settled between her legs. *What to do? She can't know. Too dangerous. She'll leave when this is finished. It was a one-off. A chance to fuck an idol.*

Celeste sipped her tea. Fat fluffy flakes of snow fell steadily, adding to the uneven drifts dotted across the valley. *Even if she wants to leave, she can't. I want more. More of her. I can control it. That hasn't happened in years. Lorraine, I miss you.* Celeste rubbed her chest. The ache in her heart, the one she kept at bay most days, rose up and choked her.

The vision of Lorraine's lifeless form swam before Celeste. A grubby man stood over her, his gun on his hip, and a smile on his face as he posed for the guide's camera. And then the aftermath: his screams, the blood, the satisfying crunch of breaking his neck as Celeste took her vengeance. But it had not brought Lorraine back. And now here she was, falling in love. Again. And risking her life. Both their lives. *What if she wants me? Would I say yes? Would I offer it? Would she want me as I am? Would she understand? Or go screaming into the night?*

She ground the beans for Eve's coffee and added them to the French press before she filled the kettle. The blue-yellow flame flared as the burner lit. Celeste was grateful once again for the large propane heater and generator that kept the house cozy and the lights on. Even without the benefit of an internet weather app she knew the storm would not end anytime soon. She knew. As she knew Eve would be arriving in the kitchen in seconds. Her acute senses and hearing never failed her. She waited until Eve entered the kitchen before she poured the boiling water over the grounds.

Eve was dressed in her own clothes, her worn jeans and form-fitting black long-sleeve T-shirt displaying her body to perfection. Celeste smiled at her. "Good morning."

"Thank you for washing my clothes. You didn't have to do that."

"I know. I had to wash my own. It wasn't a bother."

Eve rubbed the back of her neck. "I'm sorry about last night."

"Sorry it happened?" Celeste worked to keep her voice neutral and turned away from Eve to select a cup from the cupboard.

"No." Eve's voice was distant. "Not sorry it happened."

She's not telling me everything. She regrets. "Do you feel like I took advantage of you?"

Eve sat at on the tall stool next to the kitchen island, and her silence slashed Celeste's reserve like a knife.

Celeste turned to face her and placed the cup in front of her.

"I didn't say no." Eve traced the edge of the coffee cup with her finger. "I'm not sure what happened. I didn't realize I'd drunk so much."

Celeste filled Eve's cup. "I understand. It won't happen again." She turned her back to Eve and lowered her chin to her chest. *It was a one-off. Not interested in me. Other than some story to tell her friends.* "I have some work I have to attend to this morning. Shall we get back to work after lunch? Say one?"

"Sure."

Celeste refilled her teacup and left Eve there, unwilling to look into her eyes, fearful of what she would see there.

*

The room housing the small lap pool was warm, the air humid, and three of the walls were lined with plants. The overhead lighting was bright and reflected off the still water of the pool. A small glass-topped wrought iron table with two dainty chairs was to the left of the door, and Eve placed her towel on one of the chairs. She stripped out of her clothes and draped them over the other chair. Gooseflesh covered her skin. She tested the water, surprised by its warmth. Eve lowered herself into the pool and relaxed into the soothing water. She was naked and didn't care. Breakfast had been an awkward affair; Celeste was remote, and Eve had been anxious.

When Celeste offered the use of the lap pool, Eve had taken her up on the offer, already antsy from not being able to run. *Fucking snow.* The pool was on the lower level of the house. Floor-to-ceiling windows opened on one side, and the air was chill in contrast to the warm water. Eve rested her hands on the side of the pool and pillowed her chin on her hands. The snow fell steadily, and a two-foot drift rested against the base of the glass wall. *Not going anywhere any time soon. Fuck. She's as freaked out about last night as I am. No more wine for me. Unbelievably good and can't happen again. Those scars. She likes heavy pain.* A wave of sadness washed over her as she imagined Celeste bereft of a lover who she adored enough to gift her flesh and blood.

Eve lay back and floated in the pool, willing herself to relax and not think about how badly she had fucked up. Her nipples hardened as she remembered the feeling of Celeste's mouth on her, and the way she had come for her, the wanton look on her face and the way her hair had curtained them when she leaned down and kissed Eve goodnight after she carried her to her room. *Slept with a client. And not just any client, Celeste Quon. Fuck. Will we be able to get the script done? Will she send me packing? What am I going to do about the money? And the fucking rental car. Damn it. Should have gotten the insurance. What was up with me last night? What did I see? Am I losing it? Is this how it started with Mom? Would it have been different if we had caught it sooner?*

Eve closed her eyes against the memories of her mother's first break with reality, her flight from home at sixteen. She swallowed on a dry throat as she remembered the blank expression in her mother's eyes when she last visited her, and the hurt in her heart when her mother said she didn't have a daughter. *No use going there. Can't change it. Did she know it was happening? Did she ignore it? Blame it on being tired or drunk? Did she know?*

She swam over and flipped the switch to start the current for her lap swim. She settled into a rhythm as she swam freestyle and focused on her breathing as she fought against the manufactured current. The repetition of her motions and effort helped to sort her jumbled thoughts. *I can't fuck this up. Will she want more? I hurt her blaming it on the wine. Damn I want more. And then what? I go back to my life, and she stays here. She acted like she wanted more this morning. Carrying me to bed. Her kiss goodnight. No one has ever carried me anywhere. I want her. Damn it. And then I acted like I didn't want her. I'm an ass. I need to apologize.*

*

Eve had spent the rest of her morning after her swim writing out scene cards and had them spread over the library table. Lunch had been as awkward as breakfast, their sparse conversation stilted and banal. Eve prayed that working together would repair the damage to their relationship.

Celeste's hair was coiled on top of her head in an intricate braid, and she wore what Eve had come to think of as her signature outfit of black workout tights and a matching short-sleeve top. She forced her gaze away from Celeste's body, ignoring her desire to reach out, to ask for forgiveness and then trail a line of kisses along her neck and strong jaw before she lost herself kissing her plump lips.

Eve tapped the table "Where's the scene with the dog?"

"It's in the 'discuss' pile."

Celeste frowned. "That scene is vital. It makes Carly relatable, otherwise she comes across as a selfish ass."

"She is a selfish ass."

Celeste tilted her head. "Everyone has the potential to be an ass. But she's more than that. I thought you said you read my novel. If you did, you would realize Carly is much more than a woman determined to get her own way at any cost. She saves Marla."

"Yes. And then takes advantage of Marla's gratitude." Eve tapped the index card in front of her. "She seduces Marla when she's most vulnerable." Eve looked away from Celeste's hard gaze. "Carly is every person who ever helps someone and expects sexual favors in return."

Celeste lifted her chin. "Carly's hurting. Marla is a grown woman capable of saying no. It's not like she's drunk." She rounded on Eve. "Or pretends she was the morning after."

Eve pushed her hair back with both hands and exhaled sharply. "We aren't talking about the book now, are we?"

Celeste looked away. "Take it any way you want."

"I knew it was a mistake. Should we even bother to pretend to work on this? You're not going to be satisfied with anything I do. Is this why everyone else has left?" Eve's gut roiled. *Did she seduce the others who tried to work with her? Is she a predator? Am I another in a long list of conquests?*

"I am perfectly capable of continuing our working relationship. Unless you decide otherwise; I'm willing to work with you. And you are not those idiots. Nor am I the desperate slut you seem to think I am." Celeste's voice dropped to a low growl. "But I will not have my story butchered, and my characters reduced to cardboard cutouts. As far as anything being a mistake, my only regret was thinking you were someone I might be able to..."

"Might be able to what?" Eve took a step and closed the distance between them.

"Trust." Celeste looked away and stepped back.

"You can trust me." Eve tossed her pen on the desk.

"No. I can't. Not when you're not honest with me."

"I've been honest." Eve eased forward with her hand outstretched.

"No. You haven't." Celeste took another step back. "You saw. Me. The real me. And blamed it on the wine."

Eve clenched her fists. "What the hell are you talking about?"

"You talk in your sleep." Celeste walked to the window and looked out. "I heard you."

Eve scrubbed her hand over her face. "You're mad about what I said while I was dreaming?" She snorted. "That's wacky as hell."

Celeste rounded on her. "What's 'wacky' is your rationalization of things you see. Your denial."

"You don't know me."

"I know more than you think. I know your mother has been in a mental health facility for the last ten years. I know you're broke and took this job out of desperation. I know you were the most in demand Mistress, with a six-month waiting list, when you worked at the Ranch. I know you have not returned to your former profession even though it would help with paying the bills." Celeste pulled her shirt over her head and dropped it to the floor and added her sports bra to the pile. "And I know you are terrified of what you've seen."

Eve bit her lip as Celeste tugged off her pants and briefs, her mouth dry, unable to look away from Celeste's stunning physique. She held up her hand, palm out. "Stop. Please."

Celeste held her gaze. "Watch me."

Eve stared. Celeste crouched on the floor, her body glowing and her back lengthening, her skin buckling and splitting as hair sprouted and covered her body, her face morphing and changing shape as her jaw elongated. Eve covered her mouth with both hands to stifle her scream. In the place Celeste had been moments before, a Siberian tiger stood. Eve closed her eyes. *Not real. Not real. None of this is real. I'm going to wake up in my bed. Or the hospital. Or I'm dead, and this is hell.*

Fur tickled her thighs, and she opened her eyes and looked down into the upraised face of the tiger. She trembled and held her breath. Her gut roiled and bile rose in her throat. She pointed a finger at the tiger. "Not real. You. Are. Not. Real. Shoo. Go away." She stepped back and waved both hands in the air as if clearing smoke. *Can't be real. I must be losing it. This is it. Maybe they'll let me and Mom share a room.* A ragged laugh burst from her throat, and she closed her eyes. Another more insistent press of the tiger's shoulder against her thighs threatened her balance.

Her throat burned as she opened her eyes and looked into the liquid amber gaze of the tiger. Her fingers trembled as she lowered her hand and touched the tiger's head. The orange, white, and black striped fur was luxuriant under her fingertips. The tiger's ears twitched as it stared at her, amber eyes patient, fixed on Eve's face. Eve shivered even as a trickle of sweat stung her eyes. *Same eyes. Like last night. Like on the mountain. Fuck. Oh fuck.* The same eyes she had looked into last night after Celeste had made her come without even touching her clit. *Her eyes. Oh fuck.*

"Celeste?" Eve panted. "Celeste." The tiger chuffed and rubbed against Eve's thighs. "Oh fuck. You're. I..." Eve yelped. She backed away and fell over the ottoman. Sharp nauseating pain shot through her body as her elbow connected with the corner of the coffee table.

"Fuck." She ignored the searing numbing pain in her elbow and crab-walked away from the tiger. *Celeste. It's Celeste.*

She huddled against the couch and dropped her head between her knees and closed her eyes. *Not real. Not real. Not. Real.*

A cool hand on the back of her neck made her jerk away.

Celeste kneeled next to her. "I'm sorry. I didn't know how else to tell you."

Eve leaned away from Celeste. "Um. Do you...Are you a, um, what are you? A were-tiger or something?"

Celeste tucked a lock of Eve's hair behind her ear and laughed. "No. No moon needed. And I am not mindless like some of those creatures. We have been called many things. I'm a shifter. As a child I could take on any feline form I desired. As an adult, the tiger is my settled form."

Eve looked up at the ceiling. A laugh burbled from her throat. Celeste raised an eyebrow. "What?"

Eve patted her chest. "I'm not hallucinating. I'm not imagining things."

Celeste tilted her head at her. "No." She reached out and took Eve's hand and held it to her face. "Not at all. About any of this." She kissed Eve's palm. "Or about how I feel about you."

*

Celeste sat on her heels. *Too much. She's freaked. Like anyone would be. What was I thinking?* Eve's breathing was steady now. She trailed her fingers over her shoulder. "You want some water?"

Eve licked her dry lips. "Yes."

Celeste rose and walked to the desk. She poured Eve a glass of water and brought it to her. She kneeled and held it out with both hands.

Eve took the water and gulped greedily with her eyes closed. Celeste watched her throat work as she drank.

Eve finished the glass in two long swallows. She pushed a lock of her hair back over her ear and glanced at Celeste.

"More?" Celeste looked into her eyes. *Fear. Relief. Confusion.* "It's a lot to take in."

"How long?" Eve chewed her lip. "Were you born this way? Or did something happen?"

Celeste took Eve's hand. "Born this way. It's why my family left Kunming and moved to Singapore, and then here."

Eve looked away from Celeste's face. "I don't believe this. How do I know I'm not asleep? Or in the hospital like my mom?"

Celeste took her hand and held it in both of hers and placed it over her heart. "I'm real. You are not in a hospital and you are not your mother."

"But my mom sees things. She has since I was sixteen." Eve's eyes widened. "What if what my mom sees is real?" She jerked her hand away from Celeste's grip. "What if she's been medicated and hospitalized, and she's been seeing real things?" Eve stood abruptly. "What if she's not schizophrenic?"

The anguish on Eve's face made Celeste's heart ache. She rested her hand on Eve's thigh as she remained kneeling. "What does your mother say she sees?"

Eve jerked away from Celeste's touch and paced the room. "She sees animals, people, monsters." She stopped and pinned Celeste with a glare. "She hears people telling her to do things. The first time she was hospitalized, when I was a kid, she had locked my brother and me in a closet to keep us safe from giant snakes only she could see." She stepped close, reached down, and cupped Celeste's cheek with trembling fingers. "What if, instead of snakes, I'm seeing you as a beast?" Her eyes were bright.

Celeste leaned in to her touch, turned her face, and kissed her palm. She gripped Eve's hand. "Do you want to watch again? To feel it happen?"

Eve drew her thumb over Celeste's lower lip. "Can you do that?"

Celeste smiled at Eve. "My body is mine to command, unless I surrender my control to someone else."

Eve's eyebrow rose and her nostrils flared. "Someone?"

Her voice held the edge of censure and cut Celeste's submissive soul to the quick.

"You. Unless I give it to you. What would you like to see me do, Miss? Would you like me to shift for you?"

Eve rocked back on her heels and her eyes fixed on Celeste's face. "Show me the tiger again." She placed her hand on Celeste's head. Her mouth pulled into a cruel smile. "Prove it to me."

Celeste moved Eve's hand from her head and placed her elegant fingers between her teeth. She held her gaze as she focused her energy. She stretched and relaxed into her tiger, enjoying the challenge of not crushing Eve's hand in between her teeth as her body morphed, jaw and teeth changing to those of a four-hundred-pound cat.

She groaned as her spine lengthened, the pain of shifting excruciating and comforting. She chuffed as fur sprouted from her skin. Celeste looked into Eve's eyes. *No fear. Trust. Trusts me not to hurt her. Trusts my control. My submission. My gift to her. Will she want it?* She released Eve's hand, sat on her haunches, and waited for her next command.

*

The beast at her feet released her hand from between its teeth. Eve squared her shoulders. She gazed into Celeste's amber eyes. "Come back to me as Celeste. Now." The Siberian tiger lifted a paw and licked the back of it and swiped it over its face as if it were a house cat instead of a wild animal capable of shredding Eve with its massive claws. The tiger tilted its head and held Eve's gaze.

Eve stared as the air around the tiger shimmered. The beast seemed to collapse in on itself, shifting and turning until Celeste's human form filled the space the tiger had been. Eve pressed a hand to her chest and exhaled slowly. Her body tingled with the delicious gift of Celeste's submission. Overwhelming desire flowed through her at the thought of being able to control a woman with as much power as Celeste Quon possessed. A woman who wanted to surrender her control to Eve, who trusted her to keep her secret and keep her safe.

She reached out and cupped Celeste's chin and kissed her deeply, sucking her lip between her teeth and nipping it. Celeste moaned into her mouth, and Eve's body responded, her nipples tightening. She pulled back and looked into Celeste's eyes. *Desire. Want. Need.* "Why me? Why do you want to submit to me?"

Celeste looked up and into Eve's eyes. "Because you don't fear me. Because you're unafraid of your own desires. Because I know you can give me what I want." She gripped Eve's shoulders. "What I need."

Eve wrapped Celeste's braid around her hand and tugged her head back. She closed her hand over her throat and rubbed the pad of her thumb over her strong pulse. "And what do you need?"

"Pain. Pleasure. Discipline. The gift of relaxing into your control. Nothing to worry about, nothing to focus on but you and your desires. Safe in your control." Celeste's eyes were bright. "Cherished."

Eve squeezed, tightening her fingers around Celeste's throat, a hint of a threat. She released her braid and with her other hand she rolled her nipple until it was a tight point. She squeezed hard before she rubbed the tip with the pad of her thumb. She leaned down and sucked the hard point into her mouth, drawing the edge of her teeth over the tip. Celeste's chest-rattling groan filled the room. Eve lifted her head. Celeste's pupils were dilated, her body tense, and her breath rapid.

"What do you wish of me, Miss?" Celeste whispered.

Desire, rich and heady, blazed through Eve, stoked by Celeste's submission. Eve inhaled sharply and rubbed the tender skin of Celeste's throat with the back of her knuckles before she moved her hand and cupped the back of her neck. She pulled her close and brushed her lips over her mouth before she sucked her lower lip between her teeth and nipped. A rush burned through her as she savored Celeste's low moan and the sensation of her relaxing into Eve's control. Celeste trusted her, surrendered to her, wanted to give to Eve what she craved above all else. Eve's body trembled with the gift of Celeste's submission and she ached with need.

Eve lowered the zipper on her jeans.

Celeste's lips pulled back into a smile, and she swept her tongue over her lower lip. Her hands opened and closed at her sides. "Please. Let me taste you. Please, Miss." She swayed forward on her knees.

Eve slipped her hand inside her briefs and gathered wetness on her fingertips. She held her hand out to Celeste. "Do you want this? Want to suck my clit?"

"Yes. Oh please, Miss. Let me pleasure you. Please."

The neediness in her voice drove Eve to release Celeste's neck. She shoved her jeans down. She held herself open, exposing her hot hard clit to the cool air of the study. "Lick it."

Celeste scooted closer and her mouth closed over Eve's clit. *Eager. Desperate. Her mouth.* Eve groaned as Celeste's tongue swirled over her clit, delicious sensations filled her, and she rocked into Celeste's mouth, seeking more. Eve rested her hands on her wide shoulders to steady herself. Celeste tongued her, sliding her tongue over her slick lips and then inside, thrusting deep, curling her tongue and teasing her before she returned to her clit and sucked gently, her head moving rhythmically.

"Mmm. You like this, don't you? Want me to come in your mouth?"

Celeste's whimper almost made Eve come at that moment. She closed her eyes, gathered her control, and relaxed into the sensations of Celeste's mouth as she served her. She let her orgasm build, wanting it to go on. Celeste appeared to have other ideas. She edged her tongue under the hood of Eve's clit. When she fluttered her tongue over the tip softly, Eve spilled her desire into Celeste's greedy mouth. Celeste pulsed her tongue against her clit and Eve cried out and dug her fingers into Celeste's shoulders as she came again.

Chapter Five

Celeste lapped at Eve, savoring the sweet heat between her thighs, Eve's gift to her. *Her reward. Mine. To be hers. What would it be like?* Eve's hands on her shoulders pushed her away, and Celeste couldn't stifle her groan of despair as she allowed herself to be moved. "More, Miss, please. Let me give you more."

Eve's harsh laugh filled the room. "Greedy kitten. You'll have to earn it."

Celeste sat back on her heels, spread her knees wide, and lowered her head to the floor. "I am yours to command."

Eve's hand closed on the back of her neck, her grip comforting and firm. "Stand for me." Eve withdrew her touch and stood with her hands on her hips, her gaze fixed on Celeste's body as she complied with her command.

Celeste rose and stood with her hands clasped behind her back. The position thrust her breasts forward. Eve tilted her head and pursed her lips.

See me. Touch me. Celeste spread her legs shoulder width and lifted her chin. Comfortable in her skin, her body, proud of her physique, her nipples peaked under Eve's gaze. *Please touch me.*

Eve stepped close, the heat from her body washing over Celeste as she circled her, randomly skittering her fingers over Celeste's skin. Eve's power rolled off her and filled the room. She lifted Celeste's braid and draped it over her shoulder and nipped the tender skin over the curve of her neck. Celeste fought her need to kneel in her presence.

Celeste dug her nails into her palms, the sharp pain focusing her as Eve continued to ghost her hands over her skin. The gentle touches of her fingertips lingered on the myriad scars covering Celeste's back. Eve's touch stirred memories of Lorraine's single-tail whip and the exquisite torture and pleasure of her attentions.

Eve kissed her shoulder, her lips soft, and then her teeth, sharp and bruising. Celeste shuddered. Eve pressed against her back, the hard tips of her nipples contrasting with the soft fullness of her breasts. "I love your scars. They are gorgeous. Such dedication." She kissed the space under Celeste's ear and murmured against her skin. "Who did this? A lover? Or lovers?"

"Only one. Lorraine."

"Your Mistress? Are you owned?" She wrapped her arms around Celeste and pulled her tight against her.

Celeste leaned back into the Eve's embrace. "No. Not owned. Widowed."

Eve's arms tightened around Celeste. "I'm sorry." Celeste closed her eyes and raised her hand up and cupped Eve's face. She rested her cheek against her jaw. "Don't be. I'm at peace with it."

"Are you?" Eve kissed her cheek. "You're sure you want this? Want me like this?"

Celeste's breath hitched. "Yes. Please. I need. It's been too long."

Eve cupped Celeste's breasts and thumbed her nipples.

Celeste moaned and rocked her hips back, grinding against Eve. "Use me. Please."

Eve brought her lips to the shell of Celeste's ear and kissed her neck. She released her and walked over to the desk and crooked her finger at Celeste.

Celeste held her gaze as she crossed the room.

"Hands and elbows flat on the table. Spread your legs."

Celeste walked to the desk and lay down; the polished wood was cool against her nipples.

Eve drew a finger through the slickness that gleamed on Celeste's thighs. "I like how wet you are." She ground her hips against Celeste's ass. "You are wondrously beautiful like this. I don't know if I want to spank you or fuck right now." She thrust three fingers in deep, and Celeste bucked against her, her body clutching at Eve's fingers, unable to stop herself from coming as Eve fucked her.

"Mmm. You're greedy. I like that. Simply talking about spanking you makes you greedy. But you came without permission again." Eve drew back and pumped her fingers in again. "Imagine how desperate you'll be for me to fuck you after I spank you. Spank first, fuck later." She pulled her hand free and Celeste cried out with the loss.

Celeste panted and rested her cheek on the table. "Please, Miss. Please."

"Please what? Ask for what you need. Say it."

"Please, Miss. Spank me. Please."

Eve moved Celeste's braid to the side and placed her warm palm in the middle of Celeste's back, pinning her in place. "Same word?"

"Yes, Miss. Smoke, Miss."

Eve smoothed her palm over Celeste's firm ass. "Count for me, kitten. No coming without permission."

A shiver of anticipation stole through Celeste. "Yes,

Miss."

Eve's first stroke exploded against her skin. A bright flash of pain was followed by the rush of pleasure. "One, thank you, Miss."

Eve struck again, the other cheek, equally as hard, balancing the pain, and Celeste groaned. "Two, thank you, Miss."

Eve leaned over her and pressed a kiss between her shoulder blades. "Very good." She ground her hips against Celeste's ass. "You are beautiful like this. I wish you could see my marks. And how wet you are." *She's pleased with me.* Another blow, another rush of pleasure. Celeste focused on the heat of her ass, the crisp currents of pleasures suffusing her body, and counting for her Miss. *Her Miss. Does she want that? Want me?* "Three, thank you, Miss."

She arched her back and lifted on her toes, desperate for more, and was rewarded with the fourth stroke of Eve's hand on her ass. Celeste groaned. "Four, thank you, Miss."

Eve touched her fingertips to the wet heat between Celeste's legs and rubbed her clit in a slow circle.

"Oh please, Miss. I can't stop. Please let me come for you." Celeste shifted her hips, seeking relief.

Eve pulled her hand away. "Not yet. We're not through yet, kitten."

The sweet denial and promise of more made Celeste moan. She rested her cheek against the warm smooth wood of the desk.

Eve continued and Celeste gave over to the sensations, her world nothing but pain and pleasure intertwined. By the tenth blow sweat and tears stung her eyes, and her body shook with need. She wriggled and shifted her feet to press her thighs together, seeking relief. Eve stepped between her legs and kicked her feet wide. "No. Be still." Her voice was rough, and Celeste reveled in her command.

Celeste froze in place. "Yes, Miss. Sorry, Miss."

Eve dipped her thumb in and rubbed the spot that made Celeste ache for more, her fingertips brushing against Celeste's clit, edging her expertly. Giving her enough to keep her panting but not enough to send her over. Celeste rocked back into the sensation. "Oh Miss. Please. Let me. I want to come for you. Please."

"No. Two more."

"Yes, Miss." Celeste panted.

Eve withdrew her hand. The clink of a belt buckle and the rustle of clothing being removed intrigued Celeste, and she closed her eyes, envisioning Eve's body, and whined her frustration in being denied the view.

Celeste waited, desperate for the next blow, anxious for the searing pain and ultimate pleasure it would bring. She stilled, awash in the endorphins surging through her.

The hiss of leather as it swung through the air caressed her ears a second before the belt landed on her tender ass. Blinding pain and exquisite pleasure filled her. She screamed and then bit her lip to keep from coming. "Oh, thank you, thank you, Miss. Eleven, Miss. Please more."

Eve's feather-soft lips on her heated skin soothed her. "Patience."

Celeste rocked, wiggled her hips. "Please, Miss."

The stiff leather struck her ass again and she screamed long and loud. "Twelve, Miss." Celeste panted and then Eve's fingers were inside her and on her clit, and there was no helping it. Sweet pain and harsh pleasure crashed over her, and Celeste cried out and came all over her Miss's hands.

*

Eve stroked Celeste's swollen clit, drawing out her pleasure as hot liquid silk poured over her hand. "Naughty kitten. Couldn't wait. What am I going to do with you? Maybe another lesson? Let's try this again. No coming without my permission."

"Sorry, Miss. I'm sorry I couldn't stop. Let me try again, Miss. Please."

She thrust her fingers in deep over Celeste's sweet spot and jacked her clit, building her up, waiting for her to ask, to beg for release.

Celeste's body trembled and shook. Her breath came in sharp short pants. "Oh yes, please, Miss. Please. Let me come again for you."

Eve slowed her strokes. "Wait." She licked a trail up Celeste's back, savoring the salt taste of the fine dew of sweat on her skin. She held her in place with her body and fucked her slow and deep, cherishing her harsh moans as she opened to her. Eve basked in Celeste's heartrending groans as she gave herself over to Eve's attentions. Her clit was hard, nipples aching, Eve's body responding to Celeste's acceptance of her dominance. Impatient for her own release, she sped up her thrusts, building the fire between them.

Celeste clenched around Eve's fingers and thrashed her hips, her cries fierce and guttural, before she whispered, "Yes, please, Miss. Use me, Miss. Please come on me. Please let me feel you, Miss."

Eve slowed her movements between Celeste's thighs. She rubbed herself against Celeste's firm ass. The slick slide of her clit over the tight muscles of Celeste's ass made her regret she had not packed any of her favorite toys, but then she had not expected any of this, not Celeste's revelation, nor her own desire to possess her. *Hell, even if I had packed my favorite dildo, it would be in my suitcase at the bottom of the mountain. Maybe next time. Stop. This is what it is for now.*

Celeste's skin was a dull dark red from the spanking and hot against Eve's clit. She closed her eyes and imagined how it would be to sink into Celeste's welcoming body. To have it be more than a brief affair. To have more. To own her truly.

She moved her hand from Celeste's clit and lay over her, pressing her flat on the desk, holding her in place with her body. She grasped Celeste's wrists and held them with one hand over her head. Eve stretched her arms, appreciating the line and curve of Celeste's muscles, taut as a bowstring as she held on to her pleasure, waiting for Eve's permission. Eve rotated her hips wildly, desperate for her pleasure.

"Feel my clit sliding against you. Feel me come. Hold on to your pleasure. It belongs to me."

"Yes, please, Miss. Use me. Take it all, please, Miss." Celeste rocked her hips back, meeting Eve's thrusts.

Celeste's words filled her body with longing and Eve set her teeth against the soft skin over Celeste's deltoid and bit hard, rolling the muscle between her teeth, hard enough to bruise, to leave a mark, her mark. *Celeste. Mine. For now. Maybe.*

"Come for me, kitten." Eve added her own groans of satisfaction to Celeste's soft moans, reveling in her ability to make Celeste lose control. She finished against

Celeste's ass and stilled. She closed her eyes and absorbed the sensation of Celeste's strong body under her as their breathing slowed and they came down from the high of their scene. She released Celeste's wrists. She laced their fingers together and drew her hands under them, caging Celeste in her arms, yearning to have her, shelter her, keep her safe.

Celeste shivered under her, and Eve kissed the back of her neck and lay her cheek against her shoulder. "Cold?"

"A bit."

Eve released her. "Let me find your clothes." She turned from Celeste and gathered up her clothes. When she turned back Celeste was standing with her arms crossed over her body, visibly trembling.

Eve crossed to her and held out her clothes. "Are you okay?"

Celeste took the clothes from Eve and clutched them to her body. She licked her lower lip and lowered her chin to her chest. "I..." She faded out, the muscles in her throat working as she swallowed. "Yes."

Her voice was full of unshed tears, and Eve's heart cracked wide at her vulnerability. *Brave. She showed me everything. Trusted me. With her secrets. Her life.*

She stepped close and wrapped her arms around her and pulled her tight to her chest. She rested her chin on top of Celeste's head. The scent of sandalwood mixed with the heady scent of their sex play rose between them. "Would you come to my room?"

Celeste kissed the small hollow at the base of Eve's throat. "Yes." She snuggled closer to Eve as if she wanted to be inside her skin. "I'd love to."

*

They had slept in Eve's room, curled around each other. Celeste luxuriating in the closeness of Eve's body as she draped her arm and one long leg over her, possessing Celeste even as she slept. Celeste clasped Eve's hand and held it between hers, unwilling to let go of Eve's comfort even in sleep. Celeste woke first and lay there listening to Eve's slow deep breathing, marveling at the way they fit together. *Safe. Wanted. Cherished.*

Celeste luxuriated in the sensation of desire. She turned in Eve's arms and ducked her head and nuzzled her breasts, pressing her face into the soft undercurves of her full breasts. After she kissed her way down the long plane of Eve's flat belly, she licked a trail along the darker line of skin leading to the sweet temptation between her legs.

Eve moaned as she rolled onto her back and spread her legs.

Celeste clasped Eve's wrists and held them against her thighs, pinning her in place. She used her shoulders to press Eve's legs wider as she settled between her thighs. Celeste inhaled Eve's essence, her scent, and licked up the first dewy signs of her desire. She thrust her tongue deep, twitching it up and down before she drew slow lazy circles around Eve's clit with her tongue. Eve's breath came in short pants. Her hips arched to meet Celeste's attentions. "Don't stop. Please." Her voice was faint, and Celeste nipped the inside of her thigh, drawing a harsh cry from Eve.

"Why would I stop?" She licked her clit slowly and Eve groaned. "You like this?"

"Yes." She rocked her hips. "More. Give it to me." A command now. She yanked against Celeste's grip.

Celeste held fast to Eve's hands and flicked her tongue over her swollen slick flesh. "Sometimes I like to play with my food."

Eve bucked against her. "Do you know what will happen if you don't do what I tell you?"

Celeste lowered her head and blew warm breath over Eve's wet heat, delighting in the shiver it evoked from Eve. She pursed her lips and sucked Eve's hardness into her mouth, bringing her right to the edge before she stopped. "No. Tell me."

Eve thrashed under her. "If you don't get me off in the next two minutes, I'm going to show you."

Celeste laughed, tightened her grip on Eve's wrists, and lowered her head. She took her time, holding Eve in place with her body, pleasuring her, edging her twice more before she let her come.

Eve shrieked when she came and flooded Celeste's mouth with pleasure. Celeste let go of her wrists, used her hands to spread her open, and lapped at her, anxious for every bit of sweet honey from Eve.

"Come up here." Eve whispered hoarsely.

Celeste straddled her and looked down into Eve's face, studying her gleaming eyes. "Am I in trouble?"

Eve grinned. "You have no idea, my dear."

Celeste's body responded to Eve's threat, and she rotated her hips, smearing her wetness over Eve's belly. "Marvelous."

Eve rolled them quickly, and now she looked down into Celeste's face, her hand wrapped around Celeste's throat. Celeste lifted her chin, giving Eve access, desperate for the weight of her palm on her throat and the curl of her fingers around the column of her neck. Eve hummed her approval and flicked Celeste's nipple. She grasped her nipple and squeezed hard.

Celeste moaned and arched into Eve's touch.

"You want something?"

Celeste met Eve's taunting gaze. "Fuck me."

"What if I don't want to?" Eve curled her lip. "What if naughty kittens have to wait on their Miss's pleasure before they get what they want?"

Celeste bucked under Eve. "Fuck me, Miss, please. I'll behave."

"I don't believe you." Eve leaned down and drew Celeste's nipple into her mouth and bit down. Celeste writhed under her, the pain making her desperate.

"Oh please, Miss. Please. Fuck me. I'll behave. I'll do anything."

Eve trailed a finger down Celeste's firm belly, following the line of darker skin that led to the sweet treasure between her thighs. She feathered her fingers over her slick lips and parted them. Celeste's wet heat welcomed her, and she pressed inside. "You will anyway."

Celeste arched under her, seeking more of Eve's touch. "More please, Miss. I need you inside me." She met Eve's gaze, her eyes glassy with desire. "All of you."

Eve arched an eyebrow and pulled her hand free. She licked her fingers. "You're wet enough for what you're asking, but let's make sure." She lowered her mouth to Celeste's body and licked a long stroke over her clit. "Mmm. Sweet." She thrust her tongue deep.

Celeste rocked her hips on her face, desperate for more. "Oh Miss. More, please."

Eve lapped at her, relentless in her efforts, and pleasure spiraled out from Celeste's center.

"Oh Miss. Please. I can't...I'm going to come. Please may I?" Celeste panted.

Eve raised her head and slid up Celeste's body, the slow drag of her hard nipples a sensuous torture. "No.

This is mine. You save your pleasure for me." She thrust three fingers deep and swept them over Celeste's sweet spot.

Celeste rocked under her, arching into the sensation. "More. Please more. Fuck me, please, Miss." She arched into Eve's touch. Eve added a finger, the stretch and burn threatening Celeste's control. She spread her legs wider and focused on relaxing into Eve's hard thrusts. The friction on her clit from Eve's palm was elegant agony and the combination of strokes over her G-spot delicious. She clutched the bedsheets, twisting them in her hands. "Harder, Miss, please. More. Please."

Eve paused and lowered her forehead to Celeste's brow. "You may touch me. Come as you wish."

Celeste released the sheets and gripped Eve's shoulders. She drew her legs ups and wrapped them around her slim hips, opening herself to all that Eve could give her, the hard fuck Celeste craved.

Eve pushed hard and deep, her fingers drawing fierce cries and guttural moans from Celeste. Celeste lost herself, gave over to the sensation of being possessed, owned, cherished. Loved. She came hard, screaming her release as she raked her nails down Eve's back.

No. Not love. Not that. The truth edged into Celeste's consciousness and she stilled.

Eve slowed her strokes and raised her head. A frown marred her face. "Celeste? Too much?"

Celeste blinked away the reality of their situation, cupped Eve's face, and kissed her. "Just right."

She gathered Eve in her arms and held her tight, allowing herself to pretend it was more.

*

They had awoken hungry, dragged themselves from Eve's bed, and now Celeste was peering into the refrigerator. "I had a plan for dinner." She eyed the whole chicken she had intended to steam with fragrant spices. "But I'm too hungry to wait for this chicken to cook." She held up a carton of eggs. "How do you feel about omelets?"

"I'm not picky. I've been too hungry to ever refuse food." Eve leaned against the counter and traced her finger over the grain pattern disrupted by deep scratches in the wood.

Celeste placed the egg carton on the counter. "Excellent." After locating her favorite omelet pan, she placed it on the stove. "Two eggs or three?"

"Three, please. You made me hungry." Eve waggled her eyebrows.

Celeste laughed as she cracked the eggs into a bowl and whisked them briskly. "Same."

"These scratches. How did they happen?"

Celeste stopped stirring the eggs and placed the bowl on the counter as a flood of memories filled her. "Lorraine was as I am." She flushed, her body heating under Eve's observation. "Those scratches are from the night we—" Celeste turned toward Eve to study her expression. "The first time we were together.

Eve yanked her hand back. "Oh. Sorry. I was curious."

Celeste walked to the kitchen island and clasped Eve's hand. "Nothing to be sorry about. If the marks made me sad, I'd have sanded them out. There was a time when I considered it." She traced the deep scratches with her other hand. "These marks are all that remains of our time together. They're like the marks on my skin. She lives in my heart, and in my skin, and her marks on this table remind me that she was, she existed. I wasn't able to bury her. I have no grave to visit. When I want to talk with her spirit I sit here."

Eve tilted her head, squeezed Celeste's hand and released it. "Am I the first, after her?" Her voice was measured.

Celeste laced their fingers together. "Yes. Does it bother you?"

Eve raised Celeste's hand to her mouth and kissed her knuckles. "I'm honored. And curious. You seem a woman of strong appetites. Why me? Why wait?"

Celeste leaned in and kissed Eve's cheek. "That's a long answer. Let me cook our dinner and then I'll answer you."

*

Celeste lit the gas fireplace and poured them each a glass of claret.

"I will be totally spoiled for wine when I leave here. This is amazing claret." Eve took a sip of the fine vintage and patted the sofa next to her. "You promised me a story."

Celeste's smile was rueful, and Eve savored the sight of her standing limned by the firelight. She had dressed in a midnight-blue satin robe, and the color set off the pale silver of her hair and her amber eyes.

"I did, didn't I?" She sat next to Eve, with her knees folded under her on the sofa. She canted her body toward Eve and took a sip of her wine. "Where do you want me to start?" She pushed a lock of Eve's hair behind her ear.

Eve studied her face and the wary expression in her eyes. "Why no other lovers?"

Celeste pursed her lips. "Grief. At first. Fear after."

"Afraid of losing another lover?" Eve ran her fingertip over the edge of her wineglass.

"No. Yes." Celeste placed her wineglass on the end table. "I didn't want to take a chance. And there are not many of us left. And you may have noticed I live a bit off the path."

"Is it why you don't leave your estate?"

Celeste took another sip of wine. "Tigers are not social by nature, and in my human form neither am I. Lorraine and I had a bond that transcended our solitary natures."

Eve's gut roiled. "Something you could only have with someone who was a shifter too?" She gulped down the last of her wine and poured herself another glass. "I understand." *I'm something to satisfy her needs. She doesn't care about me. Not like that. I'm not her kind. Only human. Fuck me.* Celeste's hand rested on her thigh, and Eve's body responded to her nearness in spite of herself and she shifted away from her touch. *Focus, damn it. Used again. An easy way to get off. Damn it.* "Why me?"

Celeste huffed out a breath. "You're the first person who didn't grovel when you met me. The rest were fools and craven idiots. No sense of self."

"Meaning it could have been anyone who didn't cower?" Eve set her wine aside, the delicate vintage unpalatable as she turned Celeste's words over in her thoughts.

Celeste grabbed her hand and pulled it to her chest. Celeste knotted their hands together in her lap. "No. It's you. Your spirit. The first time I saw you I knew. You are the first human I have ever been with, and now I can't imagine not being with you." She raised their hands and kissed Eve's knuckles.

The tight bundle of fear and anger in Eve's chest tightened. "Sexually? Because I can get you off?"

"Not only that. I can't explain it. When I look into your eyes, I'm home. You understand me." Celeste held Eve's gaze. "You aren't afraid of me; you don't fear who and what I am."

"How did you know I wouldn't freak?" Eve lifted her hand and cupped her face. "Well, more than I did."

Celeste nuzzled Eve's palm. "I didn't."

"Why show me? Why tell me your secret? I could have left here without ever knowing."

"I had to. I want more with you. More than a fling, or affair. What I want with you is what I haven't wanted since Lorraine. I couldn't go forward without you knowing."

Eve's heart split wide. "And what do you want, Celeste?"

"You. Here with me."

"I can't stay. I have to go back. I have a life in LA."

"A mate?" Celeste lifted her chin and glared at Eve.

"No. No one special. Not for a while." Eve rubbed her thumb over the back of Celeste's hand.

Celeste lowered her chin to her chest. "I know. I know you won't stay. But you asked me what I wanted."

Eve carded her fingers through the silver strands of Celeste's hair before she leaned in and kissed her. "You are an exquisite woman, Celeste Quon. Brave. Glorious. And more than I ever imagined, or expected."

"But not enough to keep you here." The pain in Celeste's voice gutted Eve.

"I can't walk away from my responsibilities. And we have to finish the script."

"Your mother? The one who doesn't know who you are? Or cared when she did?"

"That's enough." Eve wiped her damp palms on her pants and turned away from Celeste. "Yes, that mother. Now I know about you. What if she's been telling the truth all these years and we've kept her medicated because we didn't believe her? Even if she hates me, she doesn't deserve to be locked up if she's telling the truth." Eve shuddered. "What if this is all a hallucination and I'm at home in my bed or in a hospital somewhere?"

Celeste pursed her lips. "I can't prove to you that you are not imagining this. I've shown you the truth. Would you believe it if someone else could see me? If they saw what you see?"

"Maybe." Eve held Celeste's gaze. "Who else knows?"

"My housekeeper but she won't be back until spring."

Eve laughed. "Did you ever see the movie *The Ghost and Mrs. Muir*?"

Celeste tilted her head. "Yes. Misogynistic as hell if I recall."

"Yes. But she's the only one who can see him and then he makes her believe it was a dream. She doesn't know the truth until she dies."

Celeste frowned. "For fuck's sake, I'm not a spirit."

"How can I know this is real?"

Celeste picked up her wineglass. "You are the most confounding woman I have ever met. How can I make you believe what you have seen? Touched?" She looked away and drained her glass and examined the dregs. "Fucked."

"No. Don't do that. It's more than the sex." Eve leaned over and cupped the back of Celeste's neck.

Celeste turned to her, a wary expression on her face. She placed her glass on the coffee table.

Eve brushed her lips over Celeste's mouth. "I don't know. I only know if it is a dream I don't want to wake up."

Chapter Six

Eve lay on the pool deck and watched as Celeste swam, admiring her body. The water broke over her broad back as she swam against the current in the lap pool. Her physique dazzled Eve. The stream surged around Celeste, offering a peek at her face as she turned to breathe, exposing a bit of breast here, a glimpse of thigh there, and a tantalizing view of her wickedly round ass. *What would it be like? To stay? Could I? Would I go stir-crazy? What about Mom?*

She dipped her hand in the water and spread her fingers, letting the liquid dribble back in the pool. The motor for the current stopped, and the surface stilled. Celeste swam over to Eve. She planted her hands on the pool deck, flexed her arms, and raised herself to kiss Eve, her lips wet and warm. Eve cupped the back of her neck. Celeste groaned softly and deepened the kiss. Eve luxuriated in the wet heat of Celeste's mouth, taking her time as she built the tension between them.

Eve broke their kiss to look into Celeste's eyes. "I'm hungry, kitten."

Celeste licked her lower lip. "For me?" Her tone was saucy, and her mouth pulled into a sly smile.

Eve trailed a finger over Celeste's face. Celeste opened her mouth and sucked Eve's finger into her mouth. Eve held her gaze as she slowly released her finger. Eve tipped Celeste's head up with her finger under her chin and kissed her softly. "Come up here." She spoke against her mouth before she scooted back to give Celeste space to exit the pool. Water cascaded off her body as she levered herself out of the pool. She lay on her back next to Eve on the smooth tiles. Warm water puddled around her. Eve sluiced the water off Celeste's skin with the flat of her hand. She palmed her plump mound and squeezed.

Celeste gasped, and Eve savored the quiver that chased through her body. Eve propped herself on her hand. Celeste's form was perfection. She bent her head and kissed the smooth skin over her throat, the hollow between her collarbones, the swell of her breast, and then nibbled a line down the center of her body. She teased her tongue over the crease of her thigh before she breathed warm air over her clit. Celeste's harsh breathing filled the space between them.

Eve lifted her head and parted Celeste's thick labia with her fingertips and brushed her clit with one finger, gathering the slickness between her legs. "Soaking wet. Is this from me? Or the pool?"

Celeste's eyes were closed, and her hands were clenched at her side. "You. I sensed you watching me. Your gaze following me. Your desire wrapped around me, drew me, made me ache."

Eve rubbed a slow circle over Celeste's clit, and it hardened under her thumb. "You like that, don't you? Being watched. Performing. Quite the exhibitionist, aren't you?" She jacked her clit slowly between her fingers.

"For you." Celeste arched her hips into her touch.

"Only for me?" Eve teased back the hood from her clit and touched the end of her tongue to the stiff tip.

Celeste cried out and thrashed her hips. "Only for you, Miss."

Eve slapped the outside of her thighs and Celeste hissed with the rebuke.

"Be still. Feel." Eve stood. Celeste's mouth pulled down in a moue of disappointment, and she lifted her chin and met Eve's gaze. Defiance blazed across her face.

"Spread your legs." Eve moved to stand between Celeste's legs. She nudged her calf with her toe. "Wider. I want to see everything."

Celeste opened her legs, the muscles in her thighs taut as she obeyed.

"Hands between your legs, kitten. Show me what you do when you're alone."

Celeste closed her eyes and moved her hands between her legs.

"No. No hiding, kitten. Look at me while you touch yourself. This is for me." Eve brushed her toes over Celeste's thigh.

Celeste opened her eyes and raised her chin, her expression rapt as she focused on Eve's face. Eve shifted her gaze to Celeste's hands as she drew her fingers up the soft curves of her stomach before she lifted one hand and licked her fingers. She plucked at her turgid nipples. She lowered the other hand and dipped her fingers between her legs. She made a V with her fingers, spreading herself wide and exposing herself to Eve's view. Desire gleamed on her skin and shone on her clit.

Celeste's chest rose and fell as she toyed with her breasts. Eve licked her lips, longing for the taste of Celeste. Liquid silk slicked her thighs as she kneeled between Celeste's legs and inhaled the sharp sweet scent of her want. Saliva pooled in her mouth. Celeste's strong hand slid over her clit before she slid two fingers deep. Eve failed to stifle her groan as Celeste arched into her palm and fucked herself. The wet sounds of the body clutching at her fingers as she plunged them inside herself reverberated off the tile walls.

"Please, Miss, may I come for you?" Celeste panted.

"No." Eve placed her hand over Celeste's hand and stilled her movement. "Hands over your head."

Celeste growled her disappointment as she obeyed.

Eve lay on her belly, slid her hand under Celeste's hips, and dug her fingers into the firm flesh of her ass before she took her in her mouth. She licked with the flat of her tongue and swirled a tight circle over her hard clit. She pressed forward and drove her tongue in and out, desperate for her taste. Celeste moaned and raised her hips, opening herself. "Oh Miss. That's good. Please, Miss, I want you inside me. Please."

Eve licked a wet trail up Celeste's clit. She pressed two fingers deep, curling them up and over the spot that made Celeste shake and her thighs quiver. She sucked her clit in rhythm with her strokes. Eve's heart hammered in her chest as she kept the pace, taking everything she wanted, driven by Celeste's deep groans and cries.

"Oh please, Miss, please. I can't stop. Please."

The tension in Celeste's body and desperation in her voice sent a tremor of delight through Eve. She luxuriated in her power over Celeste's body. A steady pulse of need drummed inside her, and she lifted her head and whispered, "Come as you wish, kitten, give me what's mine."

She swirled her tongue over her clit and then sucked hard. Celeste came, bucking her hips, growling her release, as her juices flooded Eve's mouth and covered her chin. She teased her with gentle thrusts, reveling in the way Celeste tightened around her fingers. Rough groans and sweet sighs filled Eve's ears as she slowed her strokes to draw out Celeste's pleasure. She hummed against her, and lifted her head to kiss her thigh as Celeste shuddered through aftershocks. Eve kissed and suckled her clit as she slipped her fingers free. She slid up Celeste's sweat-slicked body. Eve trembled as her nipples brushed over Celeste's silky skin.

Eve lowered her mouth to Celeste's parted lips. Celeste growled low in her throat and in one swift movement flipped them. She caged Eve under her body, her hand cradling Eve's head. Her eyes were luminous. Eve inhaled sharply as she stared into Celeste's face. *Adoration. Want. Trust. Love. She loves me. Truth.* Celeste rose up, lifting Eve and drawing her into her lap. Eve wrapped her legs around her waist and molded her body to Celeste.

Celeste nuzzled and nibbled at her throat the edge of her teeth sharp before she licked where she had bitten. Eve pressed her face into the strong curve of her shoulder and surrendered her attention. Celeste lowered her hand and toyed with the short hairs over Eve's clit. "May I, Miss?"

"Yes." Eve shivered, her heart aching with the sincere tone of Celeste's request.

Celeste entered her slowly. She wrapped her other arm around Eve's hips, holding her in a tight embrace.

Eve hummed her satisfaction as Celeste filled her, her palm pressing hard against Eve's clit. She fucked her slow, resisting Eve's attempts to increase the speed with a firm hand on her hip and a soft "Let me." She kissed the tender spot under Eve's ear and mumbled against her skin. "Let me, please."

Eve relaxed into her attentions, gave over, let Celeste fuck her as she wanted, as they both wanted. Celeste held her there, edged her, and the sounds of them filled the room. Eve lost herself in the experience, the magic of being held and treasured, adored. Her orgasm spun out, slow at first, and then building to a tsunami of sensation that swept her senses away. She clutched Celeste and held on tight as the last stone of the wall she had built around her heart tumbled down.

*

The hinges screamed in protest when Celeste opened the door to the playroom. She flicked the light switch and the overhead lights illuminated the space. Celeste pressed her hand to her chest, took a deep breath and blew it out forcefully. A fine layer of dust lay over the spanking bench and the St. Andrew's Cross. She placed the tote holding her cleaning supplies on the floor. Lorraine would have flogged her for letting their playroom become dusty, a delicious punishment followed by mind-bending orgasms.

Celeste blinked back the memories threatening to spill down her cheeks as she worked her way around the room dusting and cleaning away ten years of neglect. The soft scent of the lemon oil she used to polish the furniture filled the space and soothed her as she worked. She dragged the thick-legged square-backed chair with its black leather seat to the middle of the room. After wiping the dust from the chair's dark walnut wood, Celeste rubbed the seat with conditioner until it shone as bright as the wood.

Once the furniture was polished to her satisfaction, she moved to the cabinets housing the rest of the equipment and buffed the walnut wood to a deep shine.

Satisfied with her progress, Celeste washed her hands and opened the cabinet to inspect the collection of restraints and striking implements. Working quickly, Celeste cleaned the spreader bars, elbow cuffs, and shackles.

Lorraine had favored canes and crops. Celeste drew her finger along the red-ribbon-wrapped cane that had been Lorraine's favorite. The scars on Celeste's back and her heart ached with memories of their moments spent in the playroom. She picked it up, and wiped it down tenderly before she replaced it. Hanging next to it was Celeste's preferred implement, the tawse. Simple. The star of all of Celeste's fantasies from the first time she had ever been spanked with one. *Would she use it? Or does she prefer the personal connection of using her hand or her belt? Would she use it if I asked?* Celeste's body responded to the memory of Eve spanking her on the desk, and her nipples peaked hard against the fabric of her top. *Silly fantasy. She'll leave. Go back to her life. Would she stay if I asked?* Celeste snorted at her dithering. *It will be what it will be. No more, no less.*

She took the tawse from its hook, lifted it to her face, and rubbed her cheek against it. The scent of the smooth tanned leather filled her senses. Memories of belonging to Lorraine, serving her, safe in her control, fanned the flames of Celeste's long banked desire to be owned again. Lorraine's ownership had allowed Celeste to be the hard-ass woman she needed to be with the outside world, knowing she could relax into her care when they were alone. She kissed the tawse, wiped it down with the leather conditioner, and laid it over the chair seat. She glanced around the room reassuring herself all was in place, gathered her cleaning tote, and left the door ajar.

*

"What should we do this afternoon? You want to go over the dialogue again?" Eve filled her water glass and turned from the refrigerator.

Celeste stood naked in the center of the kitchen. Nestled between her breasts, suspended from a black corded necklace, was a carved jade figure. She lowered herself to her knees and clasped her hands behind her back, the image of perfect submission. "No."

Eve set her glass on the counter. She walked to where Celeste kneeled and met her gaze. "No?"

"No."

Eve traced her thumb over Celeste's lips before she drew her hand back and slapped her. "No what?"

Celeste moaned softly before she spoke. "No, Miss."

Eve bent down and kissed the red mark on Celeste's cheek from her correction. She cupped Celeste's breasts with both her hands, savoring the weight of them and the way her nipples pushed into her palms. She kissed her again, tasting her submission, deepening the kiss as Celeste opened to her desire. The sensation of her surrender burned through Eve, and she growled as she swallowed Celeste's willingness to serve.

"That's better." Eve spoke against Celeste's mouth.

Celeste panted and pulled back. "Please, Miss, may I show you my playroom? Please."

Eve cocked her head to the side and pinned Celeste in place with her glare. "Playroom? Sounds interesting. But maybe I want to have you here, right here, right now? Bend you over the kitchen table and make you beg me to fuck you. Trying to top from the bottom, impatient greedy kitten?"

Celeste lowered her chin to her chest. "No, Miss."

Eve lifted her chin with the tips of her fingers. *Fear. Not the good kind.* She softened her tone. "Why haven't you asked to show me the playroom before?"

Celeste's eyes were dark, her face expressionless. She looked away from Eve's face. "I wasn't sure I was ready. Or if you might desire it, Miss."

Eve gripped her chin, the skin blanching under her fingertips, and forced Celeste's chin up. "No hiding from me. Why now?"

"Now I want to show you everything."

Eve relaxed her grip and moved her hand to cup the back of Celeste's neck. She leaned her forehead on Celeste's. "You still haven't answered me. Why?"

"Because even if you leave, I want to give you this part of me. To give you all of me. If you want it." Celeste's teeth clamped on her lower lip but not before Eve noted the tremble.

Eve inhaled sharply. "I have to go back. I can't stay here with you, hiding from the world."

Celeste leaned into Eve's touch. "I know." She lifted the necklace from her neck and pressed it into Eve's hand. "Kuan-yin. Goddess of compassion and protection. Her compassion was so great she was put out of the underworld for fear she'd ruin it. Even if you don't return to me, I wish you only good things."

Eve clutched the small figure of the goddess in her hand. "I'll come back. Trust me?"

"With my life."

Eve kissed Celeste's forehead. "I'll keep your secret safe." She kissed her mouth, lingering on her tender lower lip. "Now, about your playroom. Why don't you crawl there?"

"Yes, Miss."

Chapter Seven

Slickness coated Celeste's thighs as she crawled to the playroom, knowing Eve was behind her, able to see how her slap and their exchange in the kitchen affected Celeste. *On display. For her. Hers.* Her breast swayed gently, and her nipples were tight and swollen. She thirsted for more of Eve's attention and deliberately moved slowly, rewarded by Eve's slap of her ass.

"Stop dawdling, kitten." Another slap punctuated Eve's warning.

The slick glide of her thighs as she crawled and the whisper of pressure on her clit made Celeste shiver. She reached the door to the playroom and sat back on her heels.

Eve's hand on her shoulder was warm. She squeezed gently and whispered. "Are you sure, kitten?"

Celeste raised her chin. "Yes, Miss."

They pushed through the half open door together. The room was warm, and the essence of the lemon oil Celeste had used to clean scented the air.

Eve pressed the buttons for the overhead lights. Celeste crawled to the cabinet. She opened it and then kneeled next to it with her arms clasped behind her back.

Eve rested her palm on the top of Celeste's head as she examined the items in the cabinet. She lifted the cane and swung it.

Celeste trembled as the sharp whistle of the thin bamboo cut the air. She groaned softly.

"Shh, kitten. We'll get there." Eve hung the cane in its place. "Look at me."

Celeste lifted her gaze to her Miss and tracked her movements as she examined the room.

Eve walked the length of the space. "Nicely equipped for a home dungeon." She smoothed her hand over the arm of the heavy chair centered in the middle of the floor and ran a finger over the top rail. "And what have we here?" Her mocking smile widened as she lifted the tawse from where it lay over the leather chair seat. "A tawse? Excellent." Eve lowered herself into the chair, imperious as a queen.

Celeste admired the way the chair fit Eve and the casual way she sat with her legs crossed at the ankle as she drew the length of the tawse through her hand. Her long fingers curled over the thick leather strap, and Celeste panted as she flashed back to herself facedown on her desk with Eve's fingers inside her, fucking her until she begged to come. The sturdy chair was the perfect height for spanking and Celeste shivered as she imagined draping herself over Eve's lap, exposed, at her mercy.

"Should I have you hold out your hands? You like to play the naughty schoolgirl?" Eve flicked the tawse. "Or should I spank you with it?"

"Whatever you wish, Miss."

Eve straightened and patted her thighs. "Come here, naughty kitten."

Celeste crawled to Eve. She rose and settled herself on Eve's lap. Eve circled her arms around her and tugged her close.

Celeste trembled in Eve's embrace. "Are you afraid, kitten?"

"No, Miss."

"You should be." Eve whispered. "Why have you kept this room from me? Denied yourself what you crave? I see how much you want this." She shifted her grip to the back of Celeste's neck. "You don't get to punish yourself. I'm in charge. I'll decide if you need to be punished. From now on."

The menace in her voice sent another wave of desire rocketing through Celeste and she squirmed in Eve's arms. Eve's grip became iron and she drew the smooth leather of the tawse over the delicate skin of Celeste's thigh and laid it over her leg, balancing it there. "Don't let it fall, kitten."

Eve's short nails scraped Celeste's skin as she traced tiny circles with her fingertips over her thigh and drew close to Celeste's wet curls. She teased a finger between Celeste's slick swollen lips and pressed forward. "Sweetness, you are my favorite flavor." Eve lifted her glistening finger to her lips and licked it. "Delicious."

Celeste watched slack-jawed as Eve sucked her fingers into her mouth before she returned and thrust her middle two fingers deep. She rested her thumb at the base of Celeste's clit and stilled. Her gaze settled on Celeste's face.

Celeste fell into the darkness reflected in Eve's gaze.

"Keep your eyes open, kitten."

Eve began with tiny presses of her fingers and thumb, barely-there sensations that peaked Celeste's nipples and made her ache for more. Celeste groaned and panted, determined to do as her Miss had asked, to stay still and take what her Miss wanted to give her. The tawse wobbled. Celeste shifted her legs, trying to keep the thick leather strap in place where it draped over her thigh.

Eve increased her touches and thrust slowly and as she brushed her thumb over Celeste's thick clit, adding to the sensations flooding Celeste's body. Eve raised a brow before she dipped her head and captured Celeste's nipple with her mouth and sucked hard.

Celeste cried out as pleasure rocketed through and her orgasm shook her body. She rocked her hips seeking more, unable to stop her response. The thunk of the tawse hitting the floor echoed in the playroom. Eve lifted her head and licked her lower lip. A feral smile lit up her face.

Eyes wide, Celeste shivered as she studied Eve's expression.

"Poor kitten. You tried so hard." Eve shoved Celeste off her lap. "Pick it up."

Celeste picked up the tawse and held it out to Eve with both hands.

Eve took it and presented it to Celeste.

Never taking her eyes from Eve's face, Celeste kissed the tawse.

Eve's nostrils flared. "Over the chair this instant." Her voice, soft with menace, ignited Celeste's need.

Celeste braced her palms on the seat of chair. Eve's warm palm on her ass made her squirm before a sharp pinch on the inside of her thigh settled her.

Eve kissed her between her shoulder blades. "Red to stop, yellow to slow down or back off."

"Yes, Miss."

The first strike of the tawse made Celeste gasp and press her thighs together.

"Don't forget to count, kitten."

"Sorry, Miss. One, Miss. Thank you, Miss."

The second strike threatened her control, and she bit her lip to stem her tears.

"Two, Miss. Thank you, Miss." Celeste spoke around the dry ache in her throat.

The third strike crashed through her and she broke, unable to hold back her tears as they coursed down her cheeks.

"Three, Miss. Thank you, Miss." Her voice wobbled.

The fourth and fifth blows landed close together. Celeste screamed. Her throat burned as fat tears puddled on the black leather seat of the chair.

"Four, Miss. Thank you, Miss." She gulped her tears. "Five, Miss. Thank you, Miss." Celeste shuddered when Eve smoothed her cool hand over the flaming hot skin of her ass. Eve fingered her, dipping between her legs and rubbing her clit. "You're soaking wet. You like being punished. Did you let the tawse fall on purpose?'

"Oh no, Miss. I tried. I couldn't help it, Miss. Please believe me."

Eve thrust deep. Celeste cried out and lifted her hips, desperate for Eve's attention. Eve chuckled as she drew her fingers free. "Not yet, kitten. Three more. Can you do it? For me?"

"Yes, Miss. Anything for you."

The anticipation and a flood of endorphins filled Celeste. She waited for the blows she knew would come, a moment, an hour, waiting as long as her Miss desired her to wait. *Her Miss.*

A sharp crack, and she panted over the burn of the tawse. A trickle of desire ran down her legs, even as hot tears scorched a path down her face. "Six, Miss. Thank you, Miss." Another blow and a deep groan as Celeste sank into the gift of her pain. "Seven, Miss. Thank you, Miss."

The last stroke fell.

Celeste screamed. "Eight, Miss." And then Eve was over her and inside her, taking everything Celeste had to give, wringing every last drop of pleasure from her.

*

Eve dropped the tawse and buried herself in Celeste's body, lost herself in fucking her, and her fierce cries as she gave Eve everything she had held on to, surrendering her pleasure to Eve. She stilled when a ragged sob broke from Celeste.

Eve tugged Celeste into her arms and sat in the chair. She gathered her onto her lap and held her tight against her chest. Celeste shook as she wept, and Eve rubbed her back. *She's perfect. And she wants to be mine. Mine.* She pressed a kiss to the top of Celeste's head and cupped her ass. The heat of her marks sent a new rush of desire and longing through Eve. "You are the most exquisite woman." *And I love you.* Eve left her thoughts unspoken.

Celeste gripped Eve's shirt in both hands and shivered.

"Is there a robe here, kitten?"

"Yes. But I don't want to move from your arms."

Eve shifted her hands to Celeste's shoulders and moved her to look in her face. "Open my shirt."

Celeste unbuttoned Eve's shirt.

Eve tugged it free from her pants and held it open and wrapped it around them both. Celeste wrapped her arms around Eve's waist and snuggled her cheek against the swell of Eve's breast over the lace of her bra.

The heat of Celeste's body against her skin and the tickle of her breath made Eve sigh with contentment. This. She could do this, only this, the rest of her life. An endless holiday. Celeste had offered. Reassured Eve she could afford it. She'd never have to work again in her life if she didn't want to. All she had to do was stay. *No. Not yet. Not until I prove every one of the assholes who said I was finished wrong.*

Celeste kissed the hollow at the base of Eve's throat. "What are you thinking, Miss?"

Attuned to Eve, Celeste had sensed her disconnect from their scene. The hurt in her voice chastised Eve. "Sorry, kitten. You deserve my full attention."

Celeste nibbled her way to Eve's ear. "Please, Miss. Let me taste you?"

Eve lifted her chin, giving Celeste access to her neck and the sensitive skin under her ear. "Mmm. You do deserve a treat. Would you like that? For me to come in your sweet little mouth?"

A shiver chased through Celeste's body. "Oh yes, Miss. Please."

Eve cupped Celeste's ass and squeezed. "Very well. Stand."

Celeste stood and stepped back to allow Eve to rise. Eve lifted her arms. "Undress me."

Celeste unbuttoned the cuffs of Eve's shirt before she smoothed her hands under the shirt and eased it off her shoulders. She folded it carefully and placed it aside. She kneeled and removed first one boot and then the other before she lined them up next to the chair. The back of her knuckles brushed against the skin of Eve's waist as she unfastened her trousers. In one smooth motion she lowered Eve's pants. Eve steadied herself with her hand on Celeste's shoulder as she raised each foot in turn for Celeste to remove her pants and socks.

Celeste looked up at her, her eyes predatory as she hooked her fingers in the waistband of Eve's briefs and tugged them to the floor. Eve stepped out of her underwear. Celeste rose and reached around and unhooked Eve's bra. With one finger under each strap she lowered it and folded it with the same care she had shown with all of Eve's clothing. She kneeled before Eve.

Eve sat. The cool leather of the chair a sharp contrast to the molten heat between her thighs. She set her legs wide and placed a hand on her thigh. With the other hand she spread her fingers in a V and held herself open. "Would you like this?"

"Oh yes, Miss, please."

Eve dipped a finger in, gathered the slickness there, and smiled to herself as Celeste's eyes glazed over watching Eve touch herself.

"Come and get it, kitten. Show me you know how to please your Miss."

Celeste closed her mouth over Eve and pulsed the flat of her tongue against her. Eve gripped the sides of the chair and slid forward to press more of herself against Celeste's mouth. Celeste's tongue traced the length of her and thrust inside, tickling and teasing. Eve's nipples ached and she raised one hand to roll and pluck at her nipple. Celeste circled her tongue around Eve's clit and sucked gently before she lifted her head. "Please, Miss, may I fuck you while I lick you?"

Eve groaned at the word on Celeste's lips. "Yes."

Celeste pushed a single finger in deep and Eve rocked her hips. "More."

"Yes. Miss." Celeste bent her head and lapped at Eve as she pushed a second finger deep.

Eve trembled as Celeste curled her fingers over her G-spot. She gripped her head with both hands and fucked herself on her face, painting her with her juices, marking her as her own. *Mine.*

Celeste purred against her and the vibrations sent Eve tumbling into pleasure. She shouted and came. Soft touches of Celeste's tongue eased her down before Celeste drove her up again and when Eve's orgasm crested all she could do was hang on and shudder through it. *Mine.*

*

Eve's satisfied sigh as Celeste kissed the inside of her thigh triggered her own moan of contentment. When Eve rested her hand on her cheek, Celeste turned her face and kissed her palm. She closed her eyes and imagined thousands of evenings spent in the service of her Miss, a lifetime, a moment in Celeste's life, a lifetime for Eve. *To be Hers. Safe in her care. Adored. Hers. Would she stay if she knew I loved her? A human. How long would I have her? Would it ever be enough? What will happen when she understands our differences? Could I cope with her aging? To know I would have many more lifetimes without a companion? Could I survive another loss like Lorraine?*

"Come up here."

Celeste sat in Eve's lap, curled herself around her, and rested her head on her shoulder.

Eve laced their fingers together. "Where did you go, kitten?" She lifted Celeste's hand and kissed her fingertips.

Celeste exhaled sharply and sat up to look into Eve's eyes. "How old are you?"

Eve frowned. "Thirty-seven, and what is this about?"

Celeste tilted her head. "Do you know how old I am?"

Eve pursed her lips. "The clips I've read have you at fifty."

Celeste snort laughed. "Do they? Hmm."

"Are you worried about the difference? I'm not some ingénue."

Celeste touched Eve's cheek. "I'm not fifty."

"Did you shave a few years off of your birth year? I don't care. My agent has celebrated her thirty-ninth birthday for years. Age is a number. I don't care."

"You might later. You know what I am. I don't age like humans."

"Are you immortal?"

"No."

"Worried you might become tired of me? Want a younger model later?" Eve's body tensed under Celeste. "Or want to save yourself the heartache of outliving me?"

"No. That's not what I'm saying. Not at all."

"What then?"

Celeste rose from Eve's lap and paced the room. "I'm saying I've never been involved with a human. I don't know how it will be when you and I don't age at the same rate."

Eve stretched her legs and crossed her ankles. "We can't know. We're like any other couple."

Celeste raised her eyebrow. "What?"

"We can't know or predict the future. Every person who attempts a long-term relationship is in the same boat. We can't know. We can only do our best." She crossed the room and wrapped her arms around Celeste. "And treat each other as best we can."

Celeste held tight to Eve. "As best we can."

Eve rubbed Celeste's back in small circles. "How old are you anyway?"

"I'm not exactly sure. We don't keep records as such. My best guess is two hundred and eighty-seven."

Eve released Celeste and held her at arm's length. "The things you've seen. No wonder your books are incredibly visceral."

Celeste tilted her head toward the window. "When I first came to this valley, it was filled with game. Plenty for Lorraine and me. We could go months without seeing humans. I've always been different, restless. I grew tired of living in the shadows. The minute my first book was published my parents abandoned me. They disapproved of my—" Celeste drew her hand over Eve's shoulder "—appetites and desire to tell stories."

"Where are they now?"

Celeste shrugged. "I don't know. I haven't heard from them in years."

"Why have you shut yourself up here? What are you afraid of, Celeste?" Eve squeezed Celeste's hand.

"Everything and nothing. I enjoyed it at first. The thrill of hunting, finding places to run wild. I got off on it. And then—" Celeste turned away from Eve. "I grew too confident. Convinced Lorraine it was safe to travel outside our range."

"It's not your fault."

Celeste spun around, her gaze piercing. "Whose fault is it? She never would have been there if it wasn't for me."

"The asshole who shot her, that's whose fault it is." Eve stared back, her gaze equally as hard. "Are you going to punish yourself by hiding out here for the rest of your life in penance? Come to LA with me. Please." Eve tugged her close. "At least until I get things settled enough to return here."

Celeste pursed her lips. "I can't."

"Why?"

"I can't imagine living in a city again. Where would I hunt? I would go mad. Risk being exposed? Hunted? Risk capture? No. I'm not going anywhere." Celeste fought the anger that flared through her as her memories of being hunted surfaced.

Eve pursed her lips. "I guess explaining a tiger sighting in LA would be difficult."

Celeste snorted. "Difficult? Try deadly. No. This is my range. I'm not leaving."

Chapter Eight

Eve folded the clothes Celeste had lent her and placed them on the dresser. She tucked the few things she was bringing back with her into her messenger bag. *Welp, no baggage fees this time. The rental car—fuck, that's going to cut into my cash.*

She touched the silk cord of the necklace Celeste had given her, the jade cool under her fingertips. Eve had hit send this morning on the email with the script they had finished with Celeste's approval. Now all they had to do was wait and see if it was acceptable to the other parties. And it was time for Eve to leave. *Leave. She doesn't believe me. Thinks once I'm out from under her beguiling presence I'll change my mind. How to make her believe me?*

A sharp knock on the door frame interrupted her thoughts.

"All packed?" Celeste's face was as neutral as her voice.

Eve pointed to the pile of clothes on the bed. "I'd like to leave a few things here if it's all right with you?"

Celeste raised an eyebrow. "Why wouldn't it be all right?"

"I'll come back."

"As you've said." Celeste gestured at the dresser. "Leave what you want. I can always send it if you change your mind." She turned and walked away.

Eve rolled her eyes at Celeste's retreating back. "Stop. Right there."

Celeste turned and cocked an eyebrow. "You need something?"

Eve rested her hands on her hips. "Yes. For you to quit acting like I'm never coming back. I can't abandon my life and Mom. I would stay if I could, Celeste."

Celeste stormed back down the hall toward Eve, her eyes dark. "I didn't ask you to abandon your life. I asked you to share mine. Here. Where it's safe for me. I get it. It's too complicated. Too much to ask. I can't change who I am. Neither can you."

"No. I can't." Eve pressed her lips together.

"Then we have nothing else to talk about." Celeste walked away, her head high and her shoulders rigid.

*

Eve backed the truck out of the garage and parked it. She climbed out and stepped gingerly over a puddle of snow melt. The door to the house opened, and Celeste walked to the edge of the porch.

Eve rounded the car and leaned against the passenger side. "I need to leave. I'll miss my flight."

"Leave the truck in long-term parking. Mail me the ticket. My housekeeper can drive it back when she returns."

"Come with me. At least to the end of your property." Eve opened the passenger door.

Celeste stood on the porch with her arms crossed over her chest, mouth pressed into a thin line.

"Please."

Celeste lifted her chin and shook back her hair. "Why?"

Eve opened the passenger car door and stood beside it.

"Because I want another fifteen minutes with you."

Celeste quirked her mouth at Eve.

Eve tilted her head. "Please."

Chin on her chest, Celeste crossed the yard and climbed into the truck.

Eve closed her door gently. *I've got fifteen minutes to convince her I'll be back. She's pissed. What to say? Tell her I love her? She's not going to believe me. Fuck. I haven't said it. Does she feel it too?* Eve avoided Celeste's eyes as she settled into the driver's seat and clipped her seatbelt. The truck engine grumbled to life, and Eve put it in gear and drove down the long winding drive.

*

Celeste turned in her seat to study Eve as she drove them closer to their goodbye. Her shoulders were rigid and her knuckles white where she gripped the wheel. Celeste mourned the loss of the easy way they had been with each other. *Goodbye. I've been saying goodbye since that first night we were together. When did I get to be a coward? Why can't I believe? What if I went with her? She's not ready. Not for me. Or a relationship. Let it go. I need to let it go. Let her go.*

They passed the twisted section of guardrail where Eve's rental car had fallen into the ravine.

Celeste noted the furrow in Eve's brow. "I paid for it."

"What?" Eve glanced at Celeste before she focused her attention back to the road.

"I paid for the rental car. It's the least I can do. You wouldn't have had to rent one if I hadn't insisted on you coming to my house. I didn't want you to be burdened."

"I could have paid for it." Eve chewed her lip. "And we wouldn't have—" Eve fought to keep her eyes on the road, desperate to check the expression on Celeste's face. "We wouldn't have had the opportunity to—" She reached over, clasped Celeste's hand, and brought her fingers to her lips and kissed them. "To get to know each other."

"I know." Celeste pulled her hand free and tucked it under her thigh to stop herself from wrenching the wheel from Eve's grip and turning the truck around to keep her from leaving.

"I'll pay you back."

"You'll do nothing of the sort. It was my fault."

"How? That damn sheep came out of nowhere."

"Not exactly." Celeste watched Eve's face as she confessed. "I was out hunting that day. The ram was going to be my dinner."

Eve grimaced. "Oh."

"I've upset you. And you're wondering if any of this will make sense once you leave. Once you go back to your life. I'll understand if you don't come back. I meant what I said—no matter what, I will always wish you safe and well." She raised her arm and pointed to a turnout. "Let me out here."

Eve pulled the truck over to the side of the road and turned on the flashers.

*

The wind lifted Celeste's hair and masked her face as she stripped off her clothes in the shelter of the passenger door. She kept her head down as she undressed, the set of her shoulders determined. Eve wanted to reach across the car and pull Celeste close, to hold her and touch her until she came undone. She bit her lip to stop herself from asking for a kiss from Celeste, unwilling to risk seeing the deep sorrow she knew haunted Celeste's eyes, not wanting grief to flavor their last kiss.

Her naked body shielded by the truck door, Celeste folded her clothes and placed them neatly on the seat. Eve watched as she crouched, her skin glowing, the air shimmering as Celeste transformed into a tiger. Her heart squeezed as she thought back to the first time Celeste had demonstrated her ability to Eve. The trust that had blossomed between them. *Love? No. Don't go there. Not now.*

Celeste turned away from the car and padded along the side of the road. Unable to look away, Eve watched in the rearview mirror as Celeste leaped over the barricade and scampered up the rocks on the embankment. After she reached the pinnacle, she turned and faced the truck. She lifted her head, roared once, turned away, and bolted back toward her home. Eve leaned across the truck and pulled the door closed. She turned off the flashers, before she eased the truck back out on the highway. Knuckles white on the steering wheel, Eve drove away from Celeste, ignoring the bonfire of regret burning in her chest.

*

The whine of the tires on the road was hypnotic. Eve's thoughts shuffled through the last eight weeks. The thought of returning to the grind of LA and the uncertainty of spec writing hung over her. *Maybe after this I could land a long-term gig, something solid. No. I promised I would come back.* Every mile she put between herself and Celeste the more her heart ached.

Working together had been magical, their styles meshing to produce a script that they both were proud of, and then there was the sex. Celeste was everything Eve had ever wanted in a partner. The perfect blend of sassy pushback and sublime submission. Eve drummed her fingers on the steering wheel. *Why? Why am I walking away from someone who loves me? Who respects me as a writer? She cares. Loves how I am. Loves me.* The road widened out as she approached the exit for the highway that would take her to the airport.

Her stomach churned as she imagined her life without Celeste, alone again in her tiny apartment. Images of Celeste's resigned look over their last breakfast together flooded her thoughts and the sound of her forlorn roar echoed in Eve's mind. The carcass of some large animal, indistinguishable in its state of decomposition, lay rotting on the side of the road. *Too short. Life is too short. For everything.* Eve stopped, made sure the road was clear, turned the truck around, and raced back toward Celeste's home.

*

Celeste snuffled through the underbrush hoping to catch the scent of something to chase, anything to distract her from the relentless emptiness creeping back to fill her soul. Eight weeks. Eight weeks of remembering what it was like to wake up and look forward to seeing someone who made her happy to be alive. Eight weeks of the heady sensation of desire and being desired, remembering what it was like to be captured by the mesmerizing gaze of a Domme who knew exactly what Celeste needed. Eve had craved Celeste's submission as much as Celeste craved surrendering to Eve. She was the perfect combination of hard and soft, as skilled at aftercare as she was at guiding Celeste to the subspace she lived to experience. *Will she return? Does she love me?* That was the question and the true reason for Celeste's melancholy.

In all their time together, they had not spoken of love, and now Celeste knew, even if she didn't want to admit it, she loved Eve. Loved her fiercely. *Why stay here and play it safe? What good is half a life?* A hare charged out from its hiding place and Celeste watched it flee. *No. Time to stop running.* She turned and loped back toward her home.

*

Eve drove down the long stretch of Celeste's driveway. In her peripheral vision she caught sight of Celeste, her lithe dark orange and white form as she ran across the field leading to her home. Eve tapped the horn twice. Celeste stopped running and turned her head toward the drive. Eve sped up until she was parallel with Celeste. She stopped the car. She met Celeste's gaze through the windshield.

Eve stepped out of the car, closed the door, and waited.

Celeste ran toward her, stopped a foot away, and shifted. Gaze locked on to Eve's face, she launched herself into Eve's arms and squeezed her tight. "Why?" Her voice was a harsh whisper.

"Love." Eve brushed her lips over Celeste's mouth and kissed her.

Celeste broke their kiss. "I'll go with you." She leaned her head against Eve's chest. "I don't want to be without you." She pulled back to look into Eve's eyes. "I love you."

Eve kissed her and nipped her shoulder. "I know."

Celeste dug her nails into Eve's back. "You are infuriating."

"I know that." Eve tipped Celeste's face up to look into her eyes. "And I love you too." She glanced at the truck. "We need to go back. I need to make some calls and then—"

Celeste stopped her with a kiss. "And then you need to remind this kitten why you came back."

THE FIRE INSIDE

Megan Hart

To Brenda for the roadtripping, brainstorming, "let's do this!" Here's to the first of many stories that begin with a "what if."

In the darkness, the sounds of moans and soft sighs drifted toward Selena's ears and sent tingling chills of arousal all through her. She could see nothing but black in front of her. The blindfold had been tied expertly, hard enough to cause her temples to throb with a faint ache. Below it, the gag in her mouth threatened to choke her as she swallowed over and over in an attempt to keep the saliva from dripping beneath it. She wasn't doing a very good job. Her chin and breasts were cold from her own spit.

She strained against the spreader bar keeping her legs at shoulder-width, but of course she couldn't move. Her arms, bound above her, had gone numb some time ago, but she could still feel her feet. The floor, firm and cool beneath her toes, promised relief—if only she could just get herself a half-inch lower. She could struggle forever but would never be able to. Her mind knew it, but her body still fought even though she was tied so tightly there was no way she could get free.

Rocking her hips, she waited for the hiss of the flogger's leather tails to signal the incoming blow. When it didn't come, she moaned from deep in her throat and forced herself to stop thrusting. She couldn't tell for sure if anyone was watching her, but she suspected there was an audience gathered. She was not an exhibitionist, but nor did she care much what anyone might think. Here in

Abyss, everyone else was living out their fantasies. She was only one of many, as anonymous as anyone could be while trussed up naked and being beaten.

Without the gag in her mouth, she'd have been begging for Miss to hit her harder. Again. Again. So far, the pain had been nothing more than a tease, sending flickering arcs of electric discomfort through her. Nothing fierce enough to chase away the mounting pleasure inside her.

Once more, she was caught in the circle. The more it hurt, the better she liked it; the better she liked it, the more pain she needed to chase away the desire. Selena shuddered in the binding ropes, wishing she could just...let...go...

Miss wasn't going to let Selena orgasm, though, no matter how she struggled. Miss would continue this teasing, the constant flick of the flogger and the subtle, terrible bite of the ropes binding Selena so tightly. Selena had to believe that. She had to trust Miss, or all of this was a waste. She *wanted* to come, but she *needed* all the rest.

Without it, bad things would happen.

That was why she'd insisted on being bound like this. On the blindfold and the gag. If the worst happened and she gave in to the fire inside her, she'd be tied up so tight she wouldn't be able to hurt anyone. It was dangerous. A risk. But one she had to take if she wanted to keep the wolf asleep.

Another moan sifted out from around the gag. Then, blessedly, came the sting of the flogger. She'd requested the tool specifically because it gave a sharp pain, rather than the dull, thuddy sort from a paddle.

I want to see you bleed.

Perdita's voice slithered through Selena's mind before she could block it out. Her body tensed, which made the flogger bite her harder. Even if Selena wanted it as much as Perdita had wanted to do it to her, Miss would not make her bleed. It was against the rules here at Abyss, and Selena had signed a contract stating she understood.

She couldn't think about Perdita now. That was the past. Selena was here, now, in this moment, her every muscle tight as she waited for another blow. Instead came the slow caress of a hand along the places the flogger had struck. Fresh pain came with the touch, and she jerked in her bonds, grateful even as she despised the way she reacted. Her thighs shook. She sagged, her toes aching, reaching for the floor and finding only air. Her shoulders and back ached from the strain of her bondage, and still, the fire inside her threatened to rise up and out of her.

When slim fingers slipped their way between her legs and into her pussy, Selena cried out around the gag. She was slippery wet, but not from being beaten. In spite of it. Because of it. In spite. Because. She no longer had any idea what pushed her body into the spiral of desire; only that no matter how much she craved orgasm, pain was the only way to keep herself from giving in to it, and to what would happen after.

Miss, *oh, please, let it only be Miss and not an onlooker,* withdrew her fingers from Selena's body. Selena strained again against the cuffs. The flogger came down again with a crack. Her back. Her ass. The sensitive backs of her upper thighs. Then, in an excruciating series of rapid, flicker blows, the flogger licked at her clit until she screamed hoarsely, over and over, around the gag.

The fire inside her never left, not completely, but it had been tamped back. Now it surged, rising. Burning.

She wrenched at the bonds keeping her in place. She bucked against them, groaning.

Then, the only sensation covering her was the cool air. No more flogger. No more fingers. Only blessed emptiness surrounded her.

*

"You have such a pretty pet," said Lady Victoria in the purring voice she affected because she thought it made her seem elegant and mysterious.

It made her sound pretentious, Clara thought, the same way the title did. Outside of Abyss, the older Domme was plain old Vicki Hanover, and although of course it was common practice for all of them to take on names while they were at the club…"Lady," really? It was because she was so into those Jane Austen novels Clara had no time for.

Clara also hated, fucking hated, the term "pet" for a human being. Refusing to even glance toward Vicki, she settled her feet shoulder-width apart and ran the ends of the flogger through her fingers. She'd used the flogger on Selena's clit, a technique that broke some subs from the torment, and although Selena could take more than any sub Clara had ever met, the flogger had nearly been too much for her. She could tell by the rising flush along Selena's pale skin. It had crept up over the sub's breasts and her throat to paint her cheeks. Selena had gone still, now, but just moments ago she'd been bucking furiously against the restraints.

"Hit her clit again," Vicki said with something like glee, a little like awe in her voice.

Clara took no pride in impressing the other Domme. It wasn't hard to do, actually. Vicki had gotten into the business for the money, and while she wasn't the only one, certainly, she'd never truly seemed to catch on to what made a real dominant/submissive relationship work. She had no imagination, no creativity. No connection with her clients. Vicki didn't admit in her outside life she was as vanilla as a soft-serve cone—not that Clara judged her for it. No, she judged Vicki for pretending she was into something she wasn't and for leading people on.

For herself, money had nothing to do with this. Both of Clara's parents had died when she was in her early twenties, leaving her with a sizable estate including property and businesses that continued to provide her with a more than living income. No, Clara did this because domination was as much a part of her as the pale-amber color of her eyes or the dark-crimson birthmark at the small of her back.

She did it for money so she could be sure she never again fell in love with her submissive.

Vicki put her hands on her hips. The boning of her corset bulged, the satin brocade tied so snugly around her ample curves, her tits heaved up and out like a shelf. She'd finished with her client about thirty minutes ago and was now bored. Clara didn't usually mind an audience, but Vicki irritated her.

"Do you mind?" Clara said in a low voice without looking at the other Domme.

"Not at all."

Clara sighed and gave a half turn. "Well, I do. Get lost."

Oh, the nonexistent-pearl clutching! Vicki's mouth twisted into the shape of a cat's anus. Clara would have laughed if she wasn't in the middle of a session. As it was, she didn't have time for such nonsense. Vicki could trot herself off and complain to the club's chatelaine. Clara did not give a single, tiny fuck.

Clara let the flogger tails drift over Selena's shoulder and over her breasts. She breathed her next words into Selena's ear. "We aren't finished yet."

In response, Selena gave a strangled groan and sagged in her restraints. Her arms and shoulders had to be killing her, but Clara had been careful to make sure she wouldn't be at risk of a dislocation or lack of circulation. Submissives, particularly masochists, could not be counted on to know their limits when they were in the midst of a session. It was Clara's responsibility to keep them safe even if she was beating them hard enough to make them pass out. Especially then.

So far, Selena had never even come close to doing that. She took whatever Clara gave her and ended each session with a request for "next time, more." Therefore, Clara was really going to put her back into it this time. See if she could get a shriek out of the woman tied up in front of her.

Selena had been very clear about what she wanted and needed, and Clara had been all too happy to give it to her. Too many times, girls claimed they wanted to be beaten, but they ended up being unable to handle more than what Clara thought of as "fifty shades of fake." A couple of swats, some nipple pinching, maybe a paddle once or twice before they begged off with their safe word. Some of them came back to Abyss but requested one of the other Dommes; some of them never came back to Abyss at all after a session with Clara.

Clara had never been with a woman, client *or* lover, who could take it the way Selena could. Now she struck, letting the flogger's leather tips strike Selena's pale flesh.

Selena's body was so lean, with so little fat, there could be no cushioning of the blow. The crack of leather on skin forced a gasp from Selena around the gag, but that was all. Clara grunted with the force of her effort and stepped back, hefting the flogger. Her muscles had strained with the effort that time. If she wasn't careful, she was the one who was going to get permanently injured.

Selena twitched in her bonds. Clara stepped closer to run a fingertip along her cleft and the slickness there. Selena cried out, her hips bucking. Sweetness trickled down her thighs. Clara let her fingers drift below Selena's nose as she whispered into her ear.

"Smell yourself. You're fucking delicious." She pinched one of Selena's nipples and bit back her own groan of arousal at how that contact pushed her into a paroxysm of twitching and writhing. No matter how turned on she got during a session, she made sure to keep her arousal under control. This was work for her. Not play. "You're gorgeous."

It was true. Selena's lithe, muscular body was perfection. Her asymmetric-cut strawberry-blonde hair fell over one eye, buzzed short around the back and opposite side. Her skin glistened with sweat and her own spit and the sweet stream of her pussy juices.

"Hurt me," she'd told Clara. "As much as you can, as much as you want. But I can't come. I mean, I don't want to come. It's important I don't."

They'd been talking over coffee, their meeting arranged for the purpose of working out all the details of this night without any distractions. Clara had made notes, scribbling Selena's desires, past experiences, her fears, at least as much as she would reveal. It hadn't been much. Selena had been insistent that she wanted, needed, and could handle an intense amount of pain but gave no reasons why. It wasn't Clara's job to analyze her clients. She was paid to provide a service, as best as she could. Clara *had* insisted on learning Selena's hard line, making that knowledge a requirement of their sessions. It turned out orgasm was Selena's hard line, something Clara did not quite understand but had agreed to do her best to abide by. Again, work, not play.

Clara had sipped from her mug, deliberately keeping eye contact with Selena for several long moments without speaking. Many of the clients who sought her out were intimidated enough by the simple action they canceled their appointments. To Clara's delight, Selena only returned the stare calmly, although her rising and falling breasts beneath the thin white T-shirt she wore suggested she was not as unmoved as she was making herself seem.

"You understand," Clara had finally said, "I can't promise you won't have an orgasm. I can, and shall, certainly make my best efforts at getting you close without letting you go over, but I'm sure you know that a climax is built as much in the brain as it is in the body. I've had subs so determined to orgasm I barely need to touch them before they're coming. Likewise, no matter how skilled I am, it's entirely possible I might not be *able* to bring you to climax, should you change your mind and want it, after all."

"It's not about what I want. I need to make sure you hurt me as much as you can, but no matter how much it seems I want to come, you don't let me. I need you to actively keep me from it. That's why I'm paying you, rather than just taking up with a lover. I need a professional, and you've got a reputation. If you don't think you're up to it—"

The offhanded comment had nearly ended their working relationship before it even began. Something had intrigued Clara enough, though, that she'd put aside her automatic reaction to the lack of obsequiousness in Selena's tone. She'd agreed to the terms. They'd signed the contract. Here they were.

Now, running the flogger's leather straps once more through her fingers, Clara debated about where to strike next. Using the flogger on Selena's clit had nearly driven her over the edge. Clara had felt the throbbing of that tight knot and the clench of her internal pussy muscles when she'd slipped her fingers inside. She respected hard lines. She wouldn't have been a very good Domme if she didn't. So, although the idea of using the flogger again between Selena's legs appealed to Clara on a personal level, she was not about to do it now.

She turned back to Selena and moved close enough to murmur into her ear. "You remember your safety signal?"

Selena couldn't speak around the ball gag, but she nodded and twisted her left hand in the cuffs. Doing the same with her right hand would mean slow down. With both hands twisting upward, Clara would stop entirely. So far, Selena hadn't so much as crooked a single finger on her right hand.

"I'm going to hurt you now. A lot."

Selena shuddered. Clara took a step back and swung the flogger so it struck her muscular ass cheeks. Selena shrieked, her agonized cry muffled by the gag. Clara struck again, focusing but also keeping her attention ready for any sign Selena was giving the signal to slow or stop. Nothing, although she did jerk and twist her body in the bonds. A guttural growling issued from around the gag. Silver drool dripped.

There were times when Clara could lose herself in this so utterly it was as arousing to her as it could ever be to the sub she was beating. The steady, relentless rhythm of each blow. The strain and work of her muscles. The smell of sweat and sex and blood. Clara had achieved multiple orgasms while beating her subs, but only those with whom she'd had a relationship, never those who hired her. She wasn't doing this for herself. This was her job.

Still, it was rare to find a sub who could take such brutality without breaking, and so far, Selena still showed no signs of it. Clara could not see Selena's eyes behind the blindfold, so was unable to tell if they were open or closed. Selena could fall unconscious without Clara knowing. She had requested as much pain as Clara could provide, but it was still Clara's responsibility to make sure Selena wasn't permanently injured.

The flogger came down again and again. Across each thigh. Over Selena's bare belly. Between her legs, targeting the tender flesh there. Moving around her, Clara struck Selena's back, shoulders, buttocks, the backs of her upper thighs.

Only when Selena's skin was crisscrossed with welts did Clara slow the flogger. Selena let out a low, agonized cry that sounded more like a protest than relief. It was time, though, to stop. Clara put away the flogger and made sure the soft towels had been spread out on the mats beneath Selena's feet. She hadn't broken the skin, so there was no need to worry about the towels sticking to torn flesh. The absorbent material would cushion and comfort Selena until she felt ready to leave the space.

Clara hadn't been noticing the music soundtrack playing over the club's speakers, too caught up in what she'd been doing. Now, the slow, sensual grind of some electronic song filtered down to her along with the grunts and moans of the club's other patrons, each enduring their own scene. With an arm around Selena's body, Clara efficiently unhooked the cuffs holding her upright. Instantly, Selena's feet went flat to the floor, holding her weight even as she sagged in Clara's grip. Clara unhooked the spreader bar and set it aside. She helped Selena lower herself onto the softness on the floor.

Clara bent to unbuckle the ball gag and set it aside too. Finally, the blindfold. Selena's eyes were closed. Her cheeks bore the imprint of the gag, and saliva still coated her chin and throat, but she turned her face into the towels to dry it.

"I'll bring you some water." Clara squatted next to Selena to put a gentle hand on her shoulder. "Stay here until you feel capable of sitting up."

It took only a couple minutes for Clara to grab a bottle of water from the mini fridge near the door to the lobby, but by the time she returned, Selena was already standing. She didn't even seem wobbly. She'd hung a smaller towel around her neck and was using a different one to blot away the sweat and other fluids that had been cascading down her thighs.

"Here." Clara pressed the bottle into Selena's hand.

Selena cracked off the cap and drank, finishing the bottle's entire contents within a couple of minutes. "Thanks."

"Are you sure you're all right? The session was pretty intense." For just a moment, Clara had a smidgen of self-doubt. She'd put her best effort into the beating, but watching Selena now, fully recovered in barely ten minutes, she couldn't be sure.

Selena didn't smile. Her dark-green eyes narrowed. She nodded and handed the empty water bottle to Clara without looking at her, without a word.

It was a paid session, Clara reminded herself. This was not a lovers' game. She and Selena were not romantic partners. There was no need for them to speak, now the session had ended. Too often, she had clients who mistook the intimacy of power exchange and a scene for a true link between them, and Clara made sure to set them straight every time.

Why, then, did this clear dismissal from Selena rankle so fiercely?

"Do you need any help?" Clara asked.

Selena shook her head as she stretched, working her muscles. She winced but seemed no more put out by the beating Clara had given her than she might have been by an intense exercise routine. "No. Thanks."

"Fine. I'll see you in the office for the post-session interview. If you're up for it." Sometimes, clients were not. Selena had agreed after the first session, but not the second. For this, their third, Clara had no idea what to expect.

Selena shrugged, looking over Clara's shoulder and not at her face. "Sure."

Disgruntled at the clear lack of enthusiasm, Clara almost said more but stopped herself. She wasn't sure what she might have said, anyway. *Look at me? How about a hug?* If her feelings were stubbed, it was her own fault for being arrogant enough to expect worship from a source not meant to provide it.

"Fine," she said. "I'll see you in the office in five. All right?"

Another shrug. The plastic bottle crumpled in Selena's fist before she tossed it into the recycling bin. Without another word, Clara strode away, determined to keep her chin up and shoulders straight, not looking back to see if Selena were watching her, or if anyone else was either.

By the time she got to her office, a small but elegantly appointed space outfitted with several comfortable chairs as well as a desk, she had managed to shake off her feeling of irritation. Not everyone realized that Dommes needed to come down after a scene too, even if not in the same way. She got herself a bottle of water and a small hand towel from the warmer. She blotted her face and throat and then finished the water slowly.

"Come in," she said at the knock on the door.

Selena came through it. "I'm actually going to head on out."

"You don't want to go over the session?" Clara clamped her lips shut on any further protest.

"Nah." Selena gave her another of those horrifyingly disinterested shrugs. "I gotta go."

Clara kept herself from blurting out a question about if Selena intended to book another session. Instead, she responded with a curt nod. Selena didn't so much as give her a glance before leaving. The door closed with a solid *snick* behind her.

"Well. Shit," Clara said aloud.

*

It had been good, the pain.

Exquisite. Intense. Prolonged.

It had not been enough.

Selena had hoped but not expected it to be. Miss Clara's skills had brought Selena the closest she'd ever been, though, to forgetting about the beast. It wasn't Miss's fault Selena needed more than any person...any human...could be expected to provide.

The pain, when it was happening, had pushed away the heat of the lurking, ever-present fire that had simmered inside her since she'd had her first period. The sinister, insistent fire that burned her from the inside out until she gave up to it and became something else.

A few scant minutes after Miss had finished, however, the gnawing ache inside, the hunger, the desperate, clawing fury, had returned. It had only been slightly appeased. Not defeated. Barely, in fact, contained, and that was because of the pleasure.

The fire fed on it the way the wolf she became fed on flesh and blood. It was all tied together. The better something felt, the harder it was to deny the fire that led to the change. Pain had been her only solution. First by using her fists to punch walls, but that had broken her hands. Cutting had been useless. She'd have had to slice herself to the bone, over and over, for it to hurt enough to force away the wolf when it was trying to get out. Selena had been twenty years old before she'd discovered there were others who sought pain the way she did, and although most of them did it for different reasons, her entry into the realm of BDSM had been her salvation.

At least so far. The longer she went without letting the wolf take over, the harder it became to hold back the fire. The more pain she needed to shove down her impulses. And, given that the pain had become inextricably linked to pleasure, she wasn't sure how much longer it would be before even this solution no longer worked.

Then what would she do? Surrender totally, first to the burning fire, then to the beast? Run as an animal full time? Selena shuddered at the thought of losing herself like that. The way she knew others had done; the way her own mother had.

She wasn't that far gone, thank the universe. So long as she could come back regularly to Miss Clara for sessions as intense as tonight's, she might be all right for a while. And if she wasn't, if she couldn't...well, she'd deal with it when it happened.

She hadn't told Miss the truth about herself, of course. Selena never told anyone. There'd been a few who'd discovered it. Perdita, for example, had uncovered Selena's affliction, but her sadism had never been tempered with common sense. She'd used Selena's secrets against her. Anyone else who'd ever known about it, and there were only a rare few, was gone from Selena's life. She aimed to keep it that way. It might be a lonely life, but at least it was a *human* life.

Abyss provided locker rooms and showers for its clientele, but although the stickiness of her sweat had dried and she probably smelled awful, Selena didn't bother with them. She had experienced her pain. Now she needed food. Sleep. Tomorrow, the urgency would start rising inside her again. It would grow every day, and she could maybe stave it off for a bit with small agonies, but then it would be back, and she'd have to return to Abyss for another session.

Miss Clara had seemed put out that Selena didn't want to have an after session, though. Selena would need to watch herself. She knew she could be blunt and come off as rude, even when she didn't mean to be. She couldn't blame it on her condition, and although she could claim it was how she'd been raised, when did it become impossible to continue blaming your childhood for the mistakes you kept making?

She might have difficulty relating to other people emotionally, but that meant she had to try harder, Selena told herself as she loped across the Abyss parking lot, heading toward home. She was not an animal. She was a woman.

On the street, Selena turned her face to the night sky and breathed deeply. She caught the scent of a food truck on the next block and headed for it at a slow jog, her stomach already rumbling and ready to be filled with ground meat and spices wrapped in fried dough. The empanadas would go down perfectly. She was going to order at least ten.

"I only have five left," the young guy behind the food truck's counter said.

Selena gestured. "Make more. I'm starving."

He was staring. He might be looking at her bare shoulders and midriff or her ass in the tight leggings, or he might be smelling the scent of sex that clung to her. Selena didn't care.

"Food," she barked.

She hadn't meant to bare her teeth. The kid didn't deserve to be terrified. She hadn't meant to threaten him. Still, he let out a low squeak and disappeared into the back of the food truck, leaving her to pace while she waited.

"Umm...?" The kid handed her a grease-stained paper plate laden with five empanadas. "The rest will be done soon..."

Selena took them, fisting two in each hand while she shoved the fifth into her mouth and chewed. Fried dough and spiced meat burst apart into delicious pieces in her mouth. She chewed. Swallowed. Bit again.

Forcibly, Selena slowed herself. She was not an animal. *Not.*

"Food's up," came the voice from behind her.

She took it. Paid. The five she'd eaten already had tempered her growling gut but, like the session with Clara, only barely. Selena didn't gorge herself right here in front of the food truck, though. She'd already given the kid enough of a show and a scare.

Selena ate the other five empanadas at a slower pace. They tasted better that way, she had to admit. By the time she'd tucked the last one into her mouth and finished it off by licking all of her fingers clean of the grease, her belly was no longer protesting, and she was almost home.

When the dark car pulled up alongside her, Selena didn't look at it at first. If someone wanted to bring her some trouble, she could handle it. She waited on the corner for the light to turn red so she could cross. As it turned out, the trouble in the car was not the sort she'd been expecting, although she supposed she really shouldn't have been too surprised.

"Think of the devil and she appears," Selena said to the woman in the front seat.

Perdita smiled. "I'm flattered you think I'm the devil."

"What do you want? It's late, and I want to get home."

"I could give you a ride."

"No thanks," Selena said. "I need the exercise."

"I could meet you there," Perdita said.

Selena shook her head. The session at Abyss was wearing off. The food in her belly was solid, making her sleepy. The woman in the car was the very last person in the world she wanted to go home with.

"I hate you," Perdita said.

"You don't hate me. Hate is an emotion, and you don't have the capacity for it. I irritate you because I won't give you what you want." Selena started walking again, smart enough to stick to the sidewalk and not step in front of Perdita's car.

The light was still red, but that didn't stop Perdita from pulling forward and following her. "You need me!"

"I don't need you," Selena shot over her shoulder. "I found someone else."

It had been either the wrong thing to say, or the best thing, since Perdita squealed away without another word, leaving only the blink of her taillights as she rounded the corner ahead. With a groan, Selena tipped her face up to look beyond the buildings and into the night sky. Maybe that would be the last of her. It wasn't likely, Selena thought, but she could hope.

*

"She's...feral. It's the only way to describe her." Clara sipped from the glass of crimson liquid Nic had handed her and made a low murmur of approval. She lifted the glass to look at it and arched a brow at her friend. "Claret? Really?"

Nic ran a hand over her bristling brush of platinum hair and gave Clara a smirk. "Sure. Why not?"

"Didn't peg you for a claret drinker, Nic."

"You," Nic said with another of those smirks, "haven't pegged me at all."

They both laughed at her smart remark. While Clara had occasionally taken on the odd male client who enjoyed being taken in the ass by a dominant woman, she'd always far preferred women and had kept her recent focus on doing only what she preferred and enjoyed. It was a perk of having made a name for herself in the business. She no longer had to take what she could get.

Now, she could take what she wanted.

"It's very good, anyway," Clara said as Nic curled her muscular form, clad tonight in a pair of faded jeans cuffed above heavy leather Doc Martens and a black button-down shirt, into the chair across from her. Between them, the fire crackled, casting red and golden light over them both.

Nic pulled out a cigar from her shirt pocket. Without offering one to Clara, she clipped the end of it and tossed the tip into the ashtray. She lit, drawing hard to get a puff of smoke before answering. "Of course it is. I know better than to serve you anything but the best. This girl, though. This feral girl—"

"She's not a girl."

"Woman, then."

Clara savored the claret's rich flavor as she shook her head and frowned. Although she never smoked herself, she adored the scent of cigar smoke, and now she breathed it in with a sigh of delight. "No. I mean, yes, of course. Selena is most definitely a woman. But she's more than that. When I say feral, I mean it. She has this passion about her that's not like anything I've ever felt. She practically prowls into the room. It's intoxicating. I can't stop thinking about her."

"Oh, shit," Nic said.

Clara rolled her eyes. "It's not that bad."

"Forgive me for saying so, but as your friend, I'm going to remind you that you've sworn off personal relationships. Not," Nic added hastily before Clara could protest, "that I think that's your best idea since you know it's my personal belief there is a lid for every pot. But you're the one who asked me to slap you down if you ever made noises about it again."

It was the truth, and Nic had done it for her a few times over the past couple of years. Clara had made the mistake of ignoring her only once, but the outcome had been tragic. "I am not in the market for another broken heart. Don't worry."

"Can't help it. If you don't look out for yourself, who will?" Nic said gruffly from around the cigar and then went silent.

Clara and Nic had been friends for ages. Since high school, back when both of them had been struggling to figure out where they fit in the world, both of them playing with gender roles and sexuality and the concept of fetish versus preference. Nic had always known she was into girls, but finally accepting she was a butch bottom had taken some time. Clara, on the other hand, had not discovered she would always insist on being the one on top until she was in college. Two decades later, she could look back on the beginnings of their friendship and laugh at how naive they'd been.

"You don't need to worry about me on this. I promise. She's a client. An interesting, unique client. No more than that." Her words tasted like a lie, even to herself.

Nic arched a brow. "She turns you on."

"That doesn't mean anything. If I never got turned on, I'd be a robot." Clara waved a dismissive hand but knew better than to think she'd be dissuading Nic's opinion. She sighed and let her head loll back as she closed her eyes. Wine sloshed a little out of her glass, sprinkling the back of her hand. "Fuck."

"You've always had a soft heart for the odd ones. Me included. How'd you meet her, anyway?"

Clara opened one eye to look at her friend and then straightened in her seat to drain the glass. She put it onto the coffee table between them. Without asking, Nic refilled it.

"She applied through the website, and Vicki passed along her information to me."

Nic paused in filling, almost adding too much claret to the glass, but stopped before it could overflow. "I thought you weren't taking on any new clients."

"I wasn't. Her application was very specific and intriguing. I had some time in my schedule, and—"

"And you were a little bored," Nic broke in with a hearty chuckle. "I know you, friend. You were looking for a buzz."

She couldn't deny it. "Selena made things very clear. She requires a strong hand. Nothing emotional, no connection. She wants the pain, and a lot of it."

"You're good at that."

"She's adamant there be nothing else," Clara said.

"And that gets under your skin, doesn't it?" Nic knew her so well.

Clara pressed her lips together. She didn't want to admit it, but yes. That was part of it. Of course, she insisted her relationships with her clients remained completely professional and not personal, but she was always prepared for the women she dominated to fall in love with her, at least a little bit.

Nic puffed again on the cigar and gave Clara a wink. "You get off on it, babe. Being wanted, being desired, being adored."

"Who wouldn't?" Clara snapped, although she had no business being irritable with Nic for pointing out the truth. They'd been friends for too long for there to be secrets...or pretenses...between them.

She sighed again, thinking of how Selena had bucked in the restraints. How the smell of her arousal had tantalized Clara, so it had become difficult, just briefly, to concentrate on what she'd been doing. She sipped more claret to keep herself from saying anything else, but of course, she didn't need to.

"She's a mystery to you, and she's given you no signs that she cares a damn beyond the scene. It makes you crazy. That's all. There's nothing special about her other than that," Nic said.

Clara shook her head. "No. I mean, yes. Of course, that's true. But it's more than that. When I say feral, I mean it. She's untamed. She's wild. There is something raw about her. I asked her what prompted her desire—you know I always ask in the first meeting. Even if they can't often pinpoint their reasons, at least it gets them thinking about it. But when I asked Selena, she answered without hesitation. She said, and this is a direct quote, 'it keeps me from being bad.'"

"No Little tendencies?"

"No. Definitely not. You know I've never been interested in being a Mommy."

Nic murmured a sound of interest. "So, a severe punishment kink. Did she say what made her bad? Or what she expected you to do to her if she was 'bad?'"

"No. She was very clear. The pain kept her from being bad. So, it's not punishment if it's a deterrent rather than the consequences. Yet..." Clara hesitated, uncertain how to describe her feelings even to her best friend. Finally, she spat them out. "She's not a masochist."

"She *has* to be. I've seen you at work. Only a masochist could possibly want you to work on them. Nobody else could handle it."

"I swear to you, Nic. It's not the pain that gets her off."

"Denial kink, then? She gets off on not being allowed to get off?"

Clara frowned, thinking again of Selena. The tension in her muscles. The grit of her teeth. The smell of her pussy, flowing with slippery honey, clearly showing she was aroused. Selena had specifically requested she not be allowed to climax.

"I can't put my finger on it, but there's something about her, and it got under my skin."

Nic leaned forward so Clara could clink her glass. "Here's to your next broken heart."

*

If you could learn how to make a fancy coffee, you'd never be out of work, and you hardly ever had to bring references. You could whip up some latte art, impress the hell out of someone, and boom. A job. It wasn't what Selena had dreamed of for herself, but honestly, had she ever bothered to dream? There hadn't been much room for it in her life, not when she was trying to keep herself off the streets. Barista jobs had kept a roof over her head, put food on her table, clothes on her back. Those gigs had paid for every community college class she'd taken. She had half a degree in half a dozen majors, and no intentions of finishing one any time soon. She just liked learning.

This coffee shop had been one of her favorites, but when she'd clashed with the new ownership, it had been time to find something new. She liked coming back, now and again, for the triple-decker deli sandwich they'd kept on the specials board, so even if the coffee itself had suffered a bit without her guiding hand, it was worth a trip to this side of the city.

"Hey, there."

A warm voice. Familiar. Unexpected. Selena turned.

"Miss!"

"It's just Clara when we aren't at Abyss, please." Clara's smile tipped up one side of her lips more than the other.

Today, Clara wore a pair of navy slim-fitting jeans, knee-high leather riding boots, and a charcoal gray sweater that hung off one shoulder to expose her dark skin. Selena had never seen or maybe just never noticed the sensuous curve of Clara's neck. It captivated her. She tore her gaze from it to meet Clara's bemused gaze.

"What are you doing here?" Selena blurted.

Clara lifted a mug. "Drinking coffee."

Of course, she was. What a stupid question. Selena frowned. "I meant here. This place."

"I like this place." Clara made a show of looking around before letting her gaze rest once more upon Selena's. Her smile hadn't faded. "It's a quick walk from my house, and they have an amazing selection of pastries."

Selena nodded. "I used to work here."

"Did you? That must have been before I discovered it." Clara's smile tipped upward again, warm and welcoming and yet not entirely unlike the firm and commanding demeanor she had when she was being Miss. "Would you like to join me?"

"Triple-deli up" came the barked words from behind them both.

Selena turned to grab the sandwich, her mind twisting. She hadn't expected to see anyone she knew, much less Clara. The invitation had been offered kindly, she knew that. To decline would seem rude, wouldn't it?

Or at least strange. And even though she didn't usually have a problem being seen as either rude or strange, it was different with Clara.

Why was it different with Clara?

The table had a space already cleared for Selena, so she slid into the chair and put the plate in front of her. Clara had pulled her laptop from the space and was busy putting it away into her bag. By the time she turned back, Selena had taken a huge bite of her sandwich. Clara blinked, looking surprised. Selena forced herself to slow down.

"How are you?" The question was simple enough, spoken in Clara's soft, melodic voice.

Even so, Selena wasn't sure how to answer. "Fine?"

"That sounds like you're not sure." Clara pulled apart a flaky croissant and tucked a piece into her mouth. She made a "yum" noise. "It's so hard to find a good vegan croissant."

"Vegan?" Selena recoiled.

Clara looked surprised again. "Yes, I'm vegan."

"Why?" Too much. Too loud. Selena covered her discomfort at her own blurted-out words by wiping her mouth with a napkin.

"I feel better when I don't eat meat. Heavy fats and animal products give me digestive issues," Clara replied.

"I could never give up meat."

"Then it's a good thing nobody would ask you to," Clara said lightly.

She didn't seem offended, so that was good. Self-conscious now, both for her overreaction and the enormous pile of flesh and bread on her plate, Selena wiped her mouth again. The coleslaw wasn't meat, so she ate some of it.

"I'm sorry if I'm making you uncomfortable, Selena. I know it can be strange to meet up outside of Abyss."

"It's fine."

Clara nodded, silent, and pulled apart another few bites of her croissant. She ate so neatly, with such grace. Selena forced herself again to take only a small bite, to wipe her mouth directly after it. To chew slowly and swallow.

"My grandmother was a terror for manners," Selena said finally. "I was never good at it."

Clara laughed. "You're fine."

They both ate in silence for a minute or so.

"Tell me about your grandmother," Clara said.

"She's dead."

"Was that sad?"

This question gave Selena another pause, although the fact Clara had even asked it as though there could be more than one answer told her something. "If I say no, will you think I'm a terrible person?"

"Are you a terrible person?"

"I try not to be," Selena answered honestly.

Clara tilted her head, and after a few seconds, she gave Selena another slow, warm smile. "That's all anyone can do, isn't it?"

It was only words, tossed at each other over good coffee at a table small enough that their knees kept bumping. Still, it was the closest Selena had felt to a connection with anyone in a long, long time. She wanted to enjoy it.

She knew better than that, though. Anyone she'd ever allowed close to her had ended up leaving or hating her or both. If that happened with Miss Clara, what would Selena do then?

"I should get going." Selena stood.

Clara gestured at the plate and the sandwich. "You haven't finished."

"I'll take it with me. I have some things I have to do."

"Ah." Clara sipped her coffee.

Selena gathered her plate and wrapped it in a couple of napkins. She was very aware of Clara's gaze upon her, but she didn't meet it. By the time she'd finished packing up her food, Clara had eaten her croissant, but she didn't get up from her chair.

"I'll see you," Selena said.

Clara nodded. "Good. I hope so."

"Soon."

"Even better," Clara said with a smile that threatened to turn Selena inside out.

She thought about that smile all the way home.

*

"Maybe you need a break." Nic said this matter-of-factly, the way she almost always said everything.

"From Selena?"

Nic shrugged and moved out of the way so Clara could get to one of the puzzle pieces strewn out over the table. "From Selena, yeah. And from Abyss. Why not take a vacation, head up to your cabin? You haven't been there in how long?"

It had been too long. Clara's cabin had always been an oasis for her, but the last time she'd been there had been with Felicity. The arguments had led to their final, and permanent, breakup. She hadn't been back since.

"I can't just up and run out of town every time I get my feelings a little bruised, Nic."

"You don't need the money," Nic said flatly, "and if the work is upsetting you, then you should definitely take a break from it."

"My clients count on me."

"You don't want to give her up," Nic pointed out and slid a puzzle piece into place.

Clara frowned and leaned back in her chair. They'd been working on this series of puzzles for the past couple of years, each a different print of a famous painting. This one was *The Starry Night*, and Nic had already claimed it for her own when they were finished.

"I don't," Clara admitted.

Nic laughed and shook her head. "And here I sit, dried up and lonely. I haven't had a decent date in months, much less found someone who could beat my ass at night and make me pancakes wearing a frilly apron in the morning."

"That's a tall order." Clara chuckled. "You know, you could make an appointment at Abyss. It won't get you a fifties housewife making pancakes in the morning, but you'll get a very decent beating."

Nic pressed another piece into the puzzle and sighed, looking pensive. Her fingers sifted through the pile of puzzle pieces, searching for the right one. She plucked a blue one swirled with gold and green and held it up. "You know Abyss isn't my kind of scene. If only relationships were as easy to put together as a puzzle."

"It's taken us three months to put this thing together, Nic, and we had to work at it little by little without giving up."

"Are you saying I give up too soon?" Nic gave her an insulted look that quickly broke into a grin. "Yeah. I give up too soon. But you…"

Clara waited, but Nic didn't continue. "I what?"

"You," her friend sighed, "you...maybe you hang on too hard, even when you know something isn't going to work?"

"Ouch."

Clara's phone saved her with the distinctive chime from her scheduling app. Abyss used a sophisticated system so each Domme could respond personally to individual appointment requests as well as check on the queries from new clients who hadn't asked for someone specific. She swiped the screen to check, biting her lower lip, but glanced up to catch Nic's eye.

"You look like the kid who got socks and underwear for Christmas."

"I don't know. Underwear can be a fun gift." Clara winked, but her heart wasn't really in the teasing.

"It wasn't her, huh?"

Clara shook her head. "No. It wasn't her."

It had been three weeks since the last session with Selena, two weeks since they'd bumped into each other at the coffee shop. Clara had returned to the shop a few times since then but hadn't seen Selena again. She didn't want to think it was because Selena was deliberately avoiding her, but that's how it had started to feel. Clara swiped again, returning a list of three dates and times she had available to the client who'd requested a session with her.

She glanced up again to catch Nic staring. "What?"

"You're smitten."

"I'm...fine. I'm smitten. She intrigues me. What's wrong with that?"

Nic shrugged. "I haven't seen you act this way about a client before. That's all."

"I've never felt this way about a client before."

This time, Nic's phone pinged. She slid it from her back pocket. Her platinum eyebrows rose. She put the phone away without doing anything else.

"What was that?" Clara asked.

"Some girl I met at the gym wants to know if I want to meet up to work out."

Silence.

Clara grinned.

Nic frowned.

"It's not like that," she insisted.

Clara discarded the piece she'd been trying to fit into an open spot and found another. This one fit. She pressed it into place and gave Nic a triumphant look.

"Or maybe, she's just the missing piece you're waiting to find," Clara said.

"Hold on, where's my wine? Because I need a glass to go with all. That. Cheese."

They laughed together at that, but Clara dropped the subject. No fair digging at Nic about something if she didn't want the same attention cast back on her. Nic's advice to take a break was sound, but she wasn't going to take it, and she didn't want to argue the point.

After Nic had gone home, Clara changed into her favorite flannel pajamas and slipped into bed with her laptop. She told herself she was checking her appointment requests, but of course that took only a few minutes. Afterward, her fingers tapped the keyboard in a few search strings, one after the other, none pulling up exactly what she was looking for.

Selena Tuller did not exist on the internet. She had no social media profiles. More digging pulled up no references of any kind, not even an address or phone number from one of those scam sites that promised to reveal every scrap of personal information, oh, but for a small fee. No birth, death, divorce, or criminal records showed up, so at least Clara was saved from having to decide if she was going to go the credit card level of stalker.

It was possible Selena was using a fake name. Some clients did to preserve their privacy, just as many of the Dommes used aliases. Selena paid with cash, also not unusual in Clara's business. She was wasting her time on a search like this.

Besides, she wondered as she closed her laptop, what would she have done if she *had* found any links to Selena's real life? Sent her a friend request? Searched her photos? Looked up all the places where she "checked in?"

The only way Clara was going to learn more about the mysterious, intriguing Selena was by asking her, and their coincidental coffee date had shown her exactly how forthcoming Selena was likely to be. *You need to stop obsessing about her,* Clara told herself and settled firmly into her pillows. It had been three weeks since their last session. Maybe it had been the last one they'd ever have.

Her phone chimed. Her heart skipped. She couldn't stop the grin spreading over her face like syrup on pancakes.

Selena.

*

Miss would not allow her to come.

Selena reminded herself of the hard line again as Miss tightened the cuffs binding her wrists to the spanking bench. She shifted, tugging, but Miss had locked the cuffs at their tightest. Already Selena's fingers tingled.

Miss cuffed her ankles next so that Selena's legs were spread, exposing her pussy and ass to the view of anyone who'd care to watch them. Tonight was an open play night, and she'd chosen specifically to come in since there'd be no chance they wouldn't have an audience. Miss had seemed surprised Selena was so insistent but had complied.

That was the only thing setting Miss apart from what Selena would have considered her true Domme. Ultimately, while Miss was the one who decided how far and how hard to take Selena during each of their scenes, in the end, it was still an agreed-upon arrangement, and Selena was the one who laid out the requirements. If this was a real thing between them, Selena would defer to Miss, no matter what, trusting her enough to know she was going to make the right choices for her.

At least, that was how Selena had always thought it should be. She'd never actually been in a relationship based on such mutual trust she could let someone else have ultimate control. What they did here at Abyss was an illusion, in the end, no matter how real it felt at the time.

"Comfortable?" Miss murmured in Selena's ear, sending a shudder through her body.

Not yet gagged, Selena answered, "Yes, Miss. Thank you. You can tighten the ankles."

"Not in this position. I don't want you losing sensation in your feet and legs, injuring yourself when you try to stand, after." Miss spoke firmly, and the no-nonsense tone in her voice sent more delicious shivers all throughout Selena's body.

She did trust that Miss Clara knew her business well enough to be sure Selena wouldn't be permanently injured. "Yes, Miss."

A warm hand rested on the small of Selena's back, just above the swell of her naked buttocks. Miss let her fingertip trail down the crack of Selena's ass and lower, to slide over her pussy from behind. She lingered, probing further to tweak Selena's clit.

"You're already wet," Miss said.

Selena didn't answer. Miss cracked a severe hand across her ass. Then again.

"Yes, Miss, I'm already wet!"

Miss leaned close again. "Lovely."

Selena closed her eyes, waiting for the blindfold and the gag. After a moment, without anything else either being put on her, nor with any touch from Miss, she opened them and looked around as best she could. Miss had stepped aside to speak with another of the Dommes, Lady Victoria. The room had been empty when Selena and Miss entered, but now people were filtering in. Some headed for the various equipment, while others took seats so they could observe. More of an audience than Selena had expected. She writhed in her bondage, incapable of doing more than a small wriggle. The tightness of her bonds gave her a sense of security she hated for allowing her to relax into the bondage.

Miss glanced at her. Selena didn't want to listen to the conversation between her Domme and the other, but she couldn't help it. The closer the wolf got to the surface, the more sensitive her hearing became. Same with sense of smell. Taste. Touch.

She'd made a mistake, she thought wildly as she subtly jerked at the cuffs on her wrists. She'd been unsettled by their chance meeting at the coffee shop. She cursed herself for being too...afraid. Too fucking afraid to meet with Miss alone, one-on-one, privately. She'd been too afraid being that close with her would lead to feelings, so she'd insisted on making sure they had their session in the most public way possible, and now look what she'd done by putting off the pain for too long.

It might even be too late.

"Of course I'm all right with it, Vicki," Miss said to the other Domme. "Frankly, I'm insulted you would even suggest that I might be unprepared for a scene."

Saliva slipped from Selena's mouth, along with a low, guttural moan. She wriggled harder. Her motions did nothing but spread her thighs wider. Raise her ass higher. All of it put her further on display.

Biting her tongue brought the pungent taste of blood into her mouth, but it also blocked out the voices and the conversation she didn't want to be overhearing. As Miss came closer, Selena caught the specific scent of her skin. Again, drool pooled on her tongue; she swallowed convulsively against the glorious odor and closed her eyes.

"Look at me, Selena."

The easy command in her voice was of a woman used to being obeyed without question, and Selena opened her eyes without hesitation.

"Are you ready?"

"Yes, Miss."

Again, Miss Clara laid a warm hand on Selena's ass cheeks. "Do you have anything you'd like to add before we begin? Beyond what we've discussed in the past."

"No, Miss."

"All right." Clara's sigh eased soft breath over Selena's skin. Her voice sounded reluctant.

Selena tensed. Would Miss refuse? Worse, would she hold back? Selena craned her head to try to glimpse her, but in this position, it was impossible. Again, she wriggled against the restraints.

Miss's hand cracked down, hard. Then again. A warning.

Relief flooded Selena. Miss would not hold back. She would hurt Selena as much as she'd requested, and if it wasn't quite as much as she needed, it would have to be enough.

Her entire body tensed at the soft sound of the crop being drawn between Miss's hands. She would beg for a blindfold, a gag, Selena thought, but before she had the chance, Miss brought down the crop against her skin. It hit in the crease just below her buttocks, finding tender flesh and setting Selena on fire.

She had no words.

A low, rasping cry arced out of her. Then another. The sounds of her own agony ought to have embarrassed her, but instead they fed the pain so it cycled in on itself. Took it higher. Fiercer.

Again and again, Miss brought the crop down on Selena's ass and thighs. Her pussy ached, her clit pulsing and throbbing. Open to the room, wet and ready for anyone who was watching. The thought of it sent a different sort of pain through her, this one stabbing deep into her heart.

"Open your eyes," Miss demanded, out of breath, panting.

Miss was aroused. Selena could smell it. The scent made her growl and buck against the cuffs as more desire swept over her. She wanted to get inside the appetizing smell, to lick and suck and nibble and lose herself in Miss's flooding juices.

"Open!"

The crop slapped and stung. Selena opened her eyes. Miss stood in front of her, gloriously naked but for the soft black leather slippers on her feet. Her dark skin glowed with dewy sweat. The fur beneath her arms was damp when she raised her hand to stroke the crop through her other palm. She gripped it with both hands. She licked her lips, and the sight of her tongue sent a spasm of longing through Selena that cut through the stinging pain left behind by the crop.

"You're gorgeous," Miss said.

Selena cried out as her body arched as best it could within her bonds. She was so close to climax the slightest touch, a whisper, a flutter of eyelashes, would send her over. Helpless against it, she rocked her hips, trying to press herself against something, anything that would provide enough pressure on her clit to get there.

She wept, unable to speak even to plead for Miss to let her come. She craved release more than the pain of being denied it. Even knowing what would happen if she was granted that pleasure, Selena couldn't stop herself from reaching for it.

"No." Miss put her hand on top of Selena's head, caressing and then entwining her fingers in her hair. "No."

"Please!" Selena barked out the plea—an actual, literal bark.

Miss grabbed her jaw and held her head in place, forcing Selena to meet her gaze. "No."

Selena braced herself for a rush of fury or violence, but warmth and calm spread through her. It tamped down the fire and held back the wolf. Every muscle had tensed, her body straining toward release, but now although she was still desperately on the edge of orgasm, she was no longer frantic. She didn't even feel the need for Miss to take up the flogger again.

Minutes later, nursing the cool bottle of water Miss had given her and resting quietly on the mats, Selena...the only way to describe it was she came back into herself in a way that had been missing for so long she barely remembered what it had been like before the wolf had started taking her over.

Miss reached a hand to help her up. "How are you feeling?"

"Fine. Great. Really great!" Selena bounced on the balls of her feet and drained the water bottle.

"Good. I'm glad. I'll give you some time to get cleaned up, and we can have a brief meeting in my office, if you like. About the session," Miss Clara said, as though she had to clarify.

Selena had avoided almost all of those meetings in the past, but tonight she wanted to talk with Miss about what had happened. What had worked so well and how she felt about it. She wanted to figure out why tonight had left her feeling so clear for the first time. For now, she gathered her clothes from the neat pile on the chair near the spanking bench.

"I'll just go grab a shower," she said.

*

It would have been arrogant to say that Clara had never been affected by a session with a sub before tonight, but it had been a long time since her own desires had overtaken her during a scene with a client. Even playtime with lovers rarely saw her lose her own control. Tonight with Selena, though, Clara had found herself almost unable to hold back from engaging personally. Only at the very last minute did the sense of desperation and terror—yes, it was far more than mere fear—rising off Selena keep Clara from tipping her over the edge and going over it herself.

Her thighs actually felt shaky as she carefully sponged herself clean of the sweat from her exertions. She slipped into her panties and bra, then the loose T-shirt dress. She brushed her teeth and touched up her simple makeup—eyeliner and gloss only. Her close crop of dark curls needed nothing more than a pat with damp fingers to be tidied, and she had no more excuses for lingering in the staff locker room.

She was hiding in there. She had to admit it. She had provided the necessary aftercare, which for Selena amounted to almost nothing other than being released from her cuffs and being offered a bottle of water and a towel. She'd made the offer, of course, to meet in her office, but...

"She never wants to meet after," Clara whispered to her reflection. She wasn't able to convince herself that was why she hadn't simply drawn on a robe and taken a drink to her office to have a quiet follow-up with the sub but was instead hiding in here to avoid what was going to be certain rejection.

You dom people so you never have to be told no.

Cruel words from a cruel person. That's what Clara wanted to tell herself, except she knew Felicity hadn't been cruel. Only honest about her feelings. She'd broken Clara's heart, but whose fault had that been, really? Felicity's, for telling what she perceived as the truth, or Clara, for not being able to be honest with her at all?

Selena had been tense, on the edge from the moment she walked into the space. Every muscle trembling. Her arousal had hovered all around her in almost-visible waves. She'd taken every blow from Clara's hand and every implement, and her body had begged for more even when her mouth only managed moans and sighs. She hadn't outright asked to be allowed to climax, but Clara had seen the raging desire all over her. How close Selena had been to it.

It would have been so easy to push her into it, to give her the release for which she was so clearly aching. Selena had been clear from the start she wanted to be hurt, but more than that, not simply forbidden to come. Prevented from it. In private, Clara always reserved the right to take her submissive's orgasm as her own tribute, no matter what they'd asked for. With clients, she practiced denial if they requested it, but she'd never had a client as adamant about it as Selena.

Tonight, Selena had been afraid. Well, so had Clara. That feral "something" inside Selena that Clara had not quite been able to describe had been there, writhing beneath the surface. It had been in Selena's gaze, unfocused and full of yearning. It had been in the waft of her breath, the silver string of drool slipping from her lips. Something inside her had been trying to get out, and Clara had been too afraid to see what it was.

Distanced from it now, she could be ashamed of herself for allowing her past to prevent her from behaving with total professionalism. Maybe Nic was right, and Clara did need a break from the woman who'd infiltrated her every thought over the past three months. Clearly, it was starting to affect her work.

The locker room door opened. Clara straightened, putting on a neutral face. She nodded toward Miyuki as her fellow Domme went straight for the water cooler in the corner to draw herself a long drink.

"Weird night," Miyuki said.

Clara faced her. "What do you mean?"

"Strange energy in the room, that's all. Didn't you feel it?"

"No. Not really."

"Huh." Miyuki shrugged and filled another paper cup of water. "Maybe it was because of Perdita."

Perdita was not a friend to either of them but was well known in their circle for having a wicked taste for granting pain. She'd been "retired" from Abyss, but only after Lady Victoria had been pressured into firing her. Perdita had put a few clients into the hospital before that. None of the other Dommes trusted her.

"What about her?" Clara served herself some water, anything to use as an excuse to linger in the locker room. *Coward*, she chastised herself.

Miyuki tossed her cup into the trash. "Oh. She tried to get in tonight."

"She's banned!"

"Tell that to her," Miyuki said.

Fifteen minutes had already passed while she camped out in the locker room, and as Miyuki tidied up and left, there was no more good reason for Clara to stay. She went to her office, breath held. No Selena. Somehow, she was both relieved and disappointed, and ashamed again of how she was letting this all affect her.

She ducked out of the back of the building using the staff entrance, avoiding the lobby entirely. She was being ridiculous. She was better than that. Furthermore, she owed Selena, at minimum, professional courtesy.

Head whirling with her conflicting emotions and self-castigation, Clara headed for her car. She paused to search through her small bag for her car keys, determined she was going to get—and keep—herself under control. First, she'd insist on a meeting with Selena, where they'd discuss their previous sessions and map out a way to transfer Selena to another Domme. Second, Clara would take a leave of absence from Abyss. Take a trip to the mountains, spend some time alone in the cabin. Get her head on straight.

"Hey there, Bitchy-Poo."

Clara stopped dead and straightened. Eyes narrowed, she searched the shadows for the source of the familiar voice. Through clenched jaws she said, "Perdita. Fuck off."

Perdita wore black jeans. Black Docs. Black hoodie. Her blonde hair flowed in a sleek ponytail over one shoulder. She stepped into the circle of light from the parking-lot lamp and grinned.

"Is that any way to greet an old friend?"

"You're not my friend, and you know it."

Perdita's laugh cut through the air between them, brittle and sharp as broken glass. "Colleague, then?"

"Don't flatter yourself." Clara lifted her chin, tense and wary. During the time Perdita had worked at Abyss, Clara had certainly seen her in action and dealt with her, but they had never been more than acquaintances. After Perdita got banned from the club, Clara had heard gossip about what she was up to but had never seen her in person. "What do you want?"

"I want to talk to you about your new sub." Perdita stepped closer.

Beneath the unzipped hoodie, her cleavage strained at the V-neck of her black T-shirt. Perdita was trying to show off the way she always had. To draw attention to her tits and hips and ass, to make sure anyone looking at her saw her as beyond desirable. It was predictable and pathetic.

"I don't discuss my clients with anyone," Clara said. "Particularly you."

"You're a fucking liar. I know you talk about your clients. We all fucking talk about our clients." Perdita's lip curled.

"I'm not discussing anything with you. It's late. I'm tired. It's cold. You shouldn't even be here."

"The parking lot's a public space," Perdita countered.

Clara laughed. "I'm sure it's not, but whatever. Fuck off, Perdita."

Perdita frowned and tutted. "Come on, Clara. Why so rude? I only want to talk to you. Think of it as a friendly warning. Between friends. Oh, and by the way, Felicity sends her regards."

At her former lover's name, Clara froze in place, her keys in one hand. She was still a good twenty paces from her car. Perdita moved a few steps closer.

"I doubt that," Clara said through clenched jaws.

Perdita's grin had become almost a snarl. "Tell you what. You give Selena back to me, and I'll make sure you get a new shot at Felicity."

She ought to have known Perdita had been referring to Selena when she demanded information about Clara's "new" sub.

"As my momma used to say, your mouth is writing a check your ass can't cash, Perdita. I don't own my clients. My subs aren't slaves. I'm not interested in, nor could I, give you anyone. Or you me."

"Felicity," Perdita said in a low, smug purr, "does anything I say. If I tell her to get back with you, she will."

Not so long ago, the thought of Felicity with anyone else, much less Perdita, would have rankled. Clara was surprised now, and glad, to feel only irritation at Perdita's bragging, as well as protectiveness toward Selena. She headed for her car again, pushing past Perdita who refused to get out of the way. Their shoulders bumped.

"Don't you fucking shove me," Perdita cried.

Clara kept moving, this time slipping her keys between her fingers to create a bristling set of brass knuckles. Perdita stepped in front of her again. Something glinted in her fist, and it wasn't a set of keys.

"What the hell?" Clara asked, backing up at the sight of the knife.

"You don't deserve her. She's mine. Nobody else can have her!"

Clara glanced around, but they were alone out here. Perdita blocked the way to Clara's car. The building was too far to run for. Perdita was fast and strong, and from the looks of it, determined to hurt her.

Perdita was very, very good at hurting people.

*

Selena had waited fifteen minutes for Miss Clara to meet her in the office, surprised at first when she didn't show. Then she had to admit she couldn't be surprised, considering every other time she'd refused to meet after a session, so why would Miss think she was going to, tonight? Selena knew she could come off as blunt or even rude, but she tried her best for self-reflection when she could. If there'd been miscommunication, she had her part to blame in it.

The crisp, cold night air tingled the insides of her nostrils, bringing with it the scents of car exhaust, frying food from one of the trucks lining the street around the corner, a puddle of dampness that was turning to ice. She never minded the cold, but the wolf inside her loved it.

She had often wished she could embrace the changes she worked so fiercely to control, but something about tonight had made a difference. For the first time in her life, Selena found herself believing she might find a way to make peace with what she was. Not to allow the wolf full control, of course. She couldn't live that way, certainly not in the city where a loose dog wasn't allowed to run and a wolf would certainly be hunted and destroyed, the way her mother had been.

Her mother had loved the wolf inside her. Of course, Selena's mother had also loved drugs and sex and grifting. She'd lived from one high to the next, always on the run. Sometimes figuratively, many times literally. She'd been shot in a suburban backyard by a man who swore he'd aimed and fired on a "giant, rabid mutt" that had been attacking his Great Dane. The fact the body in the grass was that of a forty-year-old woman had earned him time in an institution rather than prison. Selena had never blamed him for her mother's death, but she did blame her mother for never teaching her about what she was...or why.

Selena's stomach rumbled, but a sharp cry gave her pause. She turned, listening. Her hearing, this close to the wolf, was acute. She was four blocks from Abyss, but she recognized Miss's voice without trouble.

Miss cried out again. First in anger. Then, pain. The sound of her voice rang through Selena's head, echoing. She pivoted on the heel of her boot and ran back toward the club without thinking. Just moving.

She rounded the corner into the shadowy back parking lot, but didn't see Miss. She heard her, though. The soft huff of her breath. A muttered curse. Selena caught the odor of blood, the tang of sweat. Something overlaying all that too. The stink of a familiar perfume.

Fists clenched, Selena moved around a car parked in a depth of shadow. On the other side, two women grappled. The smaller had her hands around the taller's throat. Selena knew them both at once, and her heart hammered at the sight of Miss being throttled.

In seconds, Selena was upon them. She raked her nails down the back of Perdita's hoodie, shredding it and the T-shirt and digging into the skin beneath. With the other she went for Perdita's wrist. She yanked it away from Miss's throat and used the fistful of torn fabric as leverage to pull Perdita away.

With a howl, Perdita whirled, slapping and scratching, but Selena had dealt with this bitch before, and she was no match. She punched Perdita in the nose, sending her to the parking lot pavement, and then stood over her to grab the front of her clothes and jerk her upward with one hand while she used the other to punch her in the face again. The cracking sound of bone followed by the rush and heat of blood sent Selena back a step or two with her fists still raised in case Perdita decided to get back up.

She did, of course. It would never have occurred to her she might get a beating as good as, or worse than, she was capable of giving. When she came at Selena, it was with the clear intent that Selena would take whatever Perdita was getting ready to dish out. Instead, Selena sidestepped the incoming punch, ducked, and threw one of her own. Perdita doubled over, gasping and gagging. She twisted to stare up with wide, shocked eyes.

"I guess you still don't know the difference between dominating someone and assaulting them," Selena said. Her fists were still raised, but her voice was calm.

Perdita tried again, this time with a kick aimed at swiping Selena's legs out from under her. It almost worked, but Selena caught her balance. A glimmer of flame heated her insides. The wolf was waking. Perdita, she realized, was trying to taunt her through anger into changing.

"Enough," Selena said. "I don't want to have to put you in the hospital."

"Come home with me, then."

Miss Clara was still on the ground. She snorted something under her breath, and Perdita whirled toward her. She seemed to think better of attacking her, though, because Selena stepped between them. Perdita's incredulous expression said it all.

"She screams, and you come running?" Perdita snarled this through busted lips and bared, blood-stained teeth.

Gauging Perdita wasn't going to move on her again, at least for the moment, Selena bent over Miss. "Are you all right? Did she hurt you?"

"She tried." Miss Clara accepted Selena's hand and got to her feet. One eye looked as though it might be swelling, and a trickle of blood had stained her upper lip, but she looked otherwise undamaged.

Selena turned to Perdita, who had dropped her fists to her sides but was still staring with a gaping, bloody mouth. "What the hell is wrong with you? Clara, call the police. Report this bitch for assault."

"She won't do that. Can't have the police coming around her precious club. What they do in there might not be against the law, but it sure as hell doesn't need any red-and-blue lights flashing on it." Perdita spat a gobbet of blood to the side.

Clara shook her head. "She's right. We've been hassled before. I don't need to get involved with any of that. I just want to go home."

"I'll take you," Selena said. "Make sure you're all right."

"Oh. Oh, my God." Perdita's humorless laughter was as rough as concrete on a toddler's knees. "Oh, wow. Clarabell, you'd better be careful. That bitch has the hots for you. And when I say bitch, I mean it. She's a real one."

"Shut up, Perdita." Selena slipped an arm around Clara's waist.

Perdita snorted more laughter. Blood sprayed. "You have no idea what you're getting yourself into with this one! Better you let me have her. You can't handle her! What are you going to do when she starts to—"

Selena didn't punch her this time. She slapped, instead. The blow might not have hurt as much but was more of an insult. It shut Perdita up, anyway, and although her eyes blazed with fury, she tossed up her hands and backed away.

"You'll find out, I guess. Don't say I didn't warn you!"

"Which one's yours?" Selena looked at Clara and then the few cars in the parking lot.

"This one." Clara looked past Selena toward where Perdita was getting into her own car. She waited until Perdita drove away before holding up her empty hands. "I dropped my keys."

Selena scanned the ground. "I'll find them."

"Let me grab my purse, I can get my phone. Use the flashlight."

"No need." Selena couldn't see in the dark, but she— or more accurately, the wolf—had excellent night vision. She straightened, holding Clara's keys. "I'll drive."

"I'm completely capable of driving," Clara said dryly.

"You're shaking," Selena pointed out and held open her palm.

After a moment, but with a sigh, Clara handed over the keys. She even allowed Selena to open the passenger side door for her and settle her in, but when Selena tried to click the seatbelt for her, Clara put a hand up to stop her.

"Enough," she said, but quietly. Gently. "I can do it."

Selena nodded. "I know you can. I just want to take care of you."

Clara blinked rapidly for a few seconds. Then she nodded too. Selena closed the door and went around to the driver's side. She put the key in the ignition and settled her hands on the wheel.

"Show me where to go," she said.

*

It wasn't particularly late, but after what had happened in the parking lot, Clara was exhausted. She'd asked, but not expected, Selena to come inside. She had, though, and had insisted on "helping" Clara upstairs and into the bathroom for a hot shower.

Clara had assumed Selena would be gone by the time she got out of the bathroom. Wrapped in her thick fleece robe, she came into the bedroom to find a tray she'd forgotten she owned on the bed. Selena had fitted it out with a couple of mugs of steaming tea and a sleeve of saltines, along with some organic jam. Even a pair of cloth napkins.

"Wow," Clara said.

Selena had been staring out the window but turned. "I thought you might need something in your stomach."

She hadn't thought she'd be hungry again for a while, but her stomach rumbled. Clara put a hand on it. "I do. Join me?"

They sat together on the bed, Selena cross-legged and Clara in a slightly more demure position. Clara spread a cracker with jam and tucked it into her mouth with a happy sigh. She offered one to Selena, who took it.

"Thank you, Selena. For being there when I needed you. And for all this."

Selena shrugged, but also smiled. "You're welcome. When I heard you cry out, I had to run back and make sure you were all right."

"Run?"

"I was...well, I'd already left the parking lot." Selena paused to spread jam on another pair of crackers before offering one to Clara.

"How did you hear me? I wasn't screaming that loud. At least, I didn't think I was." Clara gave Selena a curious look.

"I have really good hearing."

Clara wasn't sure what to say in response. Her senses tingled with an awareness of something she couldn't pinpoint. Selena's knee nudged hers as she shifted to drink some tea, and the touch spread warmth through Clara's entire body.

"I was glad you were there. Perdita really had it in for me. I don't know why. Jealousy, I suppose," Clara said.

Selena nodded. "We were together for a bit. Months ago. Longer than that, even. Over a year. It was never as much as she wanted it to be. She's kind of a crazy bitch."

"That's a good description," Clara agreed. "Do you think I have reason to be afraid she'll keep trying?"

"If she does, I'll take care of her."

Clara pursed her lips. "Selena. I don't want you to get into trouble for doing anything to Perdita even if we both know she deserves it."

"I won't do anything unless she tries something with you."

"You aren't with me all the time," Clara said.

Selena looked her in the eyes. "Maybe I should be with you more. Enough to make sure she leaves you alone."

"That sounds like a kind offer, but I'm not sure I need a babysitter." Clara licked sweet jam from her lips. Selena's gaze followed the movement of her tongue. "You know, I was beginning to think I wasn't going to see you again. After the coffee shop, then you didn't make any new appointments…"

"I got nervous, bumping into you like that outside of the club. I liked seeing you. I like you. I like being around you."

"Why does that make you nervous?" It made Clara a bit nervous too, perhaps in the same ways. Perhaps not. *Ask her,* she reminded herself. *Ask her all the things you want to know about her.*

"Because I don't want to get attached."

Clara nodded. The tea and crackers remained further untouched, so she pushed the tray to the side. Now the bed was an open space between them. She wanted to move into that emptiness and fill it, get closer so she could be in touching distance. Kissing distance, if she was going to be honest with herself.

"You think you'll get attached to me, Selena?"

"I think it would be real easy to. Yeah."

"I often have clients who—"

Selena shook her head. "No. Not that way. I know the difference between you doing your job and it being something else. So do you."

"Do you think there's something more to us than me doing my job?" Clara's breath hitched a little in her throat, and she swallowed against the sudden dryness.

Selena kissed her. Her fingers cupped the back of Clara's neck beneath the collar of the fleecy robe. Clara, surprised, parted her lips in welcome to Selena's tongue. The kiss ended quickly, but not abruptly. Selena lingered with her mouth a breath's distance from Clara's for the span of a single heartbeat. Then she pulled away. Her blue eyes narrowed. She wiped the back of her hand across her mouth and then let her clenched fist fall into her lap.

"I don't like to get attached," she muttered.

"So, why are you here, then?" Boldly, Clara moved closer. Her robe fell open, and she didn't miss the way Selena looked into the folds of fabric to Clara's bare skin beneath.

"Because I—"

It was Clara's turn to initiate the kiss, and she made sure to do it softer than Selena had. Inviting, not taking— not that she'd minded the way Selena had gone about it. Not exactly.

"There's something between us, Selena. I don't know what it is, but I've felt it from the start. I don't get involved personally with clients, but with you, it feels different." She kissed Selena again.

Selena tensed. The kiss broke. Selena ducked her head but didn't move out of reach.

"Everyone always says that. At first, they like it. But then after a while, they don't like it anymore," Selena said.

Perdita's warning echoed in Clara's mind. Had it been more than simple sour grapes? She slid her hand across the comforter to rest on Selena's knee.

"Kiss me again," Clara whispered.

It wasn't a request; it was a command. She was used to getting her own way with partners. Selena obeyed without hesitation, taking the kiss harder and farther than Clara expected. She found herself on her back against the pillows, her robe open and Selena's hands roaming across her body.

"The tray," Clara gasped out, and Selena moved.

Lithe and graceful and fast, so fast. The tray was lifted and placed on the long dresser below the window, without spilling so much as a drop of tea. Then Selena was back on the bed, covering Clara with her body. Kissing, kissing, and her hands were cupping Clara's breasts. Her nipples tightened, aching.

The kiss deepened. Clara arched to allow Selena to pull off the robe and toss it away. Her hands found the sweet rounded curves of Selena's ass and gripped before she slid her fingers into the waistband of Selena's jeans and moved around to the front button and zipper. She got the jeans open but stopped when Selena broke the kiss to murmur into her ear.

"Let me please you, Miss. You've done so much for me already. Let me do this. Let me take care of you the way you need to be taken care of."

"Oh, God," Clara managed to say around the surge of raw lust overtaking her. "Yes. Good. Do that."

Somehow Selena rolled them both, so Clara ended up on top of her, straddling her crazy sweet mouth. Selena's hands fit perfectly on Clara's hips, but in this position, Clara had the freedom to shift and move however she liked on the insistent, delicious pressure of Selena's lips and tongue. The pleasure rose so fast inside her she was nearly mindless within minutes.

That's when Selena slowed the pace.

Clara growled out a protest, but the teasing was so glorious, keeping her right on the edge, that she didn't demand Selena lick her faster. She did slip her hand over Selena's hair to dig her fingers into her scalp, a silent but blunt reminder that, if she chose, she could grind herself onto Selena's face. Selena groaned. Her fingers clutched Clara's hips. She stopped licking altogether, merely letting her hot breath caress Clara's throbbing clit.

This time, Clara grunted. Her thighs shook. She wanted to ride Selena's mouth to orgasm...but she also wanted to savor the worship of her body from this woman who had so intrigued her for the past few months. She couldn't stop thinking of their sessions, of the beatings and the way Selena had reacted to each blow from Clara's flogger. Clara's mind filled with memories, overlaying the building explosion ready to burst inside her.

And then, yes, oh, fuck yes, she was coming. A slow, roiling surge of ecstasy became a runaway train of desire, and she was about to jump the tracks. Clara cried out Selena's name, over and over, as her body jerked and her pussy spasmed, and Selena gripped Clara's hips hard and held her mouth and tongue to all the sweet spots as Clara came and came and came.

*

"I wanted it to last longer for you," Selena said.

Clara was on her back, eyes closed, limbs sprawled in the aftermath of what had sounded like a powerful orgasm. "I haven't come with a partner in a while. I wanted to get off."

"But I wanted to make it last."

Clara opened her eyes and rolled onto her side. "So, it was about what you wanted, and not what I wanted? That's not how this works."

Selena drew her knees to her chest and linked her fingers together in front of them. Making Clara come had been amazing. The way she smelled. Tasted. The sound of her moans, the flutter of her pussy against Selena's mouth had all been a huge turn-on—but focusing on giving Clara pleasure had allowed Selena to force away the need for her own and kept the wolf from doing more than opening a single sleepy eye. She couldn't explain it to Clara in those terms, of course.

"I guess I don't know how it's supposed to work," Selena said.

Clara stretched, arching, and Selena enjoyed the thrust of Clara's breasts. Her body was magnificent, all silky dark skin and curves and softness. She looked up to see Clara had caught her staring.

"Well, generally speaking, I take care of you. You take care of me. We figure out what that means together. It's supposed to work by us coming to an agreement. The same as at Abyss, only this one would be what works for both of us," Clara said.

Selena pressed her lips together for a second. "What usually works for you?"

"That depends." Clara sat. Her fingertip drifted along Selena's calf, the touch electric even through the denim. "What about you?"

"What about me?"

Clara squeezed Selena's calf gently and leaned as though to kiss her, but when Selena didn't lean in for it, she paused. Sat back. "What can I do for you?"

"Nothing."

"I don't understand," Clara said with a frown. "You don't want to come, not even here?"

Selena shuddered. "No. Hell, no!"

Silence. Clara looked confused and a little pissed off. Selena had seen that expression a lot in her life, had regretted it every time, and still wasn't sure quite how to make it go away.

"I should go," Selena said.

Well, that hadn't been the right way.

"What? Why?" Clara demanded.

"I just should. It's late."

Clara looked less confused, which was good. Angrier, which was not. "Okay. Wow. Just like that? You fuck me, then decide you're going to leave?"

"I didn't...we didn't...I was trying to make sure you were okay! All right? So, you're fine, you're okay, so it's time for me to go," Selena retorted.

"Wait a minute. You...did you make me come out of some kind of...pity?" Clara recoiled, and before Selena could reach for her, she got out of bed and stood with her hands on her hips. She was so fucking sexy Selena's heart hurt.

"No!"

Shit, what a mess. Selena got out of bed, glad she was still fully dressed. It would make it easier to get the hell out of here. Clara came around the bed to stand between her and the doorway.

"Talk to me," Clara said in a tone that clearly meant she expected Selena to obey.

Of course, she spoke that way. Of course, she expected immediate compliance. Submission.

"I want to leave," Selena countered.

"Not until we talk about this!"

Selena moved around Clara faster than Clara could block her. "We aren't at Abyss now. You don't get to boss me around just because I went down on you."

She expected a protest, maybe more anger, but she got to the door and still had heard nothing from Clara. Selena turned. Clara had gathered her robe and put it on. She swiped hastily at her cheek and tied the robe tightly, all the way up to her throat. Silently, she gestured toward Selena with a quick, dismissive flick of her wrist.

Get out.

She didn't have to say the words aloud to make them clear. Selena was on her way out, eager to do just that, when the ratchet sound of a single sob stopped her. She hung her head.

"I'm sorry," Selena said.

"You know, just because I'm a Domme doesn't mean I don't have feelings," Clara said.

Selena turned. "I never thought that. I just don't want you to have feelings for *me.*"

"Too late."

"Please..." Her own pleading tone was unfamiliar.

She should have been out of here already. Down the stairs. Out of the front door. Gone.

Clara swiped again at tears that seemed to be making her angry. She lifted her chin. Proud, Selena realized, hating herself now for being so cold. So awkward.

"Please, don't be mad at me," Selena said.

"Is this some kind of game? Is that what you're into, Selena? Being a bratty sub? If you want me to hurt you—" Clara drew a breath and finished in a whisper. "You don't have to hurt me, first."

Selena clenched her fists, struggling for the right words. "When I came to you at Abyss, it was about getting hurt, yeah, but this wasn't."

"What was it, then? Not pity. Not poking me into punishing you. Apparently, not feelings. So. What, then?"

Clara's chin went up again, but her eyes blazed with emotion, not tears.

"I can't explain it to you."

"Try me," Clara challenged.

Selena wanted to. She wanted to tell Clara everything. How she became a wolf against her wishes. How the only way she'd found to stop herself from changing was through agony.

She did have feelings for Clara.

She could not afford to have them.

She was a monster.

"I'm not a sadist," Clara told her abruptly. "I like providing pain as a means to arousal, yes. I enjoyed disciplining my lovers and my clients. I've never gotten turned on from the act of causing pain itself, only as part of a broader range of dominance, or because seeing how it arouses my partner, in turn, gets me hot. Which is why, I think, I'm good at what I do. I can hurt someone who wants it without getting wrapped up in it, myself. I provide a service. But in a relationship—"

"That's not what this is!"

"It's what it could be," Clara said. "If we gave it a try."

"I can't," Selena told her. "I'm sorry. I just can't."

Clara, after what felt like an eternity, nodded. "Fine, then. Go."

For an instant, Selena imagined herself dropping to her knees in front of Clara. Calling her *Miss*. Begging for the back of her hand. For her kiss. Begging to taste her again.

Flames licked inside her. The wolf was waking. Selena backed up, through the doorway. There seemed to be a dozen things for her to say right then, but she couldn't make herself speak. She left in silence, and Clara didn't call her back.

*

Clara had not taken a break from Abyss. If anything, she'd thrown herself into her work harder than she ever had. Going against her usual preferences, she'd taken on a dozen new clients, most of whom weren't really into what she was best at providing. It didn't matter. She met with them anyway. Found out their desires. Did her best to fulfill them. Frankly, Clara at her worst was better than many could ever be, and if it was arrogant for her to think so, well…all she had to do was remind herself not everyone in the world thought she was all that great.

A full month had passed without a word from Selena. Clara had not reached out either. Using Selena's contact information for private correspondence was against Abyss policy. Beyond that, although Nic might be right that Clara held on too long, she'd never been one to chase. The night she and Selena had spent together had been just that. One night.

The appointment request had come in this morning, sometime in the dark before sunrise, while Clara slept. She'd woken with Selena on her mind, so the sight of her name in her app had seemed like part of a lingering dream. Yet here she was, and in a few short minutes, she would see Selena again.

"I didn't think you were on the schedule tonight." Miyuki's elegant dark brows arched as she tilted her head to look Clara up and down. "My goodness, you look upset. Are you all right?"

Clara gave Miyuki her best casual smile in their shared reflection. She touched up her lipstick, bright crimson tonight. It stood out against her dark skin, but she wanted to wipe it off almost immediately. She wanted to scrub herself down to bare flesh, to strip off her clothes to be just as naked. To start it all over again. She didn't have time for that. Selena was scheduled to be here in twenty minutes.

"I'm all right. Just had an unexpected appointment for tonight, that's all. A client I haven't seen in some time, one I wasn't sure would ever book me again."

Miyuki nodded. "I understand. I've had one like that. More than one, actually."

Unspoken questions hung between them. Clara suspected Miyuki wanted to know who the client was who'd put her in such a tizzy, but she'd see for herself soon enough. Clara, for her part, was curious if Miyuki had ever experienced a similar situation. She'd never spent much time befriending the other Dommes who worked at Abyss, and so had never hung out with any of them socially. It would be unseemly for her to blurt out an invasive question to Miyuki now, but as it turned out, Clara didn't have to ask.

"It's my own fault. I know better than to fall in love with a client. What can I say? My heart is made to love, and I love hard. I think, for me, the idea that it's something forbidden is what gets me. I know, I know. Clients aren't forbidden, exactly. They probably should be. Of course, that would make it even harder for me to resist." Miyuki lifted a shoulder in an elegant shrug.

Everything about her was elegant and smooth and left Clara feeling like the biggest sort of clumsy bumbler. Or maybe it was simply the twisting series of emotions that had been knotting inside her for the past month, during all the weeks in which Selena did not call, did not make an appointment, did not show up at the coffee shop or at her door. Clara had lost her footing because of Selena, and it was spilling over into everything else in her life.

"We're all adults, all of consenting age. Yes, we sign contracts outlining exactly what services are required and what we'll provide, but there's nothing that says we aren't allowed to also pursue relationships with each other outside of Abyss." Clara forced herself not to mess any further with her cosmetics. Her face was fine, she told herself fiercely. Everything about her was *fine*.

Miyuki laughed and leaned forward to add some mascara to her lashes before giving Clara a sideways glance. "It might not be against the rules, per se, but I think we all know it's not recommended. Right? I mean, if we fall in love with all our clients, what then? Anarchy, I'd say. At the very least a string of broken hearts, and no more clients. I don't know about you, but I need to earn a living."

"I don't need Abyss to make my living." Clara said this quietly, keeping her gaze on her own eyes in the mirror. "And I'm not in love with her."

"Are you sure?"

Clara shook her head. "No. But it can't be love. We've never even had a real date. She laid out her feelings, or lack of them, quite clearly, and that's all there was to it. So, it can't be love."

"How many sessions did you have with her?"

"Not enough," Clara said.

Miyuki shrugged again and drew a cat eye with her black liner. She didn't look at Clara this time as she said, "The heart wants what it wants, Clara. Is there anything more intimate than the things we do with clients? They fall in love with *us* all the time—"

"They fall in love with an idea of us. The concept of who they think we are. Not who we actually are," Clara interrupted, but her protest tasted futile. She shut herself up.

Miyuki laughed gently. "Do you think our hearts know the difference between falling in love with an idea and falling in love with reality? Love is love, and when you're in it, sometimes the only thing you can do about it is try to get yourself out. Or cancel your sessions with her."

"I didn't even think she'd come back around for another one. I'm not canceling tonight. I think...I think if she's here, it's because she needs it. Needs me."

"They all need it, or they wouldn't come here," Miyuki said. "The trick is understanding that maybe it's not you. Maybe it's just *someone*."

Clara shook her head. There was more to Selena than neediness. The feral undertone Clara had spoken of with Nic. The skittish way she came close and then moved away. Like an animal that needed to be tamed.

She smoothed her ebony curls away from her face and ran her hands over her red corset top, then her belly and hips beneath the sleek black leggings. She had a variety of outfits, most not much like what she chose to wear for her own comfort, but what her clients expected her to wear. Tonight's was especially Domme-tastic. "I look like a cliché."

"Think of it as a uniform," Miyuki suggested. "It's what I do."

"More like a costume."

Miyuki stood. "Or that. Good luck tonight, Clara. And hey, listen, if you want to talk, maybe you and I could grab a drink sometime?"

"Sure. That would be great." Clara surprised herself by imagining offering Miyuki a hug, but she didn't go for it. Instead, she turned her attention back to the mirror, pretending to fuss with her lipstick, until Miyuki had gone out of the dressing room. Then she put both her hands on the edge of the dressing table and stared deep into her own eyes until she lost herself in her own dark gaze.

"Not just anyone," she murmured. "Me. It has to be me."

*

The parking lot outside Abyss had been the fullest Selena had ever seen, so she shouldn't have been surprised when she got inside to find the lobby brimming with women. The atmosphere of sexual anticipation, hunger, and craving was so electric it was almost a physical charge. The hairs on the back of her neck stood up. Her nipples tightened. She could smell arousal, strong beneath the scents of lotion and perfume.

Anticipation. Everyone in here overflowed with it. Her own body ached with pent-up frustration. Every brush of another body against hers pushed more tingling sensations throughout her, even as each touch sent tingling creepy crawlies through her at the contact. Inside, low in her belly, the fire kindled. The wolf wanted out.

She shook her head to the offer of a bottle of water held out in an older blonde woman's hand. She turned away from the welcoming smiles. She shrugged off the greetings. She wasn't here to make friends. If any of them knew the truth about her, they would run, run away. No, worse. Their smiles would become sneers or grimaces. Their welcomes would turn to shouts of disgust and terror. They wouldn't run away; they would run her out.

This was a mistake. Selena's thoughts were becoming jumbled. Scattered. She wanted to get inside the play space and find Miss. She wanted to be bound, gagged, blindfolded, so the insistent press of all these sights, sounds, and smells would be dimmed. She wanted the pain to begin, so she could shove aside the rising fire already licking its way from her belly to her chest. It would reach her throat soon, and then it would start to come out of her mouth, and she would be lost.

She would become the wolf.

"I need Miss Clara," Selena said to the woman in the black catsuit guarding the door to the play space.

She wasn't a Domme. She was one of Abyss's service volunteers, and from the bored look she gave Selena, not doing a particularly good job at it. "She's not available yet. You have to wait."

"I can't wait." Selena wanted to pace but stopped herself. Held herself still. Quiet. Her muscles ached with the tension of it.

"The space isn't open yet—"

"I'm here." Clara had appeared in the doorway. She gave the volunteer sub a scathing look and reached for Selena's hand. "Come on."

Selena had been made clumsy with the effort of restraining herself. She stumbled, her toes catching on nothing. Clara clutched her arm and kept her from falling.

Clara pushed open a door, not into the vast play space to which Selena had grown accustomed, but into a smaller, private room. "Careful."

Selena had never been inside one of the private rooms. She hadn't requested one tonight either. She followed Clara inside and past her. Behind her, Clara closed the door. In front of her, the black padded walls, hung here and there with sheer crimson fabric, were a cliché, a stereotype, but also perfectly in keeping with Abyss's decor. There was something soothing about the way it met those expectations, unimaginative as they might be. About the equipment lined up throughout the space, the entirety of which looked like something from a BDSM porn set. It should have made her want to laugh at how ridiculous it all was. Instead, she stumbled, knees weak, unsteady against the pushing desire threatening to overtake her.

"Selena, have you been drinking?"

Shocked, Selena gained her feet. She twisted to look at Miss Clara. "No. Of course not. I know the rules."

Besides, she rarely drank alcohol because it made it so much harder to keep the fire tamped down. Selena straightened. Steadied herself. Breathing in, breathing out. All of her usual tricks were barely working any longer.

"You know I can't have a session with you if you're under the influence. Of anything," Miss Clara added. "Or if in any way I think you're not capable of making an informed choice."

"I can. I am. I mean, I need this. Please, Miss. I am desperate!"

Miss tilted her head to give Selena a long looking over. "To be beaten?"

"Yes. All of that. Restrained. Beaten. I need you to hurt me, Miss...or else..." She couldn't bring herself to finish. Her words tasted like iron, bitter and heavy on her tongue. She coughed into her fist.

"Or else what, Selena?"

She looked up to meet Miss's gaze. "Or else bad things will happen to me. Just...please. I need this."

"I believe you."

Relief made Selena sag, but she straightened her back and shoulders quickly again. There was a spanking bench and a St. Andrew's Cross set up, but she gestured at the plain set of cuffs set with chains into the wall. "Thank you. Please tie me up. The cuffs there, on the wall, that's all I need. Oh. My ankles too. Please, Miss."

Clara followed Selena toward the wall but held back from immediately binding her. For the first time, Selena noticed that Clara's red corset left the nape of her neck bare and lickable. Her short dark curls looked as though she'd sprinkled them with glitter. And her lips...oh, the crimson color matched the corset and set off that ripe, luscious mouth.

Selena had kissed that mouth. Tasted that skin. The memory was a bullet, shooting her dead. She stumbled again, but Miss caught her and held her up. Selena swallowed hard but found little moisture. The heat inside, of mingled pleasure and despair, was turning her into a desert.

"Now!" she cried. "Just fucking tie me up, already!"

"If you were not my client, I would discipline you for presuming to order me." Miss's tone had gone icy. She stepped back, the opposite of what Selena needed her to do.

Miss's tone sent a shudder through Selena but also another rush of heat. That fucking fire, she thought desperately. That goddamned curse, rising inside her. She swallowed hard again and again, her throat clicking dryly. Her tongue was like sandpaper when she ran it along her lips, also dry. Her palms, on the other hand, were wet and sweating.

Her pussy was wet too.

"If I weren't your client, I wouldn't be here," Selena said.

Miss flinched. Only in her eyes, no sign of any reaction in the rest of her, but Selena saw it. She hated herself for that, but she couldn't dwell on her emotions right now. There were too many physical feelings. Too much need. If she'd made a mistake in coming here, it was too late to fix it. She was already burning.

Her body jerked. She ground out words, not sure if they'd be decipherable until she managed to get them past her teeth. "We have an agreement. A contract. You have to do this!"

"Let's make one thing clear. I do not *have* to do anything. Do you understand me? Not one damned thing." The flinch had disappeared from Miss Clara's eyes, but now it came out in her voice.

Miss was clearly trying so hard not to show any emotion except maybe anger, but Selena was so far gone now, the wolf so close to the surface, that she heard everything she was attempting to hide, perhaps even from herself. She couldn't hide it from the wolf, though. Selena could smell it too. Clara's disappointment. Her hurt. Selena watched her take another step away, her expression going distant and cold, refusal written in every line of her body.

"Yes, Miss. Please, Miss. I'm sorry. You're the only one who can help me. You've been the only one who's ever been able to. That has to mean something. Doesn't it?" Selena couldn't have kept the shudder from her voice even if she'd tried.

Miss frowned. "It ought to."

"It does. Please," Selena repeated, quieter this time. "There is nobody else like you."

*

It was what Clara wanted to hear, but Selena's words didn't bring her the satisfaction they should have. If anything, they left Clara emptier than before. Feeling duped. She didn't need Selena's praise to bolster her own self-worth, dammit, or at least she didn't want to. She didn't want to need anything from Selena but an addition to her bank account, and she didn't even have to have that.

This would be their last session, Clara vowed as she pointed without a word to the cuffs Selena had requested. Fuck, this might be the last session she ever did. The pro-Domme business had been fine for a time, but she'd been a real fool to think it could replace true desire. Dominating women who paid her to do it had been exactly right for keeping Clara out of anything resembling a real relationship, but Nic was right. It was time for a break, maybe a permanent one.

She should stop this session right now, Clara thought as she cuffed Selena tightly, wrists and ankles both. Only when she'd secured her did Clara step back. Her heart was already pounding, her stomach twisting. She needed to calm herself. It was her personal policy to never, never go into a session, private or professional, without her own emotions strongly under control, and hers were anything but.

Clara opened the small lacquered cabinet. Inside hung multiple implements, tools and toys, but she stopped with her hand on the flogger she usually employed. It was her favorite for many reasons. Her fingers stroked the leather single-tail whip, instead. She took her hand away.

"Use the whip, Miss. *Please*."

Under other circumstances, Clara would have taken umbrage again to a sub making demands, but something in Selena's voice, in the way her muscles had gone so clearly tense and trembling, made the request palatable. There was more too. An underlying tension, rising. A heat radiating from Selena that pulled at Clara in many places—her gut, her wrists, the base of her throat. The places her pulse beat. She'd never felt anything like this yearning compulsion.

Clara shook her head. "I don't use the whip."

"I swear to you, I can take it. I can!"

Selena shook in her bonds. Clara pulled the whip from its hook and ran the leather through her fingers. She gave it one experimental crack. The sound echoed through the private playroom. She gave it another, relishing the feeling of the tool in her hand.

"Please." If Selena had shouted it, or in any way demanded, Clara would have unhooked her at once and sent her packing. Instead, she whispered the plea on a broken, trembling voice. She hung her head. "Please..."

Clara had not used the whip on another person in three years, but she had never stopped practicing with it. Clara could still handle this tool with as much finesse as she ever had. More, in fact, since her determination to hone her skills had kept her focused every time she used it.

Without warning her, Clara flicked the tail of the whip to lick at Selena's shoulder blades. The blow raised an instant welt. Selena bucked in the restraints but didn't scream.

It was a challenge.

Again, Clara used the whip, adding another blow within seconds of that one. Then again. Rapidly, she striped Selena's back, pausing between every third or so strike to reset her stance and make sure she wasn't tiring.

Those who'd never used a whip had no idea how much it could take out of the wielder.

At the eighth strike, Selena howled. Not a scream; Clara had been anticipating that. No, this was an actual animal howl, rising up, up, up and trailing away into a snarling, barking sob. Stunned, Clara let the whip fall at her side.

"Selena—"

"Don't stop!"

Clara did not take orders from a sub, not even one who was paying her. She went to Selena's side. Slipped her fingers between Selena's thighs. Selena was slick, dripping. Her pussy clenched hard on Clara's exploring fingers.

"When's the last time you came?" Clara asked.

Selena seemed incapable of speech. Clara let the whip fall. She put her hand on Selena's back, against the stripes, hot and throbbing. Her fingers toyed between Selena's legs, finding her swollen clit.

"If you were mine, I would make you come right now. It's what you need," Clara whispered into Selena's ear.

Selena wrenched her head away from Clara. "No! You have no idea what I need! You're only supposed to beat me. Not make me come. Not *let* me come! You're supposed to hurt me! That's it! Don't you dare let me come, Clara, or I swear to the universe—"

That was it. Clara could take no more. Her fingers worked a little faster, sliding along slippery flesh. She tweaked Selena's clit, hard, between her finger and thumb. It would take only a few more seconds, and Selena would be tipping over the edge into climax. She was so ripe, so ready...

"You," she said, "do not give me orders."

At the very last second, Clara took her hands away. To keep going would've been against not only the contract, but everything she believed about herself as a Domme. Yes, it was up to her to decide what was best for her subs, to give them what she decided they needed, no matter what they thought it was. It was also up to her to honor consent.

Shaking and sickened at her own lack of control, Clara took a step toward her. Her fingers worked the leather cuff at Selena's wrist. This session was over.

"Don't untie me!" Selena's voice shredded into a growl.

Beneath Clara's hands, Selena's body began to twitch. Her muscles rippled. Her forearm tensed, bulging with startling ferocity. Her back arched as she writhed.

Terrified Selena was having a seizure, Clara freed her left wrist, but when she went around her body to do the same to the right, Selena again shrieked out a warning. Twisting, she managed to get her left hand across her body at an angle that should have been impossible without breaking something or at least dislocating her shoulder. She grabbed Clara's hand, gripping hard enough to crack the knuckles. It didn't hurt, but only because Selena clearly pulled her grip at the last second before causing pain.

Clara stumbled back. She should scream for help. Call an ambulance.

She'd had dealt with subs who'd become ill during a scene, and almost all of them refused help. She could not abandon Selena. No matter what she was screaming, she had to be released from the cuffs and lowered to the ground. Selena needed medical attention, now.

Before Clara could get back to her, though, Selena had, incredibly, torn the right cuff from the wall. It dangled from her wrist. She bent to rip at the cuffs on her ankles, but...something was wrong with the shape of her. A hand flew up, claws instead of nails, and it was all wrong, so wrong that the floor shifted beneath Clara's feet, and she had to reach for the back of a chair to keep herself from falling.

That could not be Selena's hand.

The cuff on the wrist proved it was, or at least it had been. The shape in front of Clara now, uncuffed, free, turned. It was not Selena. It was something else, with a vaguely human shape still rapidly shifting to bend and twist into the form of something different and new and strange and terrifying, and Clara clung to the back of the chair, her lifeline, the only thing keeping her upright.

It came at her.

It was a monster.

No, sweetheart, there are no such things as monsters.

It was a monster....

She closed her eyes, and then there was only darkness.

*

Selena had been fighting the wolf since the first time it took her over at age thirteen. She'd learned tricks, over time, to stop herself before she changed. She had never, not in the thirteen years since, been able to stop the transformation once it had begun. Not until tonight.

"You should stick around until you can be sure she's all right." The service sub grabbed Selena's arm as she headed through the lobby but pulled her hand away with a hiss of surprise at the glare she got for being so fucking ballsy.

"Tell her I'm sorry," Selena said over her shoulder.

Too aware of all the eyes on her as she wove her way through the crowd of gawkers in the lobby, Selena pushed through the front doors of Abyss and into the parking lot. Then she was running, running, as fast as she could to get away. With every stretch of her legs, the pounding of her feet on the pavement, the burn of frigid air deep in her lungs, she opened herself up to any hint of pain that might help her keep away the fire and the wolf that had been clawing its way up and out of her.

It didn't help. She made it to an alley before she burned again, and this time, nothing stopped her. She dropped to her hands and knees and stopped fighting. Giving in was glorious.

In minutes, the fire had scourged away every human piece of her. She'd become the wolf. Fierce hunger assaulted her, but she'd find nothing to sate that appetite on these city streets. Rodents. Garbage. The stench of unwashed humanity drew her toward the edge of town, loping on padded paws, to the bridges and underpasses lined with tents and fires in burning barrels, but although there were those of her kind who feasted upon the homeless, Selena had never.

Would never.

Could never.

So, hungry, she went into the vacant lots and roused sleeping mice and rats and a fat raccoon, and she turned her snout and jaws to the night sky and howled, and she ached to be in the forest among the trees and in a place where she could roam without fear of being hunted down herself.

Hours passed, but time flowed differently when the wolf had risen inside her. Daylight threatened. Her body demanded sleep, but not in this form. It was too unsafe. Nor was it safe for her to travel this way in the light. As it always did when its hungers had been satiated, the wolf abandoned her and left her naked.

Fortunately, Selena was close to home and made it back to her apartment without being seen. She brushed her teeth and showered away the night's grime. Running in the city always left her filthy. Then, she crawled into her bed and collapsed.

She'd been sleeping for what seemed like a few minutes but was more like an hour when the pounding began at her front door. Selena ignored it, of course. The only time someone knocked was to deliver a package—she wasn't expecting any—or to sell something, and she wasn't interested in buying.

The knocking didn't stop, though, and despite the brief sleep she'd had, her body decided it was enough. She was hungry again. The wolf had eaten last night, but Selena had not. Muttering curses, she got out of bed and slipped into a cotton-candy-pink fleece robe patterned with doughnuts and kittens. Matching slippers protected her feet from the cold concrete floor as she went to the door and prepared to raise hell with whoever had decided to risk themselves by banging so fucking early.

Her curses died in her throat as she flung open the door to see Clara. Clad in faded skinny jeans, knee-high brown leather boots, and a matching bomber jacket with what looked like a plain white T-shirt beneath it, her glossy black curls shimmering and not a hint of makeup on her dark skin, Clara looked as different from the way she presented herself at Abyss as Selena realized she must in what she'd thrown on.

Both of them stepped back from their respective sides of the doorway looking surprised.

"How did you know where I live? Never mind," Selena said before Clara could answer. "I gave you my address for the contract. But I never thought you'd just show up here."

"Believe me, Selena, I'm not in the habit of randomly showing up at my clients' houses. Or anyone's." Clara cleared her throat but didn't say more than that.

She was waiting to be asked inside, Selena realized after an uncomfortable few seconds of silence. The idea of inviting Clara inside her space was awkward. Really awkward.

"I wasn't expecting company."

Clara gave her a long up-and-down look, taking in the robe and slippers. "I can see that."

She laughed. After a moment, Selena did too. It was the first time they'd ever really laughed together. Hell, it was the first time Selena had laughed with anyone in longer than she could remember. With a flourish of one hand and a half-bow, she stepped aside to usher Clara inside and closed the door behind her.

"Coffee? I need coffee. I need food too. I'll make some eggs."

Clara was still a few steps behind her, and now she murmured. "Oh...not for me, thanks. I'm vegan, remember?"

This stopped Selena so suddenly that Clara bumped into her back. Selena turned and ended up catching her by the upper arms to keep them both steady. Sharp contrast to the times she'd had Clara holding her upright, Selena had time to think before she remembered the night before and how Clara had fallen.

"You look okay," she said.

Clara raised an eyebrow. "I said I'm vegan, not sick."

"No. No, I mean...well, being vegan is something I can't wrap my head around, but no. You look okay. Last night, you didn't. I didn't even ask you if you were all right."

"If I wasn't all right, I don't think I'd be here now, would I?" The words might have come out sounding snarky or harsh, but the way Clara said them was calm and somehow reassuring.

"Did you get checked out? Everything okay?"

"I didn't even have to go in the ambulance," Clara assured her. "The EMTs came and checked me out. Said my blood pressure had dropped a bit. They asked me if I'd had a shock."

"What did you say?"

Selena pulled out the ingredients for pancake batter, gave the milk a second thought, and put it back in the fridge. She could make them with water. They wouldn't be as tasty, but it was the best she could do.

"I lied, of course. What could I have said, Selena? That I'd been beating my submissive, and she began to turn into...something else? They'd have taken me away, and not to the emergency room. I'm in no mood for a seventy-two hour hold in the psych ward." Clara shook her head and sipped coffee from her mug. She set it down so hard the liquid splashed. Her hands were trembling.

Selena turned back to the now-hot griddle and spritzed a few drops of water to test it. When they sizzled, she poured a small test dollop of batter. It didn't puff the same way dairy pancakes did. She'd have to be careful they didn't burn.

"I'm sorry," she said. "You were never meant to see that."

"But I did."

More silence while Selena made more pancakes. She didn't speak until she'd flipped over several and waited until they were golden before sliding them onto a plate. She put it in front of Clara but stole one for herself to start on while she finished the others. Her stomach was eating itself.

Clara waited until Selena sat across from her, both with heaping plates of pancakes and syrup. Selena added a thick pat of sweet cream butter to hers, but Clara only waved a hand when she offered it.

"Tell me what happened, Selena." Clara had not taken so much as a single bite.

Selena, on the other hand, had already gobbled up half her stack. She really wanted bacon and some eggs to go along with it, but out of respect to Clara, she'd wait. Her stomach still felt empty, but not as empty as the space around her heart at the look on Clara's face.

"Nothing happened," she said.

Clara scowled. "I'm not sure what I saw, but I know it was something. Unless you want to tell me that I'm crazy?"

"You're not crazy." Selena sighed and pushed back from the table, still hungry, but unable to finish any more food in the face of Clara's dismay.

"Then what?"

"I'm not sure how to explain."

Clara seemed to accept this for a moment. She cleared her throat. She even stabbed into the stack of pancakes in front of her, although when she lifted the fork to her mouth, she changed her mind and set it down without biting. She drew in a loud breath. Cleared her throat. Her voice, when she finally spoke, was clear and firm.

"When I was a little girl, I had a best friend named Jenny. My parents were not terribly strict most of the time, but with this friend in particular, they seemed to have some issues. They wouldn't say them out loud, but it was always harder to get permission for me to hang out with her. Of course, this only made me want to play with Jenny more."

"Of course," Selena said with a chuckle.

Clara didn't laugh. "Jenny had invited me to spend the night with her many times, but my parents had always had some reason or another as to why I would not be allowed. Finally, I became desperate to spend the night at Jenny's house. Looking back, I have no idea why it was so important. Jenny and I were friends, sure, but I had other friends I was closer with. If anything, Jenny and I were more apt to argue with each other over stupid things and go without speaking for weeks at a time, so I have no idea why I was so obsessed with having a sleepover. But finally, my parents relented, and I got my way."

"I'm not surprised. You're pretty good at getting your way."

"You're teasing me," Clara said with a small smile. She leaned forward to lightly touch Selena's hand. "I like it."

The touch tingled. Selena withdrew her hand. If Clara noticed and was offended, she didn't show it.

"What happened at Jenny's house?"

Clara spun her coffee mug in a small circle but didn't lift it to drink. She cleared her throat, her voice pitched low, and cut her gaze away. Tension crackled off her, invisible waves that nevertheless raised the hairs on the back of Selena's neck. Her own heartbeat quickened in response.

"I woke in the middle of the night to use the bathroom. Jenny was still sleeping. I stumbled down the hall, but since it was the first time I'd ever been there, I opened the wrong door. Jenny's parents were..." Clara coughed into her fist and looked at Selena with arched eyebrows.

It took her a second to get it. "Oh? Oh!"

"I knew about sex, of course. But it was the first time I'd ever seen real people doing it. I froze in the doorway. Neither of them noticed me. Her mom was on top, and I remember being surprised that a woman could be on top since I'd always imagined people only did it in one position. I didn't know what exactly was happening, but it was clear something was, for both of them. They were writhing and grunting, and it sounded like they were hurting each other, but I could tell they weren't. And then..."

Clara's gaze looked stricken. She swallowed hard. Then again, so her throat gave off a dry clicking.

"Her mother changed," Clara said.

Selena got up from the table so fast her chair fell over. Her breath caught, sharp like the slash of a razor in her chest. She tasted metal.

"Only for a minute. She looked like a woman. Then like...something else. I must have let out a shout or something because Jenny's dad looked up and saw me there. The next thing I knew, her mom was looking at me, too, and her eyes were not human. Then they were normal again, just like that, and so was everything else."

"She stopped the change?" Selena asked.

Clara nodded. Then shrugged and shook her head. "I don't know for sure what happened."

"She didn't become a wolf?"

Clara let out a shaky sigh. "Not completely. If that's what she was changing into. It all happened so fast, and I was so scared I was down the hall and back next to Jenny in her bed with the covers over my face before I knew it."

"Did they come after you?"

"Come after me? No. I mean, I know they saw me. But the next morning at breakfast, they were just as nice as could be. None of us said anything about it. I never told Jenny. I had nightmares for months, though. Of the moment when Jenny's mother turned and looked at me. How her face shifted."

Nightmares for months.

People didn't have nightmares about good things. People had nightmares about monsters. The idea that Clara might think Selena was a monster hit her like a punch in the gut.

"And your nightmare came true," Selena managed to say.

Clara stood. "I *did* see you changing, didn't I? I wasn't imagining it, just like I wasn't imagining it when I saw Jenny's parents."

"Yes. You saw it."

"I've only told one other person that story, and she said..." Clara stopped herself with a sharp shake of her head.

"She said what?"

"It doesn't matter what she said." Clara stood, pushing her chair back.

Selena wouldn't have been shocked if Clara ran away as fast as she could, never looking back. When Clara instead stepped toward her, Selena reacted with swift precision to move out of the way, so quickly her chair legs screeched on the tile floor. Clara stopped with a frown, one hand outstretched.

She hadn't been trying to hit her, Selena realized. Just touch her. Without moving, Selena waited as Clara took another step toward her to rest a hand on her shoulder. Light fingers, barely squeezing.

"You smell so good," Selena said on an exhale.

Clara blinked away the brightness in her eyes, the sheen of tears. "I was a child the first time and terrified as well as embarrassed at stumbling into something I was clearly not meant to see. I'm not a child any longer, Selena. I'm not going to have nightmares about you. I want to know the truth, that's all."

"I don't know the truth. I never have. I don't know what I am, or why it happens to me. I only know I've never been able to stop the change once it's started. Until you."

"Why do you think that is?"

Selena pressed her lips together for a moment before answering. "I don't know. I just know I've never been able to, but when I saw you faint, I knew I had to get you help. That was more important than anything else in the moment. I couldn't hold it off forever, but I was able to do it long enough."

It would have been a lot for any woman to take in, but Selena had already learned that Clara was not simply any woman.

"Come away with me. I have a house upstate. Forty acres of forest backing up to state game lands. Nobody around for miles. Come with me there," Clara said.

"Why would I do that?"

"Because," Clara said, "I asked you to."

*

"Smells funny." Selena wrinkled her nose and looked over her shoulder at Clara. "Dusty."

Clara laughed as she pushed gently on Selena's back to get her through the doorway and into the cabin's living room. "I haven't been in here in a few years, and I don't have anyone come in to clean while I'm not here. Let's make sure everything is all right before we unload the car. Although we should hurry. It looks like we got here just barely ahead of the storm."

Stepping into the cabin, Clara breathed deep, trying to smell what Selena did. She caught the scent of woodsmoke. Cedar. Furniture polish. The last time she'd been here, she'd done a deep cleaning and covered all the furniture with sheets, now lightly covered with dust. Behind her, Selena sneezed rapidly.

"It's like I knew I wouldn't be back for a long time," Clara said aloud.

Selena had been peeking into the small kitchen but turned toward her with a final sneeze. "You probably did. Even if you didn't let yourself know it at the time."

They'd talked on the two-hour drive up about the last time Clara had been here, her relationship with Felicity, and how it had ended. Selena hadn't been terribly forthcoming about her past, but she'd listened intently to Clara sharing hers.

"I'm sure that's true." Clara gestured toward her. "There's a lever beneath the kitchen sink to turn the water on. It comes from a well. I always shut it off before I leave."

"I'll check it." Selena ducked through the doorway.

Moments later, Clara heard the pipes rattle, followed by the gush of water striking the porcelain kitchen sink. She found Selena cupping her hands beneath the stream, sipping. Selena grinned, her mouth glistening.

"It's good," she said. "City water always tastes so flat."

Clara opened the cupboard and pulled out a glass, which she handed to Selena. When she took it, Clara slipped her fingers around Selena's wrist and pulled her closer for a kiss. "Everything tastes better in the mountains. Even you."

The kiss deepened. Clara caught her breath as what she'd meant as a simple embrace turned into longing. Desire flared quicker than a fire stoked with kindling. Their bodies were pressed together, Selena's full breasts an invitation to Clara's grateful palms. She cupped them, letting her thumbs pass over the already taut points of Selena's nipples through the soft fabric of her T-shirt.

Selena put the glass on the counter and used both hands to grip Clara's hips. Her fingers dented the bare flesh between the hem of Clara's shirt and the waistband of her jeans. Her mouth opened wider to the probe of Clara's stroking tongue.

Clara broke the kiss and, breathing softly, pressed her forehead to Selena's. She closed her eyes. She slid her hands along Selena's back, down to cup her ass cheeks and pull her even closer. Selena's muscles leaped and twitched under Clara's grasp.

"I take care of you," Clara reminded in a low voice. "Remember?"

Selena nodded. "Yes, Miss. And I take care of you."

"Do you trust me?"

"Yes, Miss."

They stayed like that for another few minutes. Not kissing. Simply breathing.

When the trembling of Selena's muscles eased, Clara stepped back. "First, we're going to unload the car. Then, we're going to take a bath."

"It's the middle of the afternoon." Selena's sleek golden brows arched in surprise.

Clara laughed gently and kissed her again. "And?"

"I showered this morning..." Selena sounded doubtful.

Clara kissed her again, lightly this time. "You'll understand."

Selena, typically, insisted on unloading the car without Clara's help. Not that Clara minded—watching Selena's lean, lush body work physically was a pleasure all its own. So too the idea that Selena gained her own satisfaction from serving Clara, in a way Clara had never previously thought she needed or wanted, was sufficient reason not to argue about lugging her suitcase inside. Instead, she busied herself opening all the curtains and whisking the sheets off the comfortable chairs and sofa along with putting away the groceries they'd brought with them.

By the time Selena had finished unloading all their baggage, Clara had put out a platter of soy cheese and grapes with two glasses of claret. The bottle had been a surprise, hidden in a bag with some boxes of crackers and cookies. Nic must have snuck it in there when she came over to say goodbye before they left. Clara tucked a succulent grape into her mouth as she held up a glass toward Selena, who hadn't even broken a sweat with all that labor.

"It's starting to snow. But it's *still* only the middle of the afternoon." Selena took the wine and hesitated before sipping. She licked her lips. Took another hesitant sip, obviously going slow.

It was Clara's turn to raise an eyebrow. "We're on cabin time, my dear one."

"Cabin time means day drinking and baths at odd hours?"

"It means day drinking and baths at odd hours and lovemaking whenever and wherever we choose," Clara replied.

Selena's brow furrowed and her lips pressed into a grim line, but only for a moment. Her gaze slipped away from Clara's. Her body tensed. Her tongue slipped out to slide along her lips again, but this time without the sensual tease of a few moments before.

It wasn't the time to push. Clara sipped her own wine, turning toward the platter of food. She took a grape and offered it to Selena, who leaned to take it with a kiss to Clara's fingertips. Clara opened her hand to press her palm to Selena's cheek. She relished Selena's smooth, warm skin.

"Come upstairs with me." It wasn't an invitation, and Clara didn't miss the way Selena shivered at her tone.

She had to be careful. Not push too hard. Too fast. Simply bringing Selena to this remote location, isolating them from any outside influences, had been risky enough for this relationship, as fragile as it still was. She was the Domme, yes, but that didn't give her the right to run roughshod over this woman. Selena had agreed to give the gift of...well. They hadn't fully figured out if it would be submission, but nevertheless Clara was determined to make sure she didn't forget that a gift was exactly what it was.

With Selena following a few steps behind, Clara climbed the narrow wooden staircase to the cabin's second floor. The airy loft, brightly lit from the skylights above, had been furnished with more comfortable reading chairs and lamps, all still covered with sheets. The paneled hall extended beyond the loft and led toward two generous bedrooms and a hall bath at the end.

Selena paused in the doorway to the smaller bedroom to peer inside. "Is this mine?"

"You'll be sharing with me," Clara answered calmly and reached to take Selena's hand.

She pushed Selena gently through the doorway to the master bedroom and stepped through behind her. In front of them, the king-size bed rested beneath the skylight and in front of the floor-to-ceiling glass doors leading out to the balcony. The rest of the room was sparsely furnished with comfortable pieces with clean, simple lines. In front of the fireplace, a cushiony sofa was the perfect spot to read or sip wine...or make love, Clara thought with a small thrill.

"One bed, Miss."

Clara nodded and put down her glass so she could whisk the protective sheets off the bed. Its bare mattress wasn't too impressive, but she had elegant and luxurious linen for it packed away in the closet and would make up the bed before they did anything else. She turned, her arms full of the sheets, and faced Selena.

"One bed," she said.

Selena set her still almost-full glass on the fireplace mantel. She stalked to the double doors and flicked open the latch with a strong twist. She opened them both and went out onto the balcony. She gripped the railing, her shoulders hunched as she looked over it. After a moment, she leaned back to stare up, up, up at the clear blue sky. The sight of her face in profile sent a fresh surge of thrilling desire spiraling through Clara's whole body.

Selena was so beautiful, particularly in her vulnerability. Clara had never known such a complicated swirl of emotions surrounding a relationship. She'd had lovers. She'd had submissives. She'd had clients. She'd felt affection for all of them. Love for a very few. She'd never experienced this, whatever "this" was or was trying so hard to become. All she could do now was try her best not to fuck this up.

"I love this view." Clara took her place next to Selena on the balcony. Shoulder to shoulder but not touching. She worried that the slightest brush of skin on skin would send Selena running. Outside, the late afternoon sky had started becoming dusk. Fat white flakes buffeted the windows with an occasional spatter of ice against the glass.

"It's nice, all right."

Clara bit her lower lip at the understatement. From someone else she might have taken it as an insult, but it was so typical of Selena it only made her smile. "I love how easy it is to impress you."

Selena turned slightly to face her with a frown. "I didn't mean—"

Clara kissed her.

There on the balcony, in front of the endless expanse of blue sky and evergreen trees, with nothing to witness them but the birds and squirrels, Clara let herself sink into the kiss. Yes, there was desire. Yes, passion. But more than that, she allowed herself to simply breathe with the embrace. In. Out. Taking in everything Selena would allow her to have; giving back whatever her lover would take.

"Miss..." Selena's voice trembled, but her gaze was full-on and unwavering. She put her hands on Clara's hips. "This place is incredible. Beyond beautiful. Thank you for bringing me here."

"Thank you for coming here with me." Clara stroked a hand over Selena's hair and let her fingers curl around the back of her neck.

They stayed like that for a few more moments, neither speaking. It was the most comfortable silence Clara had ever felt. More intimate than any lovemaking she'd ever shared. A rush of emotions, including terror, surged inside her, but she shoved away the fear.

"The bath," Clara said. "Now."

*

As soon as she saw the bathroom, Selena understood why Clara had been so insistent on taking a bath. The tub itself, an oversized clawfoot more than ample for the two of them, sat in front of a vast expanse of glass overlooking the forest and mountains beyond. A tiled steam shower with multiple shower heads took up one corner, one wall of it also almost entirely made of glass. A small alcove featured a toilet and bidet, and double sinks along with a long countertop ran along the opposite wall. Everything was white, crisp, clean, sleek. Selena was almost afraid to step through the doorway, wondering if she had dirt on her shoes or if she'd somehow smudge something simply by existing.

"I had this cabin built with double the recommended water tank capacity because I never want to run out of hot water." Clara twisted the faucets, and with a hiss, clear steaming water gushed out. She glanced over her shoulder at Selena and gave her the smile that had always sent tumbling swirls of desire twisting through her from their very first meeting. "Everything uses wind and solar, so even in the worst weather, we might get stuck here for a bit until the roads thaw, but we're not going to lose power."

Selena ran a fingertip along the countertop, enjoying the cool, smooth marble. She liked dark spaces, lusher surfaces. She was into crushed velvet, barn wood, candle lighting. This bright white space ought to have felt sterile to her. Intimidating. Uncomfortable. Yet, after the first few moments of uncertainty, she felt completely soothed by the open layout.

"The views. The trees, the mountains. I love that I can see all the nature. It's like it's right here with us," she said.

Clara straightened, flicking her wet fingers into the filling tub. She tilted her head to look Selena over. Then nodded. "Yes, exactly. When I'm in this space, I feel free and light."

"No worries about anyone seeing in either." A laugh slipped from Selena's lips, surprising her with its lightness.

"Anyone lurking outside this house is welcome to look at me naked. If they make that much effort, they deserve the reward." Clara tipped Selena a wicked grin.

Selena looked out the windows automatically. Clara was teasing her. She heard it in the tone of her voice. Even knowing she hadn't meant it, knowing it had to be impossible that any person would be lingering around out there in the woods, Selena searched for any signs they were being observed.

Clara joined her at the wall of glass. "I didn't mean to make you nervous."

"Not nervous. Like you said. If they make that much effort, shouldn't they get to see something?" Selena forced herself to turn away from the glass. More words rose to her lips, an explanation of why she was so continually on her guard. She quashed them.

Clara had opened up to Selena on the way here, revealing a lot about herself. Selena wished she had that confidence, but while she'd listened closely, she hadn't been able to share much, herself. She trusted Clara, yes. But not yet with this, not yet with her past and the entirety of who she was. What she was, Selena reminded herself. Not who.

What.

"Take off your clothes," Clara said quietly, but firmly, and just like that, went from Clara to Miss in Selena's mind.

Selena didn't hesitate to obey. She tugged the laces of her boots and toed them off. She stripped out of her leggings and T-shirt and folded them neatly because she knew it would please Miss if she didn't toss them onto the floor. She put the items on the countertop, the shoes neatly on the floor beneath. Standing in her plain sports bra and cotton panties, she had time to imagine what it might have been like if she'd invested in a set of pretty lingerie instead of these serviceable undergarments. She'd never asked if Miss preferred her lovers clad in sexy things. If Miss had wanted it, Selena thought, she would have said so. And, no matter how out of place Selena might have felt wearing frills and lace, she would have complied.

"Bra and panties off too," Miss said.

In seconds, Selena was naked in front of her. She'd never been ashamed of nudity, her own or anyone else's, yet at this moment with Miss's gaze on her, Selena had the ridiculous urge to cover herself. She kept her arms at her sides, although her fingers curled into fists. She lifted her chin. She'd been naked in front of Miss many times already, naked and sweating and writhing and crying out.

She didn't have to be ashamed or embarrassed or fearful for any reason here and now...except here and now, they had no witnesses. No equipment. Most importantly, they had no contract between them. It was the first time she had been naked with Miss since their relationship had changed from purely professional to something more.

"So lovely," Miss murmured. "Turn around. Let me look at all of you."

Selena spun in a slow circle. Her heart pounded. An electric taste flooded her tongue as desire coiled low in her belly, twisting tighter. Being on display always pushed something to the surface in her, but this felt different. Maybe because it was only Miss looking her over. Maybe, Selena thought, because it was Miss herself. She stopped and faced Miss.

Miss's gaze had gone dreamy, but she focused now on Selena's face. "Undress me."

The command came as a surprise, but Selena moved forward at once. She ran her hands over the front of Miss's shirt dress. Her fingers nimbly plucked apart the buttons one at a time to reveal the glory of the body beneath. Lush breasts spilled from her black satin bra. Her hips curved to showcase a rounded belly and gorgeous thighs. Matching black panties covered the sweetness of her ass cheeks, begging for Selena to grab hold.

She didn't, of course. In the past, she'd taken her lovers as fast and fiercely as she wanted to, and none of them had ever seemed to mind. She'd been gentler with Miss, that time in her apartment, but it was different here. Now. They'd talked about what would work for both of them, and Miss was in charge, on top. There was no longer a piece of paper with signatures on it between them, but this dynamic would be the same.

"I want to touch you, Miss. I mean, I want to really touch you."

"Oh. Yes. Touch me. I want that too."

Selena groaned and slipped her fingers into the waistband of Miss's panties. In moments, they were shucked down those delicious thighs so Miss could step out of them. Selena's hands fit perfectly on the soft globes of Miss's ass. Miss shivered when Selena grabbed her, and so did Selena.

"I've never been with someone like you, Miss."

Miss let her head fall back with a low, throaty chuckle before she focused on Selena's face again. "I can say the same about you."

"I *want* to please you. I've never wanted that before. Not like this, anyway."

Selena had never been in the habit of revealing her entire life's history to the women she fucked, not even the ones she slept with more than once, as few as they were. She wasn't sure she wanted to delve into it now either, but she knew there would be a time, soon, when Miss would expect her to share at least some details.

Miss wriggled in Selena's arms. "I do prefer to be set apart from all the rest."

The idea that the woman in front of her could ever, in any way, be compared to anyone else was enough to set Selena to laughing. The chuckles eased into a soft sigh as Miss let her hands drift up to cup Selena's breasts. Her nipples peaked at once.

"Nobody could possibly compare to you," Selena whispered, "and I think you know it."

"Just because I know it doesn't mean I'm not happy for you to say so."

They kissed, and Selena wasn't sure who initiated it. It didn't matter. She opened for Miss's tongue and lips; the kiss deepened. Her breath sharpened. She drew in the scent and taste of her lover. She let it cover her. Embrace. Fill.

But not overtake.

"You're trembling," Miss whispered into Selena's ear. "You're not cold?"

"No, Miss."

"Surely not frightened?"

"Not of you, Miss. No."

Miss stepped back with a frown that made Selena want to weep, if she were capable of such a thing. Instantly, Selena regretted her answer. It was honest but would lead to questions she didn't want to answer.

"If not of me, sweetheart, then what? I'm the only one here." Before Selena could answer, Miss had turned to twist off the faucets. The tub glimmered, full of steaming water. Outside, although it was still only afternoon, the sky was dark with the storm, making the windows more mirror than glass.

Selena looked away from the shadow of her reflection, sheer with the trees beyond, but rapidly filling in with darkness. "Not of you. Of...this. Of what might happen."

Miss was silent at that. She sat on the edge of the tub and let her fingers trail into the water. Her head turned, so Selena could not see her expression. Her tone, though, was calm, soothing, warm. At least on the surface. Beneath it, Selena sensed hesitation and wariness, two emotions she knew intimately.

"We'll only go as far as you want to go," Miss said at last. "We'll see what happens. All right?"

Selena nodded. She watched Miss slip into the water and joined her a moment later. The hot water lapped under Selena's chin as she sank lower, the tub's curved edge surprisingly comfortable against her back. Miss reached a bit to touch a switch. She turned out the overhead lights and left on a small series of lamps that provided a dim, golden glow. Then she, too, leaned back against her edge of the tub with a sigh and closed her eyes.

This wasn't what Selena had expected. Kissing. Touching. Not this quiet commune in the still, hot water. She relaxed and closed her own eyes.

Clara shifted in the water, so it surged and splashed over them both. She spoke quietly, her low murmur soothing as a stream chuckling over stones. "Will you tell me about yourself?"

"What do you want to know?"

"Everything. But let's start with...are you the only one?"

Selena kept her eyes closed. It was easier that way. She wished for a blindfold. "No. It's a family thing. Passed through the maternal line."

"So, if you had children...?"

"I don't know. I don't ever plan to have children, not of my own," Selena said with a fierce shake of her head. More water splashed, until she forced herself to go still. She opened her eyes. "I wouldn't subject them to this."

Clara said nothing about that, only inclined her head to study Selena's face. "How old were you, the first time it happened?"

"Thirteen. First, I got my period. Then, I started changing. Any time I..." Selena bit her lower lip, trying to think about how to talk about this. "I was touching myself the first time it happened. I didn't know what to do. I let the fire burn me up, and the wolf took over. It was a few more years before it happened again. I kept to myself, but you know, it's hard to go through life without feeling pleasure, even if you try hard to avoid it."

"A life without pleasure is no life to have," Miss said. "So. Tied to pleasure? Not the moon."

Selena frowned. "No. I'm not a werewolf. They have no choice. They change when the moon is full. But shifters *can* control it."

"As you've so well proven."

Selena flushed hot with the praise, although she didn't feel she deserved it. "I've tried my best. But even so, sometimes, I still can't."

"Why control it? Why not just do it?"

"You saw what happens when I do it," Selena said.

Clara coughed into her fist and looked uncomfortable. "Do you...hurt people?"

"You want to know if I kill people and eat them?"

"Yes."

Miss's bluntly honest reply was exactly what Selena needed to hear. "I haven't ever killed a person. But that doesn't mean it will never happen. Humans aren't the natural prey of wolves, but that doesn't stop them from hunting or killing or eating people, if they have no other choice. I'm afraid that I will, one day. Not have a choice."

"Is that why you've tried so hard to keep yourself from shifting?"

"Yes," Selena whispered. "You can't turn into a wolf in the middle of the city and not run into trouble."

"We aren't in the city now, love," Miss said.

Love. It was only a pet name. It didn't mean more than that, but it shot warmth through Selena, and her throat closed with emotion again.

"No" was all she managed to say.

"So, the fire. Tell me about it."

"It's a fire inside, a burning. It rises, and the wolf comes after it. I can't explain it better than that. I feel good, usually sexy good, although it can sometimes happen when I'm just happy or feeling good about something else. The burning feeling starts. Then I feel her waking up, and if I can't stop it, she overtakes me. I change."

Miss took a few moments to digest this. It was easier than Selena had expected, to talk about this. It helped that Miss had shown no signs of recoiling or scoffing at anything she'd said so far.

"When I come," Selena added, "I can never stop it. I can hold it off for a few minutes, but I can never totally stop it from happening."

"Even when you make yourself come when you're alone?"

"Yes. I have a room in my apartment that locks. If I need to have an orgasm, I go in there and lock myself in. If the wolf can't run, she goes away pretty quickly."

"What about when you're with a partner?" Miss asked.

Selena chose her words carefully. "I haven't allowed myself to have a partner in a long time."

"But you have had them."

"Yes. Strangers I fucked in places I could get away from fast. Once or twice, someone more like me. At least they wouldn't freak out after."

"How do you find them? Others like you?"

"How do you find lovers who are submissive?" Selena countered. "Don't you sometimes, somehow, just... know?"

"Oh. Yes. I guess sometimes, somehow, I just do." Miss paused. "Nobody long term?"

Selena gave a dry laugh. "Who'd want to live with this long term? Or even short term."

Miss fell silent at that, then said, "So you do what it takes to stop yourself. That's why you need the pain."

"Yes. It keeps the fire away and the wolf quiet."

"How did you figure that out?"

"My grandmother used to hit me."

Miss sat upright in the water. Her expression twisted. She leaned forward abruptly, reaching for Selena's hands. "You know it's different, right? Please tell me you know it's different. That someone hitting you to punish or abuse you is not the same as what we do. Please, Selena, I have to hear you say it."

"I know the difference, Miss. I learned it later, and not from her." Touched at Miss's obvious discomfort, Selena kissed her.

Oh. There. That was what she'd been expecting when they'd gotten into this tub. The kiss deepened. Selena tasted salt and pulled back, concerned. She flicked away the tears on Miss's cheeks.

"Please, don't."

"I never hit you, or anyone, out of a desire to cause real harm. Only consensual, only—"

Selena kissed her to stop the words. "I know the difference, I promise you. I learned that pain kept the wolf away, but I also discovered I liked it. It became its own sort of pleasure."

"And pleasure wakes the wolf," Miss whispered.

"Yes. It became a circle, all tangled up together, twisted tight. I needed the pain to keep the change from happening, but I craved the pain, and loved it, and so I was running, running, all the time, just trying to balance the right amount of torture and desire. It's why I only came to you when I was absolutely desperate. It's why I stayed away too. Because the more often we were together, the more ecstasy it became and the less agony." Selena kissed her again, softly.

Their foreheads pressed together as they both breathed.

"I want to make love with you," Miss said.

"I'm afraid of what will happen."

They kissed again. Miss slid a hand between Selena's thighs, her fingers warm and smooth. Selena shivered as desire began its uncoiling inside her.

"Not here," Selena said.

"Let's go to my bedroom, then."

*

"Remember," Clara said. "We stop when you want to stop. Would having a safe word help?"

"Flamingo," Selena said at once.

Clara smiled. "Flamingo, it is. I'm going to kiss you, Selena."

She did. Slowly, taking her time, letting each brush of lip on lip linger.

Selena gave a half sigh, half groan, a totally sexy sound that sent shivers up and down Clara's spine. "It's starting."

Clara saw no signs of it, no rippling of Selena's muscles, nothing like that. She believed her, though. Her own tension and anxious anticipation tried to rise inside her like her own animal. She refused to let it.

"I love you," Clara said. "I'm not going to let anything bad happen."

Love.

She'd said it to others, but never this easily or without angst and uncertainty. Never without fearing it would not be said in return. This time, the word slipped out of her as simply and sincerely as taking a breath. She loved Selena, and although she couldn't be sure when exactly her feelings had taken that turn, she'd never felt more confident in a sentiment as she did then. She didn't even worry if Selena didn't feel the same. She didn't need reciprocation. She loved Selena and wanted to help her. That was how love was supposed to feel. Like trying to make the life of the woman she loved better.

Clara kissed Selena again. This time, Selena leaned into it. They'd curled up naked on Clara's bed, the comforter and top sheet pulled down and the pillows plumped up high. She'd also lit a fire, so the room was warm enough for naked bodies not yet heated by exertion. Now, Clara settled Selena back onto the pile of pillows and straddled her thighs. The brush of Selena's pubic hair was a sensuous tickle against Clara's clit.

"Are you going to tie me up, or...?" Selena breathed the question in a low voice.

"No."

"But, Miss!"

"I love those games, you know that. Binding you. Blindfolding." Clara teased a fingertip up and over Selena's taut belly and around each nipple until they both stood up in tight peaks. "I love watching the sweet pink blush that travels up your breasts and throat as you get aroused. I love hurting you, watching how you react. Straining at the bonds. How sweet and slippery your pussy gets."

Selena groaned and tensed, rocking her hips upward. "Oh, yes. That!"

"But this isn't about any of that, love. This is about you, and pleasure, and being able to let go."

"I don't want to let go," Selena said.

Clara ran her palms down Selena's sides to let them rest on her hips. "You have to let go, sometimes. If you don't, this is going to kill you. And because I can't bear the thought of a world without you inside it, I'm going to insist that you not die."

"So...this is about you." Selena pushed up on her elbows a little, but she was smiling.

"Oh, yes. This is alllll about what Miss wants." Clara smiled, too, and cupped the back of Selena's neck as she kissed her mouth. "Are you going to be a good girl and behave for Miss?"

Selena shivered, laughed low, and shivered again. "I'm going to try, Miss."

It was a bit of a silly game, but even so, it was turning Clara on. "Good. You're going to give me your orgasm?"

"I...oh...uh..." Selena arched and writhed. She closed her eyes and turned her head. Her fists clenched at her sides. "Yes, Miss."

"Tell me you want to come for me."

Oh, yes, this. Clara had known forever that she loved being on top, but this was the moment she craved and adored. Being in charge, yes, but both giving and taking. Taking care of her lover, her sub, but gaining so much in return.

"Yes, Miss, I want to come for you!" Selena's eyes flew open.

Her nipples were rock hard, and when Clara leaned to pinch them both, Selena bucked upward. Clara gripped with her thighs against Selena's. She ground her clit against Selena's body, earning a gasp from Selena and one of her own at the sensual pleasure. She kept the rhythm going, grinding in a slow, steady circle. Sweet honey coated them both in minutes, and Selena began a low, desperate panting.

"It's not going to take you very long, is it? You haven't had an orgasm in so long." Clara's voice trailed off into a guttural sigh as her own body responded to the slow, persistent grinding. She didn't usually get off this way, but tonight it seemed like she was going to come as fast as Selena seemed she would. She wanted to close her eyes and go with it, but this was not about her own desire. Clara drew in a breath to keep her voice steady as she stared down at her lover. "Let it go. Let it happen."

"It's going to happen. The change!"

A tendril of unease drifted through Clara as the memory of watching Selena transform was overlaid with the remembered terror of the night she saw Jenny's parents fucking. Without thinking, she slowed her pace. Beneath her, Selena's hips rocked again. Clara almost moved off her but stayed put. Selena's muscles rippled and tensed. She twisted, craning her neck to the side and arching her back.

"I need you to stop," Selena rasped. "Please. I can't! Flamingo!"

Immediately, Clara eased into position next to Selena, spooning her from behind. She ran a soothing hand over Selena's body. She stroked her from shoulder to thigh, over and over, while murmuring softly. Slowly, Selena's trembling eased. They lay quietly together like that, only the sound of breathing between them.

Selena cleared her throat but made no attempt at turning over to face Clara. "I'm sorry. I wanted to."

"You never have to apologize to me for not being ready to make love. You're allowed autonomy over your own body, Selena."

"Even if I'm your submissive?"

Clara kissed her shoulder blade. "Especially then. Do you...would you like to be?"

"I'm not sure I'll be very good at it."

"Well, I'm a very, very good Miss, so I think we can work something out." Again, Clara kissed Selena's warm skin as Selena chuckled.

Selena wriggled, pressing her butt against Clara. She took Clara's hand, linking their fingers, and tucked their hands beneath her breasts. Clara snuggled closer, feeling Selena relax, then yawn. It triggered one of her own.

They drifted.

Clara woke alone. The empty space next to her on the bed was cold. Selena had been gone for some time. Clara sat, her heart pounding at the silence. Her own breathing sounded too loud in her ears. She pressed a hand to her mouth as though to stifle it but took it away at once to shake herself. She was being ridiculous.

Selena was gone, but that didn't mean she was missing. Clara tossed off the blanket to reveal her bare skin to the darkness. The room had gone chill, the fire dying down until only the dim gold-red glow of embers filtered from it. It was the sole source of light.

No moon, she thought, reminding herself it didn't matter. Selena had been insistent that her shifting wasn't tied to the moon. She wasn't a fairy-tale monster, nor any kind of monster at all. She was a woman with some baggage, but hell, hadn't Clara brought a steamer trunk of her own to this relationship? Maybe when they left this cabin, everything they'd shared would go away. Maybe their accumulated baggage would overwhelm them, and it would all be too much. Maybe neither of them would be capable of making it work outside of this idyllic refuge.

Clara put her bare feet on the chilly floor. They were here, now. Still here. Clara had held Selena while she wept over her story, and despite every rational instinct that should have told her to dismiss it all as madness and fabrication, she had promised to keep care of the woman who'd become more to her than a submissive. More than a casual lover. It could be that delusion and insanity were catching; in which case, Clara thought with a bite of her lower lip, they could go into it together.

"Selena?" Clara's voice rang out through the empty bedroom. It echoed in the hall beyond.

She got no answer. Not a hint of movement, not here on the second floor, and when Clara went into the hallway to listen, nothing from downstairs either. The cabin had its share of creaks and groans, and she knew them all. She heard nothing that would indicate the press of feet upon the floor. She heard only her own breathing and the gust of wind outside, rising, and the spat of snow against the windows and roof.

Clara called out again, louder this time. More desperate. Her voice caught, ragged and sticking in her throat. She had promised she would not abandon Selena, and she'd meant it.

It had never occurred to Clara that Selena might be the one to abandon her.

*

The snow that had been falling steadily for the past day was as deep as Selena's thighs. Her hips in a few places. She stood, naked in the frigid air, her arms outstretched, and her face tipped up to the dark sky. Cloud cover prevented even the barest glimmer of starlight, and it would be a day before the moon began to show its face again.

She had never minded the dark.

Selena had no room for regrets. When she'd agreed to come here with Clara, she had known the risks. In the years since her first change, she'd learned to control the process, but she had never been able to stop it. She had known what pain the pleasure would bring. Her only qualms now were not that she was going to shift, or that she would run through the snow and the night and slake her hunger on some hapless beast that right now was still warm and alive, perhaps dreaming, careless in feeling it was safe. No. Her fear now was that she would never again hear the sound of Clara whispering she loved her.

The guttural cry tore from her throat as Selena dropped to her knees, now in snow up to her chest. She knew it was cold, but she felt only a relentless heat. The fire inside had been stoked for a time, too short a time, but now...

Now, Selena burned.

It never got better. Never easier. Agony wracked her body as it bent and changed into its new form, but there was pleasure in it, too, and that was worse than the torment because the ecstasy was what made it so hard to deny herself.

She shrieked, spittle freezing as it left her lips. She dug her fingers into the snow, seeking the frozen earth beneath and found ground, gravel, more ice. Her nails bent and broke. Her back arched as her limbs lengthened.

There was a time, then, when Selena knew nothing else. Only the fire, burning. The hunger, fierce and gnawing, demanding to be sated.

She ran through the snow, into the forest. Branches slapped at her, but thick fur protected her. Paws slapped at the ground, plunging deep into the snow but propelling her forward. She stopped to raise her snout to the air, sniffing for prey.

That was the last coherent thought Selena had.

*

Clara had run down the stairs, through the kitchen to the back door. She'd flung open the door and, uncaring of her bare feet and nudity, ran onto the porch beyond. Marks in the snow showed her where Selena had stood. Fallen?

"Selena!" Clara shrieked her name, but there was no sign of her.

From the tree line came an eerie, ululating howl. It raised gooseflesh all over Clara's body that had nothing to do with the freezing night air. With an echoing cry, she backed up over the threshold. She slipped on the tiles, melting snow beneath her feet. She caught herself on the doorframe but could not bring herself to run out into the snow again. Already her teeth were chattering hard enough to clip her tongue. She tasted blood and swallowed.

Another howl. This one closer. There, in the trees. A flash of green light. Eyes, Clara thought in horror and wonder. Higher off the ground than they ought to be for an animal, too tall even for a human. An image came to her of a wolf on its hind legs, teeth bared, silver drool glimmering as it slavered.

Then the twin lights were gone. A third howl rose, and Clara slammed the door. Panting, every part of her tense and trembling, she went to the kitchen counter to keep herself propped up. She'd never minded being naked, especially not in her own home, but all at once she felt exposed and vulnerable.

Her mind had still been trying to deny what she'd seen in Jenny's house and the private playroom with Selena. There was no denying any of it now. Her lover had become a wolf.

Did she want to run from this? Clara backed away from the glass. She crossed her arms over her chest to stop herself from trembling. Did she want to run?

"You love her," Clara told herself aloud. Her voice sounded strong. Firm. She spoke the truth.

She did love Selena, and love did not run. Not from disagreements, not from sickness, and no, not even from this.

Clara went again to the glass and looked out, shielding her eyes so she could at least attempt to see what might be in the darkness outside. All she saw was blackness. That was all right, she told herself.

She would just...wait.

*

The wolf had feasted herself to satiation, but she still ran.

Ran and ran and ran, glorying in the cold air, the snow, the slap of tree branches on her flanks. She yipped and yelped at the moonless sky. She reveled in the freedom of this world, so different, so without the stink of exhaust and the crush of humanity.

The wolf ran.

When at last the beast had quieted, Selena returned to herself. She woke from what always seemed to be a dream but was really the wolf's memories of what she'd done. Unlike all the other times, though, now she came back with a full belly and a lightness in her heart she hadn't felt in...well. Had she ever felt it, ever in her life?

The snow and ice on the deck burned her feet as the wind whipped at her bare flesh. It was too dangerous out here for her to stay very long. She stumbled on numbed feet to the glass doors leading to the living room. Clara had left them unlocked, and that simple gesture of caretaking nearly knocked Selena off her feet.

At the sight of the warm robe, the basin of water and the soft cloth next to it, the thick fuzzy socks, all laid out on the coffee table, Selena let out a low sob. She looked up to see Clara in the doorway. Clara held a tray laid with a steaming bowl of what smelled like soup, along with a mug of tea.

"You did this for me?" Selena managed to say.

Clara put the tray on the table next to the other items. "Yes, love."

She dipped the cloth into the water and wrung it out. She approached Selena and knelt in front of her. Selena gaped, not sure what was going on—Miss, kneeling? But in the next moment, she understood, as Clara lifted first one foot and then the other, to gently wipe away the remnants of dirty snow and blood from the scratches there. She worked efficiently, then rose and did the same to Selena's hands. She put the cloth back in the water and helped Selena into the thick, warm robe and socks, before settling her onto the couch. All of this happened within minutes.

Clara herself wore comfy flannel pajamas patterned in a red and black plaid. She sat next to Selena and offered her the bowl of soup. "Do you need to eat?"

"I...ate."

A beat of silence, then another. Clara nodded and pushed the tray an inch or so away from them. She eased back onto the cushions but sat close enough to rest her hand on Selena's shoulder.

"Are you all right?" she asked.

Selena nodded, overwhelmed at these multiple shows of affection. "Why are you doing this?"

"Because I want to make sure you're taken care of," Clara said.

"I'm not used to it."

Clara smiled. "Well, let's hope you get used to it. I'm going to have a glass of claret. Would you like some?"

"No. Alcohol makes it that much harder, and I'm already too close," Selena explained as Clara got off the couch and moved toward the bar cabinet across the room.

Clara didn't turn as she filled a crystal glass with crimson fluid. She spoke in the same gentle but no-nonsense tone Selena had come to know so well. "I want you to show me."

Selena stood at once. She shook her head and backed away. "No."

The refusal stung her tongue, tasting electric. She braced herself for Clara's fury, but she merely took a seat in the chair opposite Selena and sipped from her glass of claret. Selena paced. Every time her toes, warm and comfortable in the fuzzy socks, touched the wood floor or the soft carpet, she was forcibly reminded of the feeling of snow and ice and earth and rocks beneath her feet. Of the scent of forest and wind and prey.

"No," she repeated softly, her back to Clara. "I can't let you see me that way. You would..."

"I would what?" Clara asked when Selena could not bring herself to finish the sentence. "What, Selena? Answer me."

Her tone brooked no argument, but Selena had not been a submissive long enough to ensure her immediate and automatic obedience. She shook her head, still turned away. She waited for Clara's anger, an accusation. A command, something.

Instead, the whisper-soft brush of Clara's fingertips drifted across the nape of her neck and over her shoulder. Next came the press of her hand at the base of Selena's back. Clara said nothing, but the gust of her breath, so sweet, tickled Selena's ear.

Selena drew in a breath. She closed her eyes. Her fists clenched. Her body tensed. She flinched from the squeeze of Clara's fingers on her bicep.

"What would I do, Selena, if I saw you as you are?"

"You would be afraid of me."

"Probably," Clara whispered.

Selena's tension eased. Her shoulders slumped. Tears stung her eyes but didn't fall. "You wouldn't want me anymore."

Clara's grip tightened, forcing Selena to turn. Not that Clara could have actually forced her, had Selena truly resisted, but she wanted to turn. She needed to look Clara in the face, to see the rejection. It would hurt, but at least she would know.

"Being frightened is not a reason to not want you, Selena."

Selena swallowed hard. "You would think I'm a monster. And I am. If I show you what I become —"

"What you are," interrupted Clara harshly. "What you are. *Who* you are. If you show me who you are, every part of you, do you really believe I could ever think you are a monster?"

"I am a monster!"

Clara's hand flew to the back of Selena's neck and pinched hard in that glorious and terrible way she'd perfected. Her voice went low, gruff. Terrible and terrifying in its own way. She pressed her body to Selena's.

"You," she said, "are not a monster. I will not hear you talk about yourself in those terms. Do you understand me? I won't have it."

Clara kissed her. Fierce, bruising, the slant of her lips across Selena's brought a hint of blood. They gasped together. When they broke the kiss at the same time, Selena was appalled to see the glint of tears in Clara's eyes.

"I love you," Clara said. "Whatever shape you take. I love you, Selena Tuller, and I think I have loved you since the first time you allowed me to beat you, but not because you let me hurt you. Not because you submit to me. And definitely not because you let me fuck you. I love you because with you, for the first time, I feel like I am my best and brightest self. Because when we are together, I feel like..."

Her voice broke. She fought to speak, her mouth working. She shook her head. Found her voice.

"I feel like you can be who you are too. I think it's the first time for you too. To simply be who you are, without judgment. And yes, my love, yes, I think if I see you change, I'm going to be terrified, but not because you're a monster. Because you are something beyond anything I could ever have imagined, because you are beautiful and strong, and I won't know how to keep up with you. Because I'm afraid I will fail you. But not, never, because you are a monster. Do you understand me?"

"Yes, Miss," Selena said and went to her knees. Head bowed. Her shoulders heaved as she wept. She covered her face with her hands. The heat of her tears against her palms would have shamed her in the past, but now she only felt relieved. "Yes, thank you."

"Come. Sit up." Clara led Selena to the couch, where they both curled up together.

She brushed her hand over Selena's hair, and Selena closed her eyes for a moment to push into the caress. Clara splashed a little claret onto the back of her hand. Clara laughed and lifted Selena's hand to her lips to lick it away, and that touch sent shudders of pleasure rollicking up and down her spine.

"Are you sure you don't want any?" Clara offered the glass.

Selena sipped, then grimaced and shook her head. "Gah. Okay, there's another reason why I don't drink wine. That's awful."

"No need to, if you don't like it. But not if it's only so you won't change," Clara said.

Selena sighed. "I don't want you to see me do it."

"Does it hurt you, love?"

"Oh. God, no. I wish it did. If it hurt, maybe I'd be able to stop myself from doing it more easily. It feels good, Miss. So good. But it's ugly."

"Nothing about you could be ugly, love."

"It's inhuman, then. I don't want you to see it. You say you love me—"

"I do love you, Selena, and I don't lie about that," Clara interrupted sharply.

Selena continued in a softer tone. "Not even love can stand up to something like this, Clara."

"Has nobody in your life ever loved you enough?" Clara's voice cracked and broke.

Selena shook her head. "No."

"Not even your family?"

"My grandmother kicked me out after the first time she found out it had happened. I never knew my father. I had no siblings, none that I knew of."

"You were on your own at thirteen?" Clara's eyes welled with tears again.

"A little older than that. Sixteen." It hadn't been as bad as Clara must be thinking. Selena had found her pack, a mishmash of runaways and other teens in the same situation. What her grandmother had called a curse had given Selena the strength and skills to survive. She described this briefly to Clara, but added, "There were no others like me. Shifters, I mean. There was one other girl who could set things on fire by touching them. One who could open doors, any doors. But nobody else became an animal the way I do."

"*You* are special."

Selena frowned. "I never asked to be special. I never wanted it."

"But it's what you are," Clara told her. She straightened and moved on the couch, so they were no longer touching. Her brow furrowed, and her gaze went shadowed, but after a second, she nodded firmly before lifting her chin. Her eyes met Selena's. "Tell me what it was like. Last night."

Selena thought before answering, trying to be sure she was describing it all just right. "This is the first time I've ever been able to shift in a place where I can run. And hunt. And just...*be*. I've never had that freedom. Now I've had it, I'm not sure I can go back to the way I was before. Fighting so hard, all the time. I'll lose control of it. I know I will."

"And that terrifies you."

"Of course, it does," Selena said, her voice a low growl she couldn't force herself to soften. "Surely you can understand why."

Clara shifted on the couch until her knee touched Selena's. "I know very well how scary it is to not have total control. Domme, remember?"

She laughed gently and drained her glass before setting it on the coffee table. She leaned to kiss Selena gently. Then she cupped her face with her hands.

"Your fingers are cold," Selena murmured.

"Nothing about you is cold." Clara slid her hands over Selena's shoulders and down to cradle her breasts. A flick of her thumbs brought Selena's nipples to tight peaks. She grinned at Selena's groan. "Now. Show me."

*

Clara might be ready, but Selena was clearly far from it. The moment she gave the command, Selena's entire body tensed. Her hands clenched, her nails digging into the meat of her palms. She drew in a quick, sharp breath.

"You're afraid you'll hurt me?" Clara asked.

"I won't hurt you. I would never. But the wolf might."

In truth, Clara was afraid of that too. She hadn't clearly seen the wolf Selena had become, but she'd seen the paw prints and the glare of the green eyes. She'd heard the howling. She'd seen the aftermath of her lover's night in the forest and knew there'd been carnage.

Selena's breath shuddered as she shook her head. "Miss, I've never done it in front of anyone on purpose. I've always fought so hard to keep it from happening, or I run away to keep others safe. And myself. When I'm the wolf, I'm not a person anymore, at least not the person I am now. I don't control the wolf."

"You do, though. You've been controlling the wolf for years, love. Every time you stopped yourself from changing, you controlled her." Clara had no idea if this was true, but it made sense to her. Or maybe she was just wishful thinking. Hoping.

"I controlled myself," Selena began but broke off without continuing. It was clear from the struggle crossing her expression she was contemplating what Clara had said.

"If you are the wolf, Selena, and you *are*, then when you control yourself, you also control her. If there is no one without the other, then you are in control of both. And if Selena wouldn't hurt me, then...the wolf won't hurt me either." Clara said this firmly, perhaps as much to convince Selena as she was trying to make herself believe it.

"I don't want to risk it!"

"Then you'll go outside, and I'll stay in here and look through the window."

Selena frowned and looked at the glass, now reflecting the glow from the fire and showing nothing of the night outside. "That seems so simple."

"Too much in life is made more complicated than it has to be," Clara told her.

They both laughed. The mood between them lightened instantly. When Selena moved into her arms and offered her mouth for a kiss, Clara took the chance. Lips parting, tongues stroking. She took Selena's tongue between her teeth and held it, pressing just hard enough to offer a hint of pain but no more than that. Selena moaned softly, her body melting against Clara.

Clara pushed a hand between Selena's thighs and stroked her beneath the thick robe. She used the other to grip the back of Selena's neck in the way she knew turned her on. Again, she kissed her, this time whispering into her mouth.

"You're so hot here." Clara's thumb found the sweet spot of Selena's clit.

"You make me feel so good."

Clara stepped back. Her heartbeat throbbed at the base of her throat, in her wrists. Between her thighs. Her pussy ached with arousal, but this was not about her. She gestured at Selena.

"Take off the robe."

Selena stripped with the same confident efficiency as always, but this time instead of folding her clothes neatly, she let the garments fall into a pile at her feet. She stood with her thighs slightly parted. Clara could smell her, the sweetly tangy fragrance of woman along with the special and specific scent of Selena herself.

Again, Clara kissed her. Again, she pushed her fingers between Selena's legs, this time able to seek and find the notch of her pussy and the swelling bud of her clitoris. She pinched gently with her thumb and forefinger and moaned at the throbbing there.

"Oh...oh, yeah. Yes." Selena rocked her hips forward. Her breath came in short gasps that quickly became panting.

Clara had begun to lose herself in this, so when Selena stepped back quickly and firmly, going so far as to push away Clara's hands, her first instinct was as a Domme. She bit back the barked command that had risen to her lips. The sight of Selena's wide eyes, clenched fists, and the rapid rise and fall of her shoulders with every breath made it clear she was struggling against something fierce.

"I have to go," Selena cried.

Clara swept a hand toward the sliding glass doors. "Go, love. Go. You're going to be all right. It's all going to be okay."

It was obvious Selena didn't believe her, but she let herself out through the sliding glass and stumbled onto the patio beyond. The spots she'd cleared of snow were still icy, and she slipped. Clara shuddered in sympathy at how the cold must be biting into Selena's bare feet, but she moved toward the doors only to close them. She pressed her hands to the glass, and then her face. The glare from inside made it too hard to see.

Whirling, she ran to the lights to turn them off. Only the glow from the fire lit the room now, which made it easier to peer through the glass doors. By the time she got back to her place, Selena had already started to change.

She'd been right. It was nothing like the movies. No bubbling flesh, no writhing, no bones cracking. Even from this distance with the fire's reflection between them, it was easy for Clara to see how smoothly the change took over Selena's body. She did, indeed, shift. Just like that. One second to the next, almost too fast for Clara to see the change. Selena went to her knees, her back arched, and in the next moment, her body had elongated. Her limbs bent. Her hands had become paws.

Clara had never believed in magic before tonight, but this had to be it. Selena had called herself inhuman, but even as the final wolf form coalesced into shape, Clara could not think of her lover as a beast. An animal, yes. A glorious, gorgeous animal with glowing green eyes and a shaggy gray and white pelt. The paws were the size of dinner plates.

Without thinking, she ran to the French doors and flung them open. Instantly, frigid air stung her. She stepped out onto the icy patio, a hand outstretched.

The wolf turned to face her, going for a moment onto her hind legs. Wolves didn't stand like that. Clara didn't have to be an expert on animals to know. The stance lasted for a moment before the wolf was on all fours again. Mouth open, showing sharp white teeth. Red tongue lolling.

"What big teeth you have," Clara said in a hiccupping, giddy voice.

The wolf growled.

Of all the things that flashed through her mind right before the end, the last thing Clara expected to think was the lyrics to a Meatloaf song. Yet that's what she was doing, wasn't it? Offering her throat to the wolf with the red roses, the one who would give Clara her teeth, jaws, her hunger?

The one who loved her, she thought as the massive animal bounded toward her. Its claws scratched at the layer of ice on the patio stones. Clara braced herself.

"You will starve without me," Clara said, not knowing if it was true or not. Knowing it was arrogant to say so. But that's who she was. Domme, top. Miss. She was Miss to Selena, and she would be alpha to this wolf too.

The wolf stopped just out of reach. Clara didn't try to touch her. Her body had gone from numb to burning from the cold. She couldn't stay out there much longer without causing herself permanent damage.

"Go. Run. I'll be here when you get back."

The wolf gave no sign of recognition. The gleam in her eyes was not of human intelligence. Still, the animal turned and bounded away through the snow and into the forest beyond, leaving Clara behind. She watched for a few more seconds until the freezing cold became too much for her. Then she went inside to wait for Selena's return.

*

Warm. Belly full. The crisp scent of winter air still clinging to her nostrils, Selena woke on the living room couch. Clara had covered her with the heavy knitted afghan, but Selena was naked beneath it. Her fingers and toes ached, a common enough reminder that she'd spent the night running through the forest. At least this time she wasn't covered in blood.

This time, too, she woke feeling sated and well-rested, not irritable and jumpy. She sat up and stretched. From the kitchen came the clatter of dishes and the wafting scent of coffee. Without bothering to wrap the blanket around her, Selena went naked into the kitchen to look for Clara.

This was it, she thought. Miss would surely tell her it was time for her to go. Snow and ice storm or not, she would have to find a way to get down off this mountain, and out of Clara's life.

"Good morning, love. I've made coffee, and the pancakes will be finished in a few minutes. Sit. Have some fruit. Unless you'd like to shower first?" Clara turned from the stove. Today she wore a frilly apron that barely covered her nipples on top and highlighted just a hint of her delectable pussy from below. The rest of her was gloriously bare.

Selena's stomach rumbled, and her hunger was not for food.

Clara laughed and gestured at the table, which had been set with the pretty dishes and a steaming carafe of coffee. "Sit, Selena."

She did as she'd been told and poured herself a mug of coffee. She held it in her hands, holding the warm steam to her face, eyes closed, for a few seconds. Without opening them, she said, "You saw?"

"Yes. I saw."

At the sound of a plate thumping lightly onto the table, Selena opened her eyes. At the sight of Clara's smile, she put down her mug. Clara leaned to kiss her, and Selena let her head fall back for the embrace. The kiss lingered sweetly. Heat kindled in her belly...and something else did not.

Startled at this realization, Selena opened her eyes. "I..."

"What, love?" Concern clouding her gaze, Clara pulled out the chair next to Selena's and sat. She took Selena's hands. "What's wrong?"

"Nothing's wrong. It's all...right."

Clara's brow furrowed, and she shook her head. "I don't understand."

"When you kissed me, I started to get turned on."

"Oh, good. Well, I hope that always happens," Clara replied with a smile.

Selena let out a low, throaty chuckle of relief and disbelief. "I felt good. Sexy. Turned on. I didn't feel like I was fighting the shift."

Clara took this all in without saying anything at first. Her fingers curled against Selena's. She stroked her thumbs along the backs of Selena's hands and then squeezed.

"I always felt it, as soon as there was pleasure. I mean, it's why I needed the pain so much, you know? It kept me from feeling the desire to shift. I thought pain was the only way to keep myself from losing control over it. This is the first time I can ever remember when any kind of pleasure didn't make me feel the wolf trying to get out." Selena squeezed Clara's hands too.

Then they were both laughing and crying, and Clara had pulled Selena close for another kiss. Their tongues stroked. The kiss was so fierce their teeth clashed. Clara gripped the back of Selena's neck, pinching and digging in with her fingernails until Selena shuddered with desire.

"Get on the table. I'm going to make you come," Clara ordered.

Selena knew better than to hesitate. She might forever balk at true and immediate submission, since it was not in her nature, but for Clara, she would do her best to be what her Miss needed and wanted. She got off her chair and turned to lay on the table with her ass at the very edge.

Clara stood between Selena's thighs. She ran both her hands up over Selena's hips. Over her belly. Up over her breasts, pausing to tweak the nipples hard enough to force a cry from Selena's lips. The pain was delicious. Briefly, Selena worried the pain was going to remind her too much of how it had been when she was constantly fighting the fire inside, that it would trigger her into the desire to shift, but instead her body simply accepted the sting of Clara's pinching fingers and roused to it.

The sudden, stinging spank of Clara's hand against Selena's clit brought more pain. More arousal. Her back arched as her hands slapped flat onto the tabletop at her sides. Again, Clara spanked Selena's clit, and her every muscle tensed at the combination of exquisite pain and pleasure. She cried out when Clara slipped two fingers inside her slick pussy and used her thumb to press her clit at the same time.

"Oh...yes, Miss. Ffffuck, yes. More."

She fucking loved the look on her Miss's face as she used her fingers on Selena's pussy. Fierce concentration, admiration…joy. Knowing she was pleasing her Miss with her body's reaction and appreciation of everything Miss was doing to her gave Selena even more pleasure.

"I love making you happy, Miss."

"You do make me happy." Clara breathed the words as she stroked. Her free hand pinched again, this time in a series of harsh stings down Selena's ribs and over her belly. Clara's tongue slipped out between her teeth as she worked Selena's body in exactly the right way to bring her to the precipice of ecstasy and keep her there.

"So many times," Clara murmured without ceasing the steady, relentless stroking, "you came to me and requested I hurt you, but not let you come. You were always so beautiful in your resistance, Selena. I think I fell in love with you each time you were with me, each time you gave yourself up to me and gave me your agony. But now, here, I can't imagine a time before I loved you. I can't imagine being without you. And I can't imagine not bringing you to orgasm, over and over, as many times as I desire it."

The first rush of climax hit Selena like a wave hitting a cliff. She shattered, the way the ocean breaks against the rocks. She shouted, wordless, hoarse, not knowing what she was even trying to say. Her body bucked. Her hips rocked. She came hard, but Clara didn't slow down, and instantly Selena was rising again. Up, up, and up again.

She came a second time, not as hard as the first, but the ripples from this orgasm lasted longer. Each tense and release of her internal muscles pushed more pleasure through her until she was suffused with it. Then, although she'd felt no fire inside, rising and forcing her to become the wolf, Selena howled. The sound climbed out of her throat and hung in the air for long moments, the last notes of a song she hadn't known she knew how to sing.

*

They'd brought their mugs of coffee and plates of pancakes upstairs into Clara's bed, both of them starving but also tired in the aftermath of the kitchen table romp. Selena had polished off her food, plus most of Clara's, and now lay back on the pillows with the glisten of syrup still on her lips and tempted Clara to lick it away.

"It's not totally gone," Selena said at last.

Clara sipped the last of her coffee and put the mug on the nightstand. "Would you want it to be? Now you can control it?"

"I don't know."

"It's who you are, my love." Clara leaned to brush a kiss over Selena's mouth.

Selena rolled them both until she was on top of Clara. She pushed a leg between Clara's thighs to nudge her naked pussy. "You're the only person who's ever made me feel like that was okay."

"Kiss me."

Selena did as obliged for a few moments before pulling away. "I'm sorry, Miss. I'm taking liberties."

"Just because I prefer to be on top doesn't mean I always have to actually be on top, Selena." Clara pulled her lover back for another kiss.

Selena moved her mouth along Clara's jawline, down her throat and over her breasts, pausing to suck gently at her nipples. Earlier, making Selena come, Clara had gone slick and ready herself, but they'd interrupted the lovemaking for food. Her arousal came back now, filtering through every vein and nerve along the path Selena was tracing with her lips and tongue. Down, down, over each of Clara's ribs. Lower still, along the curve of her belly. Over one hip. Then the other. Finally, Selena settled between Clara's thighs to press her mouth against Clara's clit.

Clara hissed a breath and lifted her hips a little. "Mmmm."

Then she gave herself over to the absolute pleasure of her lover's mouth. Selena was deliberately slow. Precise. She kept the pace steady and perfect, teasing out Clara's rising orgasm until it overwhelmed her. Clara came in slow, rolling ripples of ecstasy, each riding on the end of the last so it was like her climax lasted forever. When it was over, she lay limp and sprawling on the bed, incapable of anything more.

"Mmm, Miss. I love the way you taste." Selena sat up, looking pleased with herself.

Clara, still boneless and sated, managed to flick her fingers toward her lover. "Sex crater."

Selena laughed. "Huh?"

"Sex crater," Clara repeated in a dreamy voice. "You made me come so good it left me in a crater. I can't get out."

Selena, still laughing, rolled onto her back with her head on the pillow next to Clara's. Their hands found each other. Hip to hip and shoulder to shoulder, they lay in silence broken only by the soft huff of their mingled breathing.

"I love you, Clara," Selena said.

Clara had been drifting toward sleep, but she opened her eyes now. She turned her head to look at Selena. "I know you do."

More silence.

"What will we do after this?" Selena asked.

Clara twisted her body until she was able to kiss Selena's shoulder. "We love each other. Live together. And, whenever you start to feel the fire inside…"

"Yes?" Selena sounded anxious.

Clara kissed her again. "We come here. We make love. You let the wolf run free as often as she needs to. When she's satisfied, we go back to the city again."

Selena said nothing for long moments. Clara pushed up on her elbow to cup Selena's cheek. She ran her thumb along Selena's lower lip, urging her without words to open her mouth. Clara kissed her then.

"We'll have a life, my love. That's what we're going to do."

About the Authors

Megan Hart writes books. Some of them use bad words, but most of the other words are okay. Some of them hit bestseller lists and win awards and some don't, but that's the way it goes. She can't live without music, the internet, or the ocean, but she and soda have achieved an amicable uncoupling. She loathes the feeling of corduroy or velvet, and modern art leaves her cold. She writes a little bit of everything from horror to romance, though she's best known for writing steamy fiction that sometimes makes you cry.

Email:readinbed@gmail.com

Facebook: www.facebook.com/readinbed

Twitter: @megan_hart

Website: www.MeganHart.com

Brenda Murphy writes short stories and novels. She is a member of the Golden Crown Literary Society. When she is not loitering at her local library and writing, she wrangles one dog and an unrepentant parrot. She writes about life, books, photography, and writing on her blog, writingwhiledistracted.com.

I hope you enjoyed reading this book as much as I enjoyed writing it. For information on book signings, appearances, work in progress snippets, previews and sneak-peaks, sign up for my email list at:

Website: www.brendalmurphy.com

Facebook: www.facebook.com/Writing-While-Distracted

Twitter: @bmurphysideshow

Other books by this author

Dominique and Other Stories
One

The Rowan House series
Sum of the Whole
Both Ends of the Whip
Knotted Legacy
Complex Dimensions
Double Six

Also Available from NineStar Press

Connect with NineStar Press

www.ninestarpress.com

www.facebook.com/ninestarpress

www.facebook.com/groups/NineStarNiche

www.twitter.com/ninestarpress

www.tumblr.com/blog/ninestarpress

www.ingramcontent.com/pod-product-compliance
Lightning Source LLC
Chambersburg PA
CBHW032124180726
48284CB00002B/687